BEING SLOANE JACOBS

Also by Lauren Morrill

MEANT TO BE

Being Sloane Jacobs

Lauren Morrill

DELACORTE PRESS

Text copyright © 2014 by Paper Lantern Lit, LLC
Jacket art copyright © 2014 by Cindy Clarissa Tanudjaja,
Getty Images

All rights reserved. Published in the United States by Delacorte Press,
an imprint of Random House Children's Books, a division
of Random House LLC, a Penguin Random House Company, New York.

Delacorte Press is a registered trademark and the colophon is
a trademark of Random House LLC.

Visit us on the Web! randomhouse.com/teens

Educators and librarians, for a variety of teaching tools, visit us at
RHTeachersLibrarians.com

Library of Congress Cataloging-in-Publication Data
Morrill, Lauren.
Being Sloane Jacobs / Lauren Morrill. – First edition.
pages cm
Summary: Sloane Emily Jacobs and Sloane Devon Jacobs, from very
different worlds but both with problem families, meet in Montreal where
they will stay in the same hotel while attending camp, one for figure skating,
the other for ice hockey.
ISBN 978-0-385-74179-8 (hardcover : alk. paper) –
ISBN 978-0-375-98712-0 (ebook)
[1. Interpersonal relations–Fiction. 2. Camps–Fiction. 3. Family problems–
Fiction. 4. Ice skating–Fiction. 5. Hockey–Fiction. 6. Montreal (Quebec)–
Fiction. 7. Canada–Fiction.] I. Title.
PZ7.M82718Bei 2014
[Fic]–dc23
2012046889

The text of this book is set in 12-point Cochin.

Book design by Heather Daugherty

Printed in the United States of America

10 9 8 7 6 5 4 3 2 1

First Edition

For Adam and Lucy, the best family a girl could have

Being
Sloane
Jacobs

CHAPTER 1

SLOANE EMILY

*T*he music in my head swells to a crescendo, the timpani rolling like a summer thunderstorm. I push hard
into the ice and turn, the wind whipping pieces of hair into
my face. I position my arms for an arabesque. I look over
my shoulder. I bend low at the knee, suck in a deep breath,
and leap, spin, spin . . .

And land hard and fast to a cymbal crash only I can hear.

"Damn," I mutter. I wanted a triple, but once again, I
missed. I wussed out at the last second and doubled it, a
move that is quickly becoming my signature. *And* the landing was total crap. I can practically hear my mom's voice in
my head, bemoaning yet another failed jump.

I stand up straight and skate a wide circle around the
center of the ice with my hands on my hips, shaking first
my right foot, then my left, my standard "Get it together,
Sloane" move. In two hours of practice, I only managed to

get two halfway-decent triples, and both times I was sure I was going to snap my leg in two with the force of the landing.

The fear I've had since I started practicing again a few months ago is becoming more and more real: I lost it, and it's not coming back.

I execute a low, fast camel at dead-center ice, as if the physics of the impossibly fast spin will send the fear and doubt flying out into the empty seats above me. I straighten up from the spin a little bit dizzy and am immediately annoyed that I didn't spot properly, something I learned to do when I was just six years old. What is wrong with me?

A beam of light pours down from an open door high in the last row of the stands. I see Henry shuffling down the stairs from the mezzanine level in his standard-issue jeans and threadbare wool sweater. His gray hair peeks out from a black wool beanie, and I wonder, as I often do, if it's the same one he's been wearing since I started at this rink when I was five or if he replaces it every few years. Even though it's a balmy eighty-two-degree Washington, DC, day, Henry wears long pants and wool year round, and he's never without his hat. I guess that's what comes of a lifetime maintaining an ice rink.

He makes his way down the stairs, until his nose is nearly pressed up against the glass that surrounds the rink. I pick up the pace and go for one last triple, just for him. I barely land and have to step out of it a half second after I hit the ice, but Henry applauds anyway.

"Hey there, Little Bit," he calls to me, his pet name for

me from back when I actually *was* a little munchkin of a skater. He doesn't care that now that I'm five four, one of the taller skaters out there, and sixteen years old, the name no longer applies. "It's closing time. Off the ice." Henry may be my biggest fan, but he's also a stickler for the rules.

I skate toward him, then throw a hard hockey stop like James taught me when I was little. The blades give a satisfying *SSSSSCHICK* across the ice as I skid to a stop inches from where Henry stands. "Okay, okay, I'm going!" I'm breathing hard from the last jump, which was probably one too many for this session. I can feel my thighs starting to turn to jelly.

He just shakes his head and smiles, then opens the little door to let me out of the rink. "Don't you have school tomorrow?"

"School's out, Henry," I say. "Last week."

"So I guess I better get used to shooing you out at closing for the next three months, huh?"

"Nope," I reply. "In fact, this is the last you'll see of me, Henry. I'm off to Montreal in the morning."

"They shipping you off to some fancy finishing school or something?" Henry chuckles. He likes to pretend I'm some prim and proper lady circa 1955, and I like to pretend like I'm some kind of rebel skate punk. He's a little closer to the truth than I am.

"Worse. Skate camp. 'Four intensive weeks of training with former Olympians, surrounded by more than fifty promising young athletes,'" I say, quoting the brochure.

"A fate worse than death, I'm sure. For someone who's here every dang night, isn't skate camp the perfect summer plan?"

"Here the only person I have to impress is you, and you've been clapping for me since I first learned to skate backward," I say.

"You put too much pressure on yourself," he says. He lays his heavy hand on my shoulder. "It ain't a big deal. Either you love it or you don't. Either you can do it or you can't. And, kid? I been watching you for years, and I know you can do it. The question you gotta figure out is, do you love it?"

It's a wonder my jelly legs don't collapse beneath me immediately. Henry knows the question is way too big for me, though, and he doesn't even wait for an answer. He steps onto the ice behind me and makes his way slowly to where the Zamboni lives.

In the locker room, I remove my skates, then strip off my leggings and leotard and replace them with a pair of holey jeans and a white T-shirt. After spending hours spinning in spandex, there's nothing better than throwing on baggy, soft, comfortable clothes. Actually, there's one thing better, and that's slipping into a hot bath. But according to the voice mail Mom left for me earlier, that's not on the agenda tonight.

I wad up my skating clothes and wedge them into the front pocket of my black skate bag, making a mental note to take them out when I get home so they don't ferment. I pull the elastic out of my bun and check the mirror to see if I can do anything with what I see, but my long black hair, normally shiny and stick straight, is a sweaty, frizzy mess. I wind it back up into a pseudo-bun and secure it with the elastic. Mom will be here to pick me up any minute, so there's no time for the shower and blowout I'm sure she'd prefer.

With one final look in the mirror, I lug my bag over my shoulder and push through the heavy blue door that leads into the lobby. I walk across the shiny linoleum and out the front door, but there's no sign of the shiny silver sedan Mom drives, a gift from Dad on their twenty-fifth anniversary. I dig my phone out of my bag and see that she still has ten more minutes. Mom is always Right On Time. She's always right, period.

I head back inside to wait.

I settle in on one of the benches in the narrow corridor across from the trophy cases. I've probably spent days of my life sitting here. Between my lessons and training sessions and James's hockey games, I feel like the rink is my childhood home, not the two-story brick colonial in Alexandria. I root around in my skate bag, searching for my summer reading book, but it's not there. In my mind's eye, I can see my copy of *A Portrait of the Artist as a Young Man* on my nightstand. I hate being without something to read. I get up and wander across the floor.

The trophy case takes up an entire wall of the lobby, and even though I've looked through it a hundred times, I can't stop myself from scanning the photographs of various skate teams from the past decade. A small, gangly girl grins cheesily in every one, a mile-wide gap between her two front teeth. Her jet-black hair, cut in a severe wedge, shines in every shot. In some she's raising medals to the camera, in others she's executing spins, and in one she's even mid-salchow. In all of them, she looks completely blissed out, like she's the queen of the ice.

I step back and shudder at the pictures of my tween-age self. Thank God for a growth spurt, several thousand dollars' worth of orthodontia, and finally ditching that awful bob haircut my mom always said was "so CUTE!" If I had more of a juvenile delinquent bent, I'd break the glass and burn those pictures. I can just imagine what the papers would have to say about *that*.

The last picture is of me at sectionals, age thirteen. I'm wearing a navy-blue dress with tiny silver rhinestones around the collar and a short, flouncy skirt. It was my lucky dress, I had decided, because it brought me a first place at regionals. I'm holding a bouquet of red roses nearly bigger than I am and hoisting a gold medal over my head.

I'm glad there's no picture of me from junior nationals that year. It would show me in that same navy dress, skidding across the ice on my butt after failing to land a double—*a double!* And that moment, three years ago, was the end of my competitive career—until now.

My mind is already going there, to that disastrous routine. I'm picking up speed, I'm bending, I'm leaping, I'm spinning, I'm—

Honk! Honk!

I turn around. Through the glass doors I can see my mom's silver Mercedes. I shake off the memories, grab my bag, and rush out to the car.

"Sloane Emily Jacobs, do you have to dress like a street urchin every time we go to dinner?" Mom swings the car out onto the road and instantly hits traffic. Her voice is high and severe, the way it always gets in DC gridlock when she has somewhere *very important* to be.

I would love to know the last time my mother actually encountered a street urchin, but I keep that comment to myself. It would most certainly be followed by a remark about my "smart mouth."

When I don't say anything or apologize for my appearance, I see her hands tense on the steering wheel. "Honestly, why can't you just play along this once? It's our last dinner as a family before you go off to camp."

I flinch at the word "camp," which for me does not conjure up images of archery and swimming and making fun arts and crafts with glitter. No. This summer is going to mean blisters, ice packs, morning workouts, tights and leg warmers and gloves and earmuffs, trying to stave off runny noses during eight-hour sessions on the ice. It will mean pressure from coaches, pressure from fellow campers, and even worse, pressure from myself. There *will* be glitter, but it certainly won't be on fun arts and crafts.

"Is James coming?" I ask.

"Yes, James is coming, he's a member of this family,

and apparently the only one who knows how to dress like a civilized member of society." She sighs.

If James is coming, then this dinner is definitely *not* about celebrating my trip to the Glitter Gulag. James has been unofficially exiled from family dinners lately, ever since he announced his plans to double major in biology and international affairs with a goal of achieving "a green and peaceful future." When my parents aren't screaming at him about a lifetime as a broke hippie tree-hugger or "what it looks like" for my father, they're simply swimming along in total denial. In Dad's latest appearance on Fox, he told that uppity Nina Shelby with her crisp suits and her helmet hair that James was premed.

So this dinner may be about family togetherness, but only the kind that looks good in front of cameras. My stomach tightens into a knot. We're putting on a show for the press, probably to help certain blind items on Washington gossip sites about a senior senator getting frisky with a pretty young female staffer.

This is the kind of togetherness that makes my family feel like it's splintered right down the middle.

"Please, Sloane. Can you just . . . fix this?" Mom waves a hand in my direction. I'm not sure whether she's signaling my outfit or me, generally, as a person.

But there's no use in arguing. There's never any use in arguing with my parents. Besides, Mom has enough to deal with. I almost feel sorry for her.

I hunt in my bag until I find a plaid wool blazer and a

camel-colored pashmina, both only slightly wrinkled. It's the best I can do considering the circumstances of the surprise dinner. Mom glances over from the driver's seat and simply snips, "When we get home, those jeans are going straight into the trash."

There's no point in telling her the holes were placed there, strategically and fashionably, by the fine people at J.Crew, and that in fact I paid *extra* for the holes. But if she had absolutely no problem tossing a pink leather Marc Jacobs miniskirt that cost enough to feed a family of four for a month, she won't think twice about my eighty-nine-dollar jeans. Like I said, I *almost* feel sorry for her.

I wind the scarf around my neck and nearly strangle myself with it as Mom banks a hard right onto Pennsylvania Avenue, floors the gas pedal, then screeches to a halt at the valet stand outside the Capital Grille. In one quick move she's out of the car, slipping her purse over her shoulder, handing the keys to a red-vested attendant. I unfold myself from the passenger seat. My muscles are already starting to tense a little after all those jumps and landings.

The valet pulls the car away, and Mom, clad in an impeccably tailored ivory pantsuit, gives me a final up-and-down. I get the anticipated sigh, this time with a bonus eye roll. "Button up that blazer," she says, then whirls on her heel and steps through the revolving door.

Before I can follow her, though, I take a deep breath, square my shoulders, and try to ignore the bad feeling coiled in my stomach. Jacobs family dinners tend to look pretty good from the outside, but they feel like a Guantá-namo interrogation to the insiders. Two hours of Dad. Two hours of Mom and Dad.

Thank God I'll have James.

Inside the dimly lit restaurant, I head toward the big table near the center of the dining room but close to a large window facing the street. It's the place to see and be seen, and it's been our regular table since Dad graduated from junior senator status five years ago. I rush for the coveted "hiding seat," the one whose back faces the window. Here, I can usually prevent my photograph from being taken. Luckily, James still isn't here or he would have snatched it. We used to spend hours wheeling and dealing over who'd get the chair. I usually won, but I did a lot of laundry and washed a lot of dishes to make up for it. Never mind that my mom employs a full-time maid; Dad says chores build character.

As if he knows *anything* about character.

Mom is situating herself in her usual seat to Dad's right (his seat is the one that faces the window, all but guarantee-ing a photo). Dad is across the room chatting up one of the many silver-haired donors and "family friends" who will no doubt interrupt our dinner tonight. The waiter is already pouring Mom a glass of her favorite pinot gris.

I reach for my water goblet and start chugging. That workout really drained me. I catch my mom raising a brow at me across the table and remember that it's not ladylike to drink as if I've been lost in the desert for days, so I restrain myself. Resistance is futile tonight. I just have to get through it. It's almost enough to make me want to go away to skate camp.

Almost.

"Seej!" I turn at my nickname since birth, the vocalization of my initials, S.E.J., since my four-year-old brother either couldn't, or wouldn't, say "Sloane." I look up and see James making his way through the restaurant, and true to form, he's dressed like a civilized member of Washington society in khakis, a gingham oxford (sleeves rolled up, of course), and tasseled leather boat shoes. He's got that windblown look of someone who spent the day on a schooner off the coast of Martha's Vineyard, and if it weren't for his jet-black hair and the gap in his front teeth, you might mistake him for a member of the Kennedy clan. I have to suppress a giggle imagining him at a meeting of the Georgetown chapter of Greenpeace. He must fit right in.

He tugs on my messy bun, then plops down in the chair next to mine, opposite Mom. After Dad's seat, it's the chair that's most likely to land you in a newspaper photo above a caption about "meeting and greeting" or "lobbying" or some other Washington euphemism for raising money.

"Good to see ya, kid," he says. He scoots his chair in and smooths a white linen napkin over his lap. "Though I hear I won't be seeing much more of you. Skate camp, huh? I thought those days were over."

Mom nearly chokes on her sip of wine but manages a more dignified hiccup. "Your sister was taking a little hiatus from skating to focus on school, but she's been desperately missing the ice. She's ready for her big comeback."

I barely manage to suppress an eye roll. Across the table, James winks at me. I'm pretty sure those exact words are on a press release somewhere, right below "Senator Jacobs Kicks Off Reelection Campaign."

"Well, go for the gold, Seej," James says. He waves the waiter over and orders a beer. My mom quickly adds, "In a glass, please." Before the waitress leaves, we place our orders: wedge salad and baked chicken for Mom; a fish entrée that James confirms is sustainable; the usual—steak, medium-rare—for Dad; and a hamburger, fries, and salad for me (with a side of eye roll from Mom).

Dad finally takes his seat next to Mom. I can tell his mind is still with the man at the next table, thinking about money or policy or . . . oh, isn't it all just about money? "So what is everyone having?"

"We already ordered, Dad," I say, avoiding eye contact. "You missed it."

"I ordered you the steak," Mom adds, and puts a heavy-bottomed glass of whiskey in his hand.

"Good to see you, James," Dad says between sips of his drink. "How were finals?"

"Great," he says. "I did really well. I think I'll make the dean's list again."

"Excellent. I'll pass that along to the staff to add to the newsletter," Dad says. I stifle a groan. "Started looking at med schools yet?"

"No, Dad," James says. His smile hasn't faltered. James has an uncanny ability to ignore Dad's bait and instead hear only what he wants to hear, as if the father he sees sitting at the table came straight out of some evening sit-com (and not one of the dysfunctional ones). I don't know how he does it. I shouldn't be surprised, though. Dad does the exact same thing. "But I have started looking into public policy programs where I can focus on environmental policy. You know, the Kennedy School has a great program."

Dad instantly perks up at the mention of Harvard and politics, and the strained conversation picks up a little. It's shocking how he seems to be talking with a totally different son, imagining a political dynasty while James chatters on about clean-water policy in the third world as it relates to the United Nations.

The food comes, and I tear into my burger. The only redeeming quality of these dinners is that the burgers here are possibly the best things I've ever put in my mouth. A couple of years ago I discovered that I could get the chef to put avocado on them, and it's made the whole experience of family dinner much more bearable. With the first bite, a thick stream of meat juice and grease runs down my chin and onto my napkin. Heaven.

"Sloane, isn't it about time you got back to your training diet?" Mom says. Her face is screwed up in disgust. "Lots of fruits and vegetables, some lean protein, right? Your body needs good fuel to perform at its peak."

"Sure," I say between bites. "I bet there will be plenty of that at camp."

"Well, you might want to get started early," Mom replies. She pushes the cherry tomatoes around on her plate a bit, then finally spears one and brings it to her lips. I swear, she will spend at least five minutes chewing that one tomato, and by the time she's done, I'll have wolfed down almost my entire burger.

"Oh, leave her alone," James says. "She looks great. And besides, she's an athlete. She can eat whatever she wants."

"Thank you, James," I reply, and take another monster bite of burger.

"You *are* beautiful, darling," Dad says, and Mom sighs and takes a sip of wine, clearly annoyed that Dad hasn't taken her side and encouraged my "healthy" (no-fat, no-taste, no-fun) diet. "Which is why she's got Preston on the hook. When are you two finally going out?"

"Um, never?" I reply. My parents exchange a look. It's the first time they've made eye contact tonight. Neither of them appreciates my sarcasm, which is why I usually keep it corked up. At least they can bond over that.

"Preston's a nice young man, Sloane," Mom says.

Actually, Preston Brockton-Moore is a reptile. A slimy, disgusting, slithering snake of a guy who wants nothing more than to hiss his way into a Congressional seat, and also the pants of every female offspring of every politician this side of the Potomac.

Dad, of course, loves him, mostly because his father

is Archibald Brockton, who possesses the delightful dual attributes of having more money than God and being the owner of a media company. Free press and free money? Throw in a tax cut and it's my father's version of heaven on earth.

"I think you two make a great pair," Dad says. "And Archibald said Preston is off to Princeton in the fall."

"Okay," I say, dropping my eyes to my plate. I can't look at Dad directly. I haven't been able to look at him for months.

"Well, you're interested in Princeton, aren't you?"

"I want to go to Brown," I reply. "Or Columbia."

"But you'll apply to Princeton, too, of course. And if Preston is already there, I'm sure that will help you with your decision."

"Yeah, in that you'll decide to stay far, far away from Princeton," James stage-whispers to me. I'm thankful he said it so I don't have to.

"Oh, honestly, Sloane, you act like the boy is an ax murderer," Mom says. She raises her glass to take another sip of wine but finds it empty, so she raises it toward the waiter and gives a little wave. "He's smart and handsome and comes from a wonderful family."

"Mom, he backed me into a corner at that benefit and tried to molest me. He was stealing drinks from the bar all night."

"That benefit was lovely. Preston's mother wore the most beautiful Monique Lhuillier," Mom says, once again steamrolling over what I have just said. "What was it for, again?"

"The sexual assault crisis center!" I practically shriek.

"Keep your voice down, dear. So inappropriate." *Wait, that's inappropriate?* The irony escapes her entirely, or maybe she just doesn't care. Next to her, Dad is buried in his phone, texting God knows who, and James is focused on his fish.

I can feel the blood rise past my neck and start thudding in my ears. I want to shout something at her about how taking her relationship advice would be like learning to put out fires on the *Hindenburg*. The only thing keeping me from a full-on scream is the threat of another diner whipping out an iPhone and recording the whole thing. Living through this dinner once is bad enough; I definitely don't need to relive it for all eternity on YouTube.

"Guess your standards are lower than mine" is what I finally mutter. James elbows me in the ribs at the exact moment that Dad chokes on a bite of steak, and when I look up, Dad's staring at me hard. For the first time all night, he's actually heard what I was saying.

James gives me a nearly imperceptible shake of his head that I know means *No, not worth it, abort.* I can't believe I said it, in public, no less. Jacobses don't—*I* don't—lose control like that. I turn my eyes back to my burger. I take another bite, but suddenly it tastes like sawdust and sand. I have to take a gulp of water to get it down without choking. This meal, for me, is over.

♡ ♡ ♡

After dinner, James takes a cab back to his dorm, and Dad heads to his office to proof some press releases. That leaves me and Mom in the car on our way home to Alexandria. The monuments whiz by as we make our way out of DC proper. At this point, I can't wait to get to Montreal. I want to be anywhere but here.

Mom rambles on about a packing list, wondering if I'll need two formal dresses or three. I turn away from her, press my cheek against the glass, and stare up at the night sky.

"I had Rosie pull out your navy strapless and that lovely champagne-colored one. Do you think you should take that pink one with the ruffle down the front too?" Mom asks. I don't answer, which is good, because she apparently doesn't need me to. She's already moved on to shoe options.

A streak of light bursts across the darkness. A shooting star. It's rare to see a star so bright in DC because of all the light pollution. For some reason, it makes me want to cry. I haven't seen a shooting star since I was a little kid—since Mom and Dad were my heroes. Since I believed in them. Since they believed in me.

I close my eyes tight and make a wish.

I wish to be somebody—anybody—else.

CHAPTER 2

SLOANE DEVON

I can feel all eyes in the arena on me. The fans, my teammates, everyone. But there's only one set of eyes I care about.

Coach Butler is pacing the sidelines. His eyes keep flickering back and forth between me, the puck, the goal, and the scoreboard. My skates, beat-up but perfectly broken in, are positioned for a shot. The puck floats on top of the ice just off the toe of my right skate. The Liberty High Belles' goalie is twitching back and forth in her red and blue jersey, ready to block my shot. The period clock ticks down and the score shows a tie game.

This is it. I can do it this time; I can shake whatever this funk has been these last few weeks. All I needed was a do-or-die situation like this one. I got this. *I got this.*

But when I try to take a deep breath, the air comes too fast and I gasp like I'm drowning. And then I feel them.

They start in my shoulders and wash down through my arms into my fingertips. The nerves are starting. Suddenly I can't focus. Tingles. Pins and needles. Whatever you want to call it, it's all I can feel, all I can think about. *I have to do this. I can't do it. I have to. Shake it off. It's all mental. It's in your head.* I lower my eyes back down to the puck, raise my stick back, pivoting at the waist, and — BAM!

I'm on my face, kissing ice. I roll over onto my back. My vision starts to swirl into a tunnel of bright white light, and for a second all I can see is a red and blue jersey bearing the number 22 skating away. She throws a quick glance over her shoulder at me. I turn to see Coach Butler shaking his head.

I lie there for a second, wondering whether I should be pissed that she blindsided me or thankful that I didn't have to take — and inevitably miss — that shot. When I try to breathe, something catches in my lungs. There's no air. I blink a few times until everything comes back, and I see my teammate Gabby Ramirez, number 63, appearing over me. She lifts her helmet until her bleached-blond ponytail comes tumbling out.

"Hey, girl, you dead?"

"Air," I gasp. "I need —"

Gabby stands up and calls to the sidelines, "She just got the wind knocked outta her! She's okay!"

When I finally catch my breath, Gabby takes my big sweaty glove in hers and drags me to my skates. "Slow breaths," she says.

Then I see number 22 on the Belles, helmet off like she's just out for a leisurely skate, waving her stick toward me, doubled over laughing.

"Screw her," Gabby grumbles, following my gaze. "Dirty player. You totally had it, dude."

"Yeah," I mutter, but I'm still staring at 22. When she catches me looking, she sneers at me. I feel whatever was wound up in me unraveling fast. I feel loose, like nothing is holding me back.

I fling off my gloves. Gabby tries to grab the back of my jersey, but I'm too quick. My shooting may be off, but I can still sprint like a speed skater. In two blinks I'm in front of her, and in three I drag her to the ground.

"What the hell!" she screams.

"Dish it out but can't take it?" I shout. I draw my arm back to deck her. This time? No tingles.

My fist connects with her face, and her head jerks back onto the ice. I see blood, but I can't tell if it's coming from her or me. I try to look at my fist to see if I cracked a knuckle or something, but hands grab my shoulders and suddenly I'm being dragged across the ice. Coach Butler is yelling, something about discipline, maybe having it, maybe needing it? I can't tell; he's yelling too fast and too loud. The rest of my team is staring, mouths open. When we get to the bench, Coach nearly shoves me over the wall.

"Locker room," he growls.

"Game's not over, Coach," I pant. Shouldn't I just be parked in the penalty box?

"Go," he says, then turns away from me.

I burst through the metal door and lean back hard against the Hornet, a chipped yellow and black mural that's been on the wall of our locker room since medieval times. Within seconds I hear a buzzer and cheering from the side of the arena. The wrong side. We lost.

"Dammit!" I shout, then yank my helmet off and hurl it across the room. It slams into a yellow locker, leaving a small dent. I shuffle across the rubber floor on my skates and pick it up, then go hide in one of the shower stalls. The team will be in any minute, and I can't face them.

It takes more than half an hour of crouching in the handicapped stall in the dark corner of the locker room before I hear the last player drag her bag out the door. I wait a few more beats to make sure it's quiet, then make my way back out to my locker to change and get out of here. I sink down onto one of the ancient wooden benches and start unlacing my skates.

I hear the door squeak open halfway. "Jacobs, you in there?"

I suck in a breath, wondering if I can make it back into the handicapped stall before Coach Butler sees me. But with my skates half unlaced and him halfway in the door, it's pretty unlikely.

"Jacobs, I didn't see you come out, and your team didn't either. You're in there, and I'm coming in. If you're not decent, speak now."

I could shout something about being in my underwear,

but it's no use. I'm going to have to take the lecture from him at some point; might as well be now. "Come in," I finally call back.

Coach Butler strides in, marches across the floor, and sits down on the bench across from me. He takes off his yellow Hornets ball cap and leans down until his elbows are resting on his knees. Then he looks me dead in the eyes.

"I don't know what you could have *possibly* been thinking out there. That kind of crap does not fly on my team," Coach says. His voice is even and completely cold. It's worse than yelling. "I'm ashamed of the way you behaved." He shakes his head. "I didn't train you to play like that."

"I'm sorry," I say. I feel a lump rising in my throat, but I gulp it down. There's no crying in hockey, not for me, at least. But I feel like I've been punched square in the sternum. We sit in silence for a few moments. Coach stares hard at me, and I keep my eyes firmly on the ground.

"Jacobs, you're benched."

My gaze snaps to his. "But the season's over," I say, my voice going shrill.

"Well, I'm coaching next year, and unless you plan on moving to another school, you better plan to park your butt on the bench for the first three games next season."

"You can't do that!" Three games? That's a lifetime! That's when the scouts come, when college visits start. *Benched?*

"I can, and I will," he says. "I won't tolerate fighting. You could have really hurt that girl."

"She came at me," I reply, but immediately I know it's the wrong thing to have said.

"It was a legal hit. I watched it. You were too busy reciting Hamlet's soliloquy or some crap while you were lining that shot up. What were you expecting, an engraved invitation to the goal?"

I drop my eyes again. I can't even begin to come up with an explanation. Not without exposing my secret. He's right, of course. Had I been paying even a sliver of attention to what was going on around me instead of freaking out, I would have seen that girl coming a mile away. I was too busy thinking about *not* making the shot—again.

I try to take a deep breath, but I choke on a sob. It comes out as a strangled noise that I turn into an angry string of curses. Coach has heard me swear before; it's either swear or break down in tears, which is *not* an option. Coach just watches me. His gaze is intense, his eyes narrowed in a mixture of confusion and something I can't read.

"I don't know what's gotten into you lately, but you need to get it together. Figure out a way to control yourself, or I won't have you on my ice," Coach says. He runs his hand through his hair, then fits his ball cap back on his head. "Now go get showered and get out of here. Go home."

♥ ♥ ♥

I leave the corner bodega and shuffle home with my hands in my pockets, my hockey bag over one shoulder and a plastic bag holding a frozen pizza bouncing awkwardly against my thigh. I try not to think about the game, the fight, the suspension . . . and definitely not the tingles. Because if I start thinking about any of it, especially the tingles, my brain will simply follow the path to its natural conclusion, which is that hockey is over.

And if hockey is over, then my life is over.

No hockey means no scouts. No scouts means no college scholarship, which means no life outside of this stupid neighborhood that's half row houses bursting with kids and grandparents and aunts and uncles and half UPenn hipsters turning the Laundromats into brunch spots with all-you-can-drink mimosas. It's only a matter of time before our landlord hikes our rent so high we can't afford to live here anymore. And no college and no house is not a pretty equation.

As I round the next corner, I lower my head and prepare to walk the gauntlet of homeboys and hoodlums hanging out on a stoop two doors away. If they're deep into whatever club or girl or hot new track or illegal activity du jour, I can usually get by with barely a whistle. As I get closer, I see a couple empties in brown paper bags littering the stoop, and I know right away that tonight I won't be so lucky.

"Hey, girl, you wanna bring that pizza and that fine ass over here?"

"Mmm-hmm, hard to tell which I want to taste first." *Oh ick.*

There's a round of high fives and "aww yeahs." I can

feel the thudding in my ears again, the heat rising up my neck, but if I jump these guys like I did 22, it'll be the cops and not Coach Butler pulling me off. That's if the home-boys don't give me a concussion — or worse. Out here is not like the controlled, contained world of the rink. Out here it's the wild. Out here I have to control myself.

"Screw off," I mutter, and then double my pace until I'm past them. I hear the laughing and the catcalls until I've turned the next corner onto my street and slid my key into the lock on the front door.

Inside, I drop my skate bag at the bottom of the stairs and leave my keys on the table next to a pile of unpaid bills and take-out flyers. I don't hear the TV, so I call, "Dad!" He should be home from work by now.

"Kitchen," he calls back.

Dad's sitting at our little blue chipped Formica kitchen table. He looks tired, but that's not new. Ever since Mom left last month, I don't think he's slept at all. And if he is sleeping, I don't think it counts if it's on the couch in front of the television.

"We need to talk, Sloane," he says, and that's when I see that underneath the exhaustion, there's something else. The last time we had to *talk*, Mom was already gone for her ninety-day stint at Pleasant Meadows or Calming Breezes or whatever pseudo-cheery name the place is called. All I remember is the pamphlet Dad slid across the table at me. The front of it showed the name in loopy blue script over a picture of a pair of smiling people who looked nothing like the disaster my mom had become, having a picnic somewhere green that looked a world away from Philly.

"Yeah, okay," I say. I slide the pizza box out of the bag, then wad the bag in my fist. "Let me just pop this in the oven."

"The pizza can wait. Just sit down."

I leave the frozen pizza on the counter and slump down in the seat across from his, bracing for the news.

"Coach Butler called," he says, his voice gruff. "Says you got in a fight. Again. He said he suspended you starting next season."

I'm so shocked, I can only stare. Coach Butler never rats us out, not ever. Not when Julie Romer got a hornet tattoo on her lower back (though he made the nurse look at it to make sure it wasn't infected), not when he caught us in possession of Middlebury High's disgusting stuffed bulldog mascot (we had to take it back), and not even when Madeline Gray showed up to practice so hungover that she barfed on the ice during sprints (she had to do five morning makeups and sign a no-alcohol pledge). We trust Coach Butler. How could he do this to me?

"Sloane, I tolerate a lot from you." Dad sighs. He picks at a spot on the table where the blue Formica is so chipped that particleboard is starting to show through. "That hoodlum musician boyfriend, your middle-of-the-road grades. I let you get away with a lot, because you've got hockey. It's your ticket. You know we can't afford to send you to college. You won't go to college without it. I don't want that for you, and you don't want that for you, so what in the hell are you doing getting yourself suspended going into your senior year?"

"But she came at me! And that ref was totally from Liberty! He was biased!" It all comes tumbling out, all the words I can say to hide the ones I can't. I can't tell him about the tingles, not when he's just laid out all the repercussions of biting it in hockey. *Oh, sorry, Dad, it's just that I was so freaked out about not being able to hit the broad side of a barn with a four-square ball that I ended up tackling some blond bimbo from Liberty High. So you see, no big deal! Either way, my hockey career is over!*

As I'm rattling on about how I barely even touched her, Dad holds up his hand. "Save it."

"See? You don't even want to hear my side." I cross my arms over my chest and slouch further into my chair.

Dad ignores the remark. "Luckily, your coach is looking out for you, and he called with a suggestion," Dad says. "He thinks you need a change of scenery. One of his old college buddies runs a hockey camp up in Montreal, and he made a phone call on your behalf. You'll leave tomorrow. You finish the summer with a good report from this camp, you can start the season with your team next fall. No harm, no foul."

It's so much information, I don't know what to process first. I'm not benched? But I have to go to hockey camp? The coaches are going to see that I can't make a shot. I can hide it for maybe a week, but after that someone will notice.

And then that someone will call Coach Butler. They'll call Dad. And then I'm screwed.

But that's not what I land on first.

"I can't leave tomorrow!" I burst out. "It's *summer*. I have plans! I was going to apply for a job at the Freeze and save up. And I can't leave Dylan!" As soon as I say it, the part about Dylan, I realize it's hardly true.

"Fine, skip hockey camp. But you're not playing the start of next season. And the scouts aren't seeing you, and you've got a suspension on your record, and then college falls off the radar."

I shake my head, even though I know he's right. "I can't believe you're doing this to me."

"We make our own choices, Sloane," Dad says. "And frankly, you're lucky you've got a coach willing to compromise and make phone calls on your behalf."

"This is bullshit," I say.

"Knock it off, Sloane. Honestly, what would your mother say if she was here?"

"Well, she's not, because she obviously made *her* choices," I retort. "But you sent her away too, so I guess I shouldn't be surprised."

I see the pain start in Dad's eyes, then ripple outward like a stone disturbing the water. Immediately I feel guilty. He doesn't say anything, just stands up from his chair. He stares at me hard. "You've got a nine a.m. bus, so you better pack," he says, then walks out of the kitchen. I hear him shuffle up the stairs. A few minutes later his bedroom door slams shut.

I stomp back to the front of the house where I dropped my bag and dig my phone out of the front pocket. Because I don't know who else to talk to, I text Dylan, jamming on the keys so hard I worry my thumb is going to come out the other side.

Awful day. Need to talk asap.

I drag my bag up the stairs and into my room, then heave it onto my bed with enough force that the sound echoes my level of anger. I. Am. Pissed.

At the Vid with guys. Come out.

Great. He knows I don't have a fake ID, and even if I did, he knows I wouldn't go to the Vid and hang out while a bunch of his friends get trashed. Idiot. Life sure is a hot fudge sundae with a cherry on top, isn't it?

I pull my big black duffel down from the top of my closet and start throwing clothes inside, not even paying attention to what I actually need. A handful of sports bras, a couple of pairs of jeans, some jerseys, some T-shirts . . . Who cares? I'm not going to make it past the first week anyway. Maybe after they throw me out I can just hit the road, trade in my return ticket for somewhere warmer. Somewhere hockey doesn't even exist.

I hear the scritch-scritch of little feet coming up the stairs; then a fuzzy black face pokes inside the door. I jump up on my bed and pat my comforter. "C'mere, Zaps."

Zaps is the only good thing that ever came out of Mom's drinking. One evening, after finishing a bottle of some cheap red, Mom was flipping through the channels and saw one of those über-sad ASPCA commercials where a nineties pop starlet is warbling her old hit while pictures of abandoned and injured animals flash across the screen. Ten minutes later, Mom and I were on a bus to the local shelter, and less than an hour after that, we were getting out of a cab in front of our doorstep with Zaps, a terrier mix on a bright red leash. His name is actually Zapruder, after the guy who made that infamous Kennedy assassination film. Nerdy, I know, but it was Mom's choice. She loved history. Maybe she still does. It's hard to see where her affections lie beyond an empty glass or bottle.

Zaps jumps up on the bed and nuzzles my armpit, then starts furiously licking my face. "Down, boy!" I cry, but pretty soon I've dissolved into giggles. I can't believe I've got to leave this moppet behind tomorrow. Is Dad even going to remember to walk him?

Thinking of Dad brings back that awful guilty feeling. I shouldn't have accused him of sending Mom away. It was all her. She chose to become a drunk. She chose to drive after drinking not one but *two* bottles of wine. And it wasn't the first time, either. It wasn't even surprising when she finally hit something. Luckily it was just a city mailbox on the corner and not a small child on the sidewalk. Which means it was her choice to go to rehab, even if it seemed like the court didn't give her much of one.

She chose and she chose and she chose until she was gone.

I sigh into the scruff of Zaps's neck. Mom hasn't always

been like that, though the past three years have been so miserable that it seems like forever. She always enjoyed a glass of wine or two, but when I was in eighth grade she left her job teaching social studies at a magnet school in town to take care of Grandma Rosa, who had been diagnosed with lung cancer. It wasn't easy for Mom, leaving a job she loved to watch her mother get sicker and sicker. I didn't blame her when she drank . . . at first. As sad as I was when Grandma Rosa died last year, I was hopeful that maybe things would go back to normal. But at that point Mom was just too far gone. She couldn't get her old job back, and she couldn't get herself together to apply for something new. Everything went downhill fast after that.

I curl up on my pillow, hugging Zaps, until I've fallen asleep and am dreaming of somewhere far away from Montreal, far away from Philly, even. Somewhere far away from hockey and far away from home. Dreaming of being someone—anyone—other than me.

CHAPTER 3

SLOANE EMILY

We've reached the point of no return.

"Sloane, I want you to take this seriously. If you work hard, you'll get back everything you lost and then some. You're a beautiful, talented young woman, and I know you can achieve great things."

"Okay, Mom," I reply. I adjust my tote bag on my shoulder and look at the growing line at security. "I'll do my best."

"Good, better, best, never let it rest . . . ," Mom quips, her photo-op smile spreading across her face.

". . . until your good is better than your best," I finish. If the Jacobses have a family motto, that's it. Mom and Dad have been repeating it since I was five.

Mom puts an arm around my shoulder and sort of pats me on my back twice. Her version of a hug.

"Excellent. Oh, and your father wanted me to give you

this." Mom reaches into her ivory quilted Chanel handbag and pulls out a crisp white envelope from the office of Senator Robert Jacobs of Virginia. I look down at the envelope and see the seal of the commonwealth in the upper right-hand corner. The envelope is sealed, and he's signed his name across it like a recommendation letter.

"Have a wonderful summer," she says. There's a brief pause where I think she might try to hug me again, but instead, she just sort of pats me on the shoulder. We're not much of a hugging family. Encouragement toward excellence, yes. Public displays of affection? Not so much.

"Better be getting to your gate," she says finally. "Boarding starts in an hour, and the line is getting long."

"Okay," I reply. Another pause. "Bye, Mom."

I make it through security without getting felt up by the agents, then bolt for the bathroom. It's cavernous and bright white. The door slams behind me and the sound bounces off the porcelain and tile. There's only one other woman at the sinks, reapplying eyeliner. Her eyes flit over to me, then back to the mirror. I wheel my carry-on skate bag into the handicapped stall at the end of the row and do the little dance that's required to get all my luggage in with me and still get the door closed.

Once I'm closed in, I sit down on top of my suitcase and pull the envelope out of my tote. There could be a confession in here, or an apology . . . or both.

I run my index finger under the seal, tearing through his name, and my hands are shaking so bad that I give myself a paper cut. But when I get the envelope open, I don't find the confession I was hoping for. Or even an apology. In fact, there's no letter inside at all. Instead, there's just a fat stack of crisp fifty-dollar bills.

Confused, I flip the envelope over to see if there's anything I missed, maybe a message or a note. But all I see is my name scrawled across the front in heavy black ink from one of his fancy fountain pens. As I look closer, I realize that the handwriting isn't his. It's fat and loopy, like a woman's. He had one of his assistants prepare it. And the only other thing I can find is a note that he actually wrote himself, just under where his signature was on the back of the envelope. "For emergencies," it says.

I flip through the stack of bills again, counting quickly to myself. So a thousand dollars is what my dad thinks I need for *emergencies*. More likely that's what he thinks my silence costs. If only he knew that I'd be happy to keep my mouth shut for free. I have no interest in even *thinking* about what I saw in his office two weeks ago, much less talking about it.

I take a deep breath and count backward from ten. There's nothing more embarrassing than crying in an airport bathroom over daddy issues. Once I'm sure I'm not about to be the basket case of Terminal B, I put the money back in the envelope and shove it back into the tote as deep as it can go, this time not so I don't lose it, but so I don't have to think about it. One of the reasons I agreed to go this summer was to get as far away from my dad as possible. Now, knowing that that envelope is sitting at the bottom of my bag makes it feel like I'm carrying him around with me, or at least a heavy dose of his guilt. I'm not stupid enough to throw away a thousand dollars, but I'm not going to look at it if I don't have to.

"Out of sight, out of mind" is another one of my family's mottos.

♡ ♡ ♡

It will take me two planes, a layover in Toronto, a trip through customs, and one very shiny town car to get to the hotel where I'll be staying for my first night in Montreal. Move-in day at camp isn't until tomorrow afternoon, but my parents booked my flight for a day early. Mom claimed it was so I could have a day to relax from travel before diving in, but more and more I'm starting to think that Dad just wanted to be rid of me a day earlier.

I'm pissed. Totally pissed. Pissed because of what my dad did, pissed because I saw, and pissed that my father thinks he can give me an envelope of cash and get me to shut up, as if I'm one of those political gossip bloggers (who, from what I've heard, are very easily bought).

The hours of travel have done nothing to quiet the mass of misery whirling around inside my brain. All they've done is switch my anxiety gears from the past to the future, because the reality has started to set in: Skate camp. A comeback. Junior nationals. Ugh. I spend the car ride from the airport to the hotel coming up with creative yet totally impractical plans to break one of my legs.

The car pulls off the street into an overhang driveway crowded with bellmen speaking French. A young blond bellhop takes my hand and guides me away from the car onto the patio in front of the hotel. "Checking in?"

"Yes," I reply, and give him a slight smile. I'm exhausted, and I smell like airplane. I'm in no mood to flirt.

"Name? And perhaps your phone number?" The bellhop is giving me the kind of crooked grin that looks all too practiced. I scowl at him.

"Sloane Jacobs," I say, "and no." The bellhop chuckles as if I'm playing hard to get and scribbles on a luggage tag, which he affixes to the handle of my suitcase. He makes another for my skate bag, and then reaches to take my tote off my shoulder. I instantly think of the envelope of cash and pull back.

"No thanks," I reply, and grip the handle tighter. "I'll keep this one with me."

"I will personally make sure it arrives in your room," the bellhop says, in a way that makes it clear he's used to getting girls to hand over much more than their bags. He pulls on the handle, which slips off my shoulder, and the tote tumbles to the ground. A couple of books, my phone, and a collection of ChapSticks go skittering everywhere.

"I'm so sorry!" The bellhop's face loses all the confidence. He immediately goes into panic mode. He drops to his knees and chases after a tube of cherry ChapStick.

I reach down and snatch my bag, standing up so fast I

have to take a quick step back. My foot lands on something other than the ground. It's soft and lumpy and gives way underneath me. I feel my ankle wrench to one side, and I start to pitch backward.

My hand closes around a fistful of fabric, but it's only a temporary save. I'm on the ground, lying on top of some kind of oversized duffel bag that smells like a foot, while a dark-haired girl next to me is on her butt on top of my suitcase, glaring. She's wearing an oversized hoodie and loose jeans.

"What the hell?" She tosses her long black hair out of her face as she stands up, wincing.

"I'm sorry." I pick myself up, rotating my ankles to test for pain. "I was falling and—"

She cuts me off. "You didn't care who you took with you? Why don't you watch it next time?"

"I'm so sorry, it was an accident," I say. What is her problem?

"Whatever," she snaps, then shoots me a look that contains so much venom I'm shocked I don't fall over dead on the spot. Suddenly, with that look, all the exhaustion and anger of the day comes rushing into my chest. Even though every part of my brain is screaming at me to just turn around and let it go, the next words are out of my mouth before I can even stop them.

"Well, I wouldn't have tripped if you hadn't left your luggage on the ground. Seriously, who does that?" I say in my nastiest mean-girl competition voice. She doesn't even blink. Something tells me I'm not even close to the baddest person she's ever encountered.

She takes a step closer. I may be in over my head here. "*Most* people watch where they're going, princess."

"Well, *most* people are more mindful of others . . . jerkface."

"'Jerkface'? What are you, twelve?" she sneers.

I'm halfway tempted to deck her. Not that I really know how. But maybe getting in a catfight on the street will be enough to get me deported back to the States.

"*Mesdemoiselles*, can I help you?" A tall, thin man with a very silly, totally not-ironic mustache appears before us.

"I was just checking in when that girl knocked me on my—" the dark-haired girl says, just as I start speaking over her.

"Well, she just abandoned her bag on the sidewalk, and I—" I start to say.

The mustachioed man holds up a slender hand.

"*Mesdemoiselles*, let me help. My name is François, and I am your concierge. Please forgive my staff for creating this little pileup. I will send your luggage upstairs, and will be happy to treat you to dinner in the restaurant this evening. Just give Jeffrey here your names"—he nods almost imperceptibly at one of the bellhops—"and he will ensure that your bags are waiting for you and that the hostess has your name for your meal."

The bellman (luckily not the sleazy one) whose name is apparently Jeffrey steps up with a handful of luggage tags and looks expectantly at me.

"My bags are already tagged," I say.

"Then you can go right to the desk to check in," François says in a smooth voice. He gestures to the revolving door. I breeze past the other girl and push through the door without looking back.

CHAPTER 4

Sloane Devon

*D*ad drops me off at the bus station first thing in the morning. We haven't spoken since our fight last night, and standing in front of the shiny silver bus, I'm feeling more than a little bit sorry for what I said. But I'm even sorrier about where I'm heading. The fact remains that I can't play, and I have eight hours on a bus to think about it.

"I know this isn't what you wanted for the summer, but it'll be good for you," Dad says, as if he's reading my mind. Or maybe he's reading it all over my face. I never was good at hiding my emotions. I know he's thinking not just about my future, but also about Dylan. He's never liked him, not since the first time Dylan came over to dinner and called my dad "Pops." Dad's referred to him as "the Fonz" ever since, and that's when he's being nice. It's usually something closer to "hoodlum" or "greaseball," and sometimes just "that boy."

"Whatever," I mutter.

The driver opens the storage compartments, and my fellow passengers start shoving their bags in. Dad takes my gear bag and places it underneath along with my duffel, leaving me my backpack for the ride. I give him a nod, then turn to climb onto the bus. He grabs my arm.

"Sloane, please," he says. He looks exhausted. "Don't leave mad. We're all we've got."

I feel a lightness in my chest and the start of a lump in my throat, and I shake my head to suppress it. "Bye, Dad," I say.

"Wait. I have something for you," he says. He pulls out a folded twenty-dollar bill and presses it into my palm. I open my hand to see it unfold into five twenties. One hundred dollars.

"Dad, I don't need this," I say, trying to give it back. He presses it back into my palm, then wraps his hands around mine.

"For emergencies, Sloane," he says. "You're going to be in a foreign country. You never know."

Looking down at the folded bills makes me instantly sad. I know the cash is probably the last he's got until payday next week. I wish I had restocked the freezer with pizzas before I stomped out in a huff this morning.

"Thanks, Dad," I say, then give him an honest-to-goodness hug. I turn and climb the steps of the bus. I make my way halfway down the aisle to an empty row. I fling my backpack into the rack overhead and plop down in the window seat. I see my dad standing there in the crowd, hands in his pockets, watching me. I know he'll stay there until the bus finally pulls away.

By the time we get to Montreal, my legs feel like they've been infested with a thousand grasshoppers. The bus ride was *eight hours:* eight hours on a bus sitting next to a man who smelled like Robitussin and tuna fish. Eight hours listening to the girl in front of me yap her way through two cell phone batteries. Eight hours of pure, unadulterated transportation hell. Nine if you count the hour we spent at the border, where we all had to file off the bus and stand there while the border patrol made sure we weren't trying to smuggle in six pounds of amphetamines in our luggage. I almost wished I'd forgotten my passport, which until now I'd used exactly once, to attend a hockey tournament in Toronto. It doesn't even have any stamps.

The bus station is eleven blocks from my hotel for the night, but the thought of boarding another bus makes me stabby, so I opt to haul my gear bag, my duffel, and my backpack the rest of the way on foot. When I finally get to the hotel, I drag my bags through the maze of cars and limos, looking for the entrance along the vast stone façade. Already, I can tell this place is ten times nicer than anywhere I've ever stayed. My cousin Theresa is a concierge at the Westin in Philly, so she hooked me up with a room with the same company for almost nothing. All around me, bellhops in crisp uniforms dart from car to car, opening doors, smiling, taking bags off shoulders and depositing them on carts, but not one throws a glance my way. Typical. They can probably sense that I don't belong here.

My duffel starts to slip off my shoulder. By now, my shoulders are aching, so I drop my duffel, then start to ease off my backpack. I feel a hand tug on me. And before I know it, I'm going down. I land hard on my elbow and let out a grunt.

I look up to see a skinny, dark-haired girl in pristine clothes pulling herself up from the ground and brushing invisible dirt off her jeans.

"What the hell?" I toss my hair out of my face so I can get a good look at her.

"I'm sorry. I was falling and . . ." She trails off with a shrug. Like it was no big deal. She's not even looking at me. I see her rotate a thin ankle and rub a spot on her shiny gold flats.

"You didn't care who you took with you?" I say, finishing her thought. "Why don't you watch it next time?"

"I'm so sorry," she says. She finally looks at me, and I see a brief look of horror cross her face. I'm probably not looking so pristine after my eight-hour journey. "It was an accident."

"Whatever," I say.

"Well, I wouldn't have tripped if you hadn't left your luggage on the ground. Seriously, who does that?"

I can't believe it. Now *I'm* rude? "*Most* people watch where they're going, princess."

"Well, *most* people are more mindful of others . . .

jerkface." She looks so proud of herself, I can't help myself. I burst out laughing. What is this, the playground?

"'Jerkface'? What are you, twelve?" I'm half laughing, half shouting at her. I see the girl ball her hands up, but I know she won't do anything. She'd be too afraid to mess up her outfit. I could totally take her.

A stuffy bellhop—he must be the big cheese, because he's wearing a crisp black suit—interrupts us and starts ordering us around, snapping his fingers to get tags on our bags and directing us to our rooms.

When Miss Priss has finally made her exit, I slowly start to calm down. Jeffrey, a skinny, freckled, trembling bellhop who I could probably bench, shuffles closer to me.

"Your name, miss?"

"Sloane," I reply. "Sloane Jacobs."

"Okay, Miss Jacobs, I'll put these tags on your bags and have them sent up to your room," he says. "You can head through the doors to check in."

I wait a few beats just to make sure Miss Priss has had time to clear out and head up to her room—I have no desire to see her again. Then I head into the hotel and across the vast lobby floor. But with each step I feel a pain in my knee, just below the kneecap, zapping up the inside of my leg. By the time I'm at the door I'm practically limping. I know that pain. I've felt it after long workouts and particularly rough games, and even sometimes when it rains. It's left over from a nasty hit I took last season. Great. I'll have to take my delicious nap wearing my massive knee brace.

While the woman behind the counter types away in her computer to check me in, I shift my weight to my good leg and look around. An enormous crystal chandelier hangs over my head, and water rushes down the black stone wall behind the desk in some kind of silent water feature. Looks like I'm in for one night of peace and happiness before moving into the dorm at hockey camp and subsequently getting exposed for the big athletic fraud that I am, then slinking back to Philly for a future as a waitress with an anger management problem.

I know Coach Butler would be pissed if he knew that within an hour of being on Canadian soil, I nearly got into a fistfight with some pretty princess. There would be no hockey camp in my future then. Probably just jail. But maybe that would be better?

My room is on the fifth floor, and it is tiny. Like, *tiny.* It's actually about the size of my room back home, only my bedroom doesn't have a bathroom *inside it.* One whole wall is a window looking out onto the city, while the opposite wall makes up the sliding-glass door of a blue-tiled shower. The bedside table is glowing white and oddly shaped, and when I get closer I realize that the cover slides off to reveal the sink.

Despite the fact that it's the size and shape of a studio apartment in a tenement slum, the place still looks pretty amazing. Everything is white and blue, and the light shining from hidden fixtures makes it all look like I'm in a spa on a spaceship. The bed takes up most of the space, and just like I expected, it's crisp, white, and fluffy.

"Nap!" I cry out loud, then dive into bed, forgetting my knee until even the soft landing of my heaven-sent bed sends a shooting pain up my leg. "Ugh," I grumble into the comforter. "Find brace, *then* nap."

I roll over onto my back and pull my jeans up over my knee, which is unfortunately swelling like a water balloon and sporting the beginnings of an ugly purple bruise. Forget the knee brace, I need to wrap and ice this thing before it swells too big to get my pants on.

I gingerly climb out of bed, then hop over to the dresser, where I grab the blue Lucite ice bucket, then limp into the hall. I look left, then right, but I don't see anything providing any direction toward an ice machine. I choose left, away from the elevators, and hobble down the plush carpet.

I spot an alcove at the end of the hall and double my pace so I can return to my room, but in my frenzy for ice I don't notice a door open to my right. A modelesque woman in a little black dress, a good six inches taller than my five-foot-four-inch frame, strides out into the hall, barely looking in either direction. I have to hop out of the way to avoid yet another collision. Do none of these people watch where they're going?

"Excuse me," she says, giving the first word about four extra syllables. She says it in a way that implies there's clearly *no* excuse for me. I'm suddenly aware of the smell of musty bus air and stale Doritos that seems to be all over me. Before I can say anything, the model is gone.

I manage to get my ice without further incident. Returning to my room, I see my suitcase has at last been delivered. I unzip it and hold my breath, expecting the funk of my gear bag to come wafting out. But all the air rushes out at once when I see not my ratty old black and white hockey skates, but a pair of bright white figure skates. And from the smell of the leather and the shine of the blades, they're brand-new, or at least *really* well cared for.

"What the hell?" I say. Now I see that the duffel bag only looks superficially like mine. It's much newer and much nicer. I reach for the rolling suitcase, black like mine but without the peeling duct tape on the corner. It's also much newer and has about ten more pockets than mine has. I heave it onto the bed and unzip it to find not my favorite jeans or my stack of practice jerseys, but a collection of neatly folded and rolled garments made of a fabric that looks like it should be worn by pixies or woodland fairies.

Lots of pastels, gauzy materials, and even a few sequins. And unlike my bag, which smells like Irish Spring and athletic tape, this bag smells like it's been hanging out with whatever mythical creature wears the clothes inside it: fruity and floral and generally girly. I promptly break into a sneezing fit.

I throw the cover back over the suitcase to close it, then check the tag. It's got my name on it.

"Dammit, Jeffrey!" I mutter. The idiot must have switched the bag tags. The screechy girl from the lobby must have my bags. Great, and I was hoping to never have to see her again.

I go to grab the phone to call downstairs and again forget my knee, which wastes no time in reminding me that I landed on it wrong just half an hour ago.

I flop backward onto the bed. I close my eyes and take slow, deep breaths until the pain subsides. And then it dawns on me: you can't spend the summer playing hockey when you can't walk across your hotel room. For the first time all day, I feel comforted. Can't play hockey . . . because my *knee is injured.* Huh, maybe things finally are looking up. Maybe they'll even send me home. It's not too late to apply at the Freeze.

And at least Pretty Princess girl has to sleep with my stinky skate bag in her room. I twist up the plastic bag inside the ice bucket and tie it in a knot so I won't wake up in a puddle. I wince as I place the bag on my throbbing knee. Getting it back can wait. I snag one of the seven extra pillows from the other side of the bed, wedge it under my knee for some elevation, then promptly fall into the first peaceful sleep I've had in forever.

CHAPTER 5

SLOANE EMILY

"**M**a'am, I'm lost. What do you mean you don't play hockey?"

Deep breaths. Don't be rude. Kindness goes a long way. The desk attendant, whose shiny brass name tag reads "Monique," stares at me blankly from underneath a sweep of blond bangs. It's the first time she's actually looked at me. For the duration of this conversation, she's kept her eyes glued to the computer embedded in the desk. It's time to try a new tack.

"I know this isn't your fault. I'm just trying to explain what's going on, in an effort to get my own luggage back," I say. I smile and arrange my face in a categorically-not-angry-with-you expression.

"So you're saying you have Sloane Jacobs's luggage in your room?" The desk attendant narrows her eyes and wrinkles her nose as if I've just asked her to solve some kind of crazy logarithm.

"Yes," I reply.

"And you *actually* need Sloane Jacobs's luggage instead?"

"Yes," I say. I try to push my hair back from falling over my face. I wish I had a hair tie to secure it, but those are all in my *actual* luggage. "Look, maybe the bellhop swapped the tags. Or duplicated them. Or maybe there are two of us!"

"Two Sloane Jacobses?" She laughs at my bad joke. "I sincerely doubt that. Two Jane Smiths? Yes. Two Sloane Jacobses? No."

"Well, then you need to find the girl who checked in at the same time as me this afternoon, because she has my bags, which includes a very expensive pair of custom figure skates. She's about my height," I say, "and she has long dark hair and dark eyes."

"So she looks like you," she says.

"No. I mean, barely," I say.

"So *you* have my bags, then," a voice says behind me. I whip around and see the girl from earlier today, still wearing the black and orange hoodie with the weird logo on the front and what I assume are the same pair of baggy, holey jeans.

"And you are?" The desk attendant leans over the counter. This is probably the most excitement she's had all day.

"I'm Sloane Jacobs," she says, and if I were drinking anything, I'd do a spit take.

"*You're* Sloane Jacobs?"

"Yeah, and who are you?"

"*I'm* Sloane Jacobs," I say. I expect the girl to look surprised, maybe even pass out from shock, but she just frowns.

"Is this some kind of joke?" she asks.

"Does it seem funny to you?" I snap. Then I take a deep breath. "Look, can we figure this out? I'd really like to get my bags back so I can change out of these airplane clothes."

"Your name is really Sloane Jacobs?" She gives me an up-and-down assessment.

"She *does* look like you," the desk attendant says, still listening in.

"She looks nothing like me," the nasty girl says, and from the way she's eyeing me, I think it's an insult.

"Whatever, can I please have my bags?" I say. I'm already tired of this conversation. I was looking forward to tonight being a stay-in-and-veg-in-my-awesome-hotel-room before-I-get-thrown-to-the-wolves-tomorrow. This insanity is seriously cutting into my junk-food-and-movie time.

"Ladies, I see you've come down for your dinner." The squeaky, clipped voice of François cuts between us.

"We didn't —" I start to protest, just as Sloane says, "That isn't —"

But François ignores us. He glides behind the counter and leans toward Monique, who whispers in French. François nods almost imperceptibly, then steps back out from behind the counter. With some kind of smooth French Canadian magic, he takes us both by our elbows and leads us into the dining room.

He breezes past the hostess stand and guides us to a large table covered in a crisp white tablecloth in the corner of the room. A white light fixture hangs down over our heads, and I want to grab it, point it at this girl's face, and start interrogating her about the location of my bags.

"Please enjoy anything you'd like, compliments of the hotel," François says, and when I open my mouth to ask about my bags, he holds up a thin hand to shush me with all the experience of a man whose job is to cater to people's every whim. "Please accept my sincerest apologies for your luggage mix-up. While you are dining, I will have one of our bellhops switch your luggage. I do apologize for the inconvenience."

"Excuse me, but we're not together," the other Sloane says.

"I am so sorry, *mesdemoiselles*, I thought you knew each other," he says, looking from me to her. "Unfortunately, the restaurant is booked up for the night. This is the only table I have."

"Well, I'm starving," she says, and plops herself onto a chair. She glares at me, as though daring me to back down. Jerk. I hesitate for only a second.

"Me too," I reply. I take the empty chair across from her. I'll just call this practice for skate camp and step up to the challenge.

A waiter hurries over and puts oversized menus in our hands, and I realize that in all the confusion, I haven't eaten since I was on the plane. My stomach growls as I look over the dishes.

"Um, I can't read this menu. What is this, Spanish?" I peek over my menu to see Sloane glaring menacingly at hers, as if she could threaten English out of it.

"Well, it's an Italian restaurant, so the dishes are in Italian, and we're in Montreal, so the descriptions are in French," I say, trying to sound helpful, but from the way she glares at me, I realize I probably just sound snotty.

"Great, two languages I don't speak," she mutters.

"Two languages I do," I reply. "Well, one and a half. My Italian is rusty. I haven't used it since last summer, when my parents took me along on a trip to Rome."

"Gosh, I haven't visited Venice in years, so my Italian seems to have escaped me," she says, in what skips sarcasm and goes straight to nasty. She squints at the bottom of her menu. "*Tomate,* that's 'tomato.' I know that one. I just don't want to end up eating dog."

"I can help," I say. "What do you want to eat?"

"I don't know, spaghetti sounds good, I guess." This place isn't exactly a spaghetti-and-meatballs kind of joint, but I scan the pasta section for something she might like.

"Are you a vegetarian?"

"Hell no!" she says.

"Okay, okay, chill out," I reply, skipping over the leek confit entrée for her. The waiter sidles up just as I settle on dinner for the two of us.

"Bonjour. Qu'est-ce que vous voudrais aujourd'hui?"

"*Je voudrais les cavatelli al pomodoro et olive avec un verre d'eau, s'il vous plaît. Elle aura le pappardelle con polpettine di vitello al sugo di pomodoro et*—what do you want to drink?" I can't help but smile. My French is back after a momentary lapse. Madame LeGarde would be proud.

"Water's fine," Sloane says, avoiding my eyes.

The waiter nods, takes our menus, and hurries back to the kitchen to report our order.

"You ordered me dog, didn't you?"

"Spaghetti and meatballs, basically," I say. "But the meatballs are made of kitten. I hope that's okay." I fold my napkin in my lap. Across the table I see Sloane start to tuck her napkin into her shirt. The couple at the table next to ours, both dressed head to toe in sleek black, a giant diamond gleaming from the woman's left hand, shake their heads. I make a show of smoothing mine across my lap, and Sloane quickly drops hers into her lap too, a little red creeping into her cheeks. I pretend not to notice.

For a minute we sit in awkward silence. The waiter comes back with a pitcher of water and fills our glasses. "I was pretty freaked out when I opened my bag to find it wasn't actually mine," I say finally.

"That makes two of us," she says. She takes a gulp from her water glass, then sets it back on the table with a little too much force. Water sloshes over the side and pools on the table. A busboy appears out of nowhere and wipes it up. "I'm glad we're switching back before I actually have to wear anything in there."

"My clothes are cute!" I protest.

"Look at me," she says. She gestures to the logo emblazoned across her chest. "Do I scream 'cute' to you?"

"I guess not," I say.

"Discussion over. I'll get my bags back as soon as this meal is done."

More silence. Sloane busies herself looking out the window. I've never met someone more antisocial than she is. Finally, the waiter arrives and sets warm plates down in front of us. From the way Sloane dives in, it's clear I've made a good choice for her. We chew in silence for a few minutes before I can't take it anymore.

"So what's your middle name?"

She looks up midbite, only slightly confused. "Devon," she says.

"Well, at least *that's* not the same," I say. "I'm Emily, named after my grandmother."

"I don't know where Devon came from. I know my mom got Sloane from this old movie, *Ferris Bueller's Day Off*." A mini storm crosses her face, but as quickly as it came, it's gone.

"Sloane was my grandfather's name," I reply.

"You were named after your grandfather?"

"Family names are really important in my—well, in my family." Thinking of my family makes my stomach seize up.

"Why?" Sloane raises her eyebrows. "Are you royalty or something?"

"My dad's a senator," I say, and get the standard moment

of discomfort I feel every time I say it. The last thing I want to talk about right now is my dad's political career. There's a moment of silence. Sloane seems to sense my discomfort. I'm relieved that she changes the subject.

"So, I saw you have skates," she says. "You in Disney on Ice or something?"

"Figure skater," I reply, ignoring her sarcasm.

"And that's not the same thing?"

"Not even close," I say. "One's a sport and one's not."

"Are you kidding me? Figure skating's not a sport any more than synchronized swimming is."

"Well, I know plenty of Olympic athletes who'd disagree with you," I snap. "On both counts."

She just shakes her head, smirking. Seriously, I can't believe I share a name with this ray of sunshine.

"And you play hockey, I'm guessing?" I say. "At least, that's what the stench from your bag and your giant shirts says."

"Damn right," she says. "Now, *that's* a real sport."

"Right, because being one of twenty people whizzing around on the ice barreling into people is so high-pressure," I retort.

"Twenty? Have you ever *seen* a hockey game?"

"It was *hyperbole*. My brother played hockey in high school, so I've seen a few games. Doesn't look so hard to me."

"Oh yeah, definitely not as hard as skating around waving your arms and smiling for the camera."

"Maybe when you're five. More like a crowded arena, a spotlight on you, flinging yourself through the air, and trying to land on a blade thinner than a kitchen knife while a bunch of judges score your every move." Just saying it out loud makes the sweat start to form behind my ears, and I feel my pulse pick up a bit.

"Yeah, that's definitely easier than lining up for a game-winning shot in front of hundreds of people while four giant girls skate toward you as fast as they can with a singular goal of leveling your ass," she says. "I'd much rather face a bunch of judges than a bunch of hit men on ice."

"You couldn't last one day in my skates," I say.

"If I can't last a day in yours, I give you four minutes on the ice in mine. You'll pee your pants and cry for your mama after one check into the boards."

"Oh please, I'd much rather hide out on a team than spend my summer with all eyes on me," I say, and I realize I'm not just talking about skating. I reach into my bag and pull out the brochure for the Baliskaya Skating Institute of Montreal. The cover features a picture of the main dormitory. It's a gorgeous stone mansion with a terra-cotta tile roof and sprawling gardens in front, all surrounded by iron gates. The property is made all the more beautiful by its setting, smack in the middle of the city.

"Are you kidding me? You're spending your summer *here*?" She takes the brochure and gazes at the cover.

"Yep, four weeks." I sigh.

"I don't know why you sound so depressed. This place

looks amazing." She starts flipping through the brochure. Images of smiling skaters are interspersed with pictures of the dorm rooms and the dining hall. It looks like Harvard meets Hogwarts. She points at a photo of a room with two queen beds and an overstuffed chair by a bay window looking out over a lush garden. "Are you kidding me?"

"If you like it so much, why don't *you* go?" I say. "You seem to think figure skating is such a breeze, after all."

"Don't tempt me," she mutters.

I pick at my entrée, twirling pasta around on my fork. The brochure just reminds me of what will be expected in the next four weeks: perfection. And if there is anything I am not, it's perfect. I'll spend my summer falling on my butt while I attempt jumps I can't do anymore. I'll eat tasteless food in the name of fitting into yet another leotard. I'll pretend to be friends with the cutthroat competitors who are my fellow campers. I'll be reminded of three years ago, when I ate ice at junior nationals, ending my season and possibly my career.

A real dream. I'd give anything not to have to do it. I'd even —

And then it hits me. Like an elbow straight to the stomach.

"You could do it, you know," I blurt out.

"Yeah, right." She flips back to the page showing the dorm rooms and sighs. The next page shows a girl outfitted in red sequins and rhinestones, and Sloane starts laughing. "Can you imagine me in this?"

"Actually, I can," I say.

"What are you talking about?" Sloane stares at me.

I don't answer right away. The puzzle pieces are just slotting together in my head. Even though it sounds slightly insane, it could work. I look over at Sloane, with her long black hair, her athletic build. We are the same height. She can skate, we know that. So it's a different kind of skating — who cares? And if she fails, at least she figures out that it's not so easy. Everyone always thinks it's so easy to be me.

"We look alike. Even that desk attendant thought so," I say, as much to myself as to her.

Sloane blinks at me from the other side of the table, staring at me as though I've gone insane.

And maybe I have.

But the idea won't let go: Here it is. My chance to be somebody else for a bit.

My chance to switch.

CHAPTER 6

Sloane Devon

I get it now: This girl, this other Sloane, is totally, completely, and inarguably crazy. Not cuckoo-homeless-man-on-the-bus crazy, but crazy in a way only rich girls can be.

She can afford to risk her whole future on a whim, because there will always be someone to clean up her messes and pay for her mistakes (literally).

It doesn't sound half bad to me.

I look from the brochure to Sloane and back, and a little beat of temptation starts drumming in my brain. Figure skating is way easier than hockey. No one is trying to break your legs or bash your brains out when you're figure skating. There are no shots to take or miss, which means no tingles. And there are no scouts or coaches expecting me to be a hero, thus there's no way to fail.

I look up at Sloane Emily again. "You really think we could pull this off?"

She breaks into a huge grin. She must take my question for an agreement, because the next thing I know she's dragging me out of my chair—she's surprisingly strong—and up to her room to plot.

When we get to her door, Sloane bumps it open with her hip. Inside, she flings her purse onto the table, then turns around to face me. "You coming in?" she says.

The sight of the room before me stops me in my tracks. So this is what you get when you're actually *paying* for a room at a hotel like this. It's a giant loft space on the top floor, corner of the hotel, with everything in one oversized room. Floor-to-ceiling windows that have to be at least twenty feet high overlook the entire city. In one corner are two fluffy queen-sized beds like the one I have crammed in my teeny tiny room. In another corner, an L-shaped bank of couches faces a massive flat-screen TV. Partially hidden behind a privacy screen is a glassed-in shower large enough to host my entire hockey team, a Jacuzzi for nearly as many, and an expansive tile countertop with not one, not two, but *three* sinks. What do you even need three sinks for? And there's another massive television facing the Jacuzzi, so you can watch TV while taking a hot soak. The only thing this place is missing is a rapper, his entourage, and several bottles of expensive champagne.

Sloane heads straight to a mahogany cabinet near the couches and flings open the door to reveal a minibar that is anything but mini. The door of the cabinet is stocked with tiny liquor bottles, wine, water, and cans and jars of various nuts and other snacks. There's a glass-front fridge filled with sodas and sparkling water and beer. Sloane slides out a deep drawer underneath the fridge filled with enough candy to help a kindergartner achieve liftoff. It probably costs enough to send that kindergartner to Harvard. There are no prices on anything, but I can imagine. I remember the time my parents took me to New York for Christmas to see the Rockefeller Center tree when I was eight. We stayed at a Marriott in Times Square, and back then I thought it was a palace. I ate a jar of jelly beans from the minibar, and my dad nearly had a heart attack over the fourteen-dollar price tag. And that place wasn't even half as nice as this.

"Candy bar?" Sloane says. She riffles through the stock and pulls out a Butterfinger for herself.

"Snickers," I say, and she tosses a king-sized bar at me. "Aren't those things like, twelve dollars each?"

"It charges to the room, which charges to my parents' credit card, which means all of this is fair game."

"Won't they be pissed?" I ask, but I waste no time in peeling back the wrapper and taking a giant bite.

"My mom will be mad that I ate my weight in sugar, but Dad couldn't care less. Eat up—we'll need fuel to pull an all-nighter." For a second I detect a trace of bitterness in her voice, but it's quickly gone, and she breaks into a smile.

She throws a bag of Bugles at me, followed by a Coke in a glass bottle. Then she kicks off her shoes and settles into the corner of the couch.

"Now let's talk terms."

"Terms? Okay, Senator," I reply. I plop down next to her, not bothering to remove my sneakers before propping them on the oversized ottoman.

"Hey, if we're going to do this, we're going to do it right," Sloane says between mouthfuls of candy bar.

"I don't even think we've established that we're definitely *going* to do this. And there's pretty much no 'right' way to pretend to be someone else while spending a summer participating in a sport you've never played, in which the other person is supposedly a pro."

"False," she says. She pulls the last of the Butterfinger out of the wrapper, pops it into her mouth, then reaches for a sleeve of Reese's Cups. "We are both excellent ice skaters. Our skills just lie in different areas. And everyone at this camp knows I've been out of the game for three years. I—I mean *you*—are going to be rusty. If you're as good as you say you are at hockey—"

"Hey, I'm good," I snap, but almost immediately I start to feel a tingle in my shoulder. I shake it off. "I can skate."

"Well, to get good at hockey, I imagine you have to be a hard worker. You have to take feedback and listen to your coaches. And you can do all that at my camp, and who knows, maybe there are some latent figure skating skills hiding underneath those baggy clothes."

"I doubt it," I say.

"I'll be the judge of that," Sloane says.

"Aren't you forgetting something?"

"What?"

"Uh, how am *I*"—I gesture to myself—"supposed to get mistaken for you? Aren't all those skater girls going to see through me in a second?"

"I've been out of the game awhile," she says. She pulls out her laptop. "Let's just say I've changed." She opens iPhoto and scrolls through to some old pictures of herself in spandex on the ice. She double-clicks on one, making it full-screen. I practically leap back.

"Jeez! Plastic surgery much?" I lean back in, squinting at the tiny face, trying to find some of the dark-haired beauty in front of me.

"No," she snaps. "Just puberty, braces, and a decent haircut, thankyouverymuch. Now back to business."

For the next hour, Sloane teaches me the basics of figure skating. She pulls out her shiny MacBook and plays YouTube videos of her old programs. She makes me raise my arms, then molds them into what she calls "ballet arms," with my fingers all raised and sculpted like it's teatime or something. I feel ridiculous. But every time my arms droop, Sloane Emily slaps me on the back and tells me to tighten up. I listen to the music for her long and short programs on a continuous loop, and when I think I'm about to pull my hair out from hearing *Madame Butterfly* one too many times, we switch to a hockey tutorial.

I clear off the desk, and using the mini liquor bottles, I show her the positions and set up plays. I tell her about practices, training, and drills. I demonstrate some of the basic hockey skills off skates, and I even pull up some clips of old Flyers games on YouTube. By three a.m., we've devoured nearly the entire contents of the candy drawer, sampled all the nut varieties, and polished off the sodas. All we're left with now is the sparkling water, which tastes gross to me, and the unopened bottles of liquor, which she doesn't offer and I definitely avoid.

"I think I'm going to be sick," she says. She drops a wadded-up Skittles bag on the floor, then lines it up with my hockey stick to practice her slap shot into the over-turned trash can.

"I told you to stop with the king-sized bag of peanut butter M&M's, but you wouldn't listen," I say. I'm clicking through old videos of Olympic programs, watching Tara Lipinski and Sarah Hughes grin and spin their way to gold medals.

"Ugh, don't mention candy." She shanks the bag to the left, where it bounces off the desk chair and rolls under the minibar. "Damn," she mutters. She uses the end of the stick to rescue the Skittles bag and takes a second shot. This one lands squarely inside the trash can. "Yippee!" she shouts, jumping up and down with the hockey stick hoisted over her head, then falls backward onto the bed in victory. "Did you see that? I did it!"

"Sloane, you're going to need to dial back the perky about six notches if you want to make it in a hockey game. 'Yippee'? Are you kidding me? No one, and I mean *no one*, is cheesin' out there on the ice. That's how you lose your teeth."

"I can be tough," she says, and I can't contain the snort. "I *can*!"

"Then let me slap you in the face."

"What? No!"

"C'mon, let me slap you in the face." I march up to her and lean over, hands on my hips.

"Why?" She shields her face with a pillow in case I launch some kind of sneak attack.

"My teammates and I do it all the time before games. Most people freak out about contact sports because they're afraid to get hit. They work it up in their brain that getting hit is awful and unbearable, but it's really not that bad. And when you get slapped in the face, it sort of recalibrates your toughness."

"You're crazy." She throws the pillow at me. I bat it to the floor.

"And you're doing it," I say. I grab her by the shoulders and pull her up, then position her right in front of me. "I'm not going to make you bleed or anything, I'm just going to give you one good slap, okay?"

She takes a deep breath. "Okay," she says. I raise my hand, but as soon as it's near my shoulder, she flinches and ducks.

"Hold still!" I scold, but I'm laughing. "I can't believe in the cutthroat world of ice dancing or whatever that you've never been slapped in the face."

"Figure skating," she corrects. "We're much classier. Hence, no face slapping. Just do it."

"Okay." I smile; then *I* take a deep breath to prepare, but she closes her eyes and shouts, "Now! Now! Do it now!" so I haul off and slap her. I don't give it everything I've got, but it's enough that the palm of my hand stings a little. Her eyes open, then grow wide. For a minute, I worry she's going to cry, or maybe even slap me back. But I watch the smile grow until her entire face cracks and she's got the most insane case of the giggles I've heard this side of first grade.

"Don't tell me I slapped you silly," I say, watching her, now crumpled on the floor, clutching her stomach and gasping for breath. But within seconds, I'm laughing too, and we're both down on the floor in a heap of oversugared teenager. It takes a few minutes before we've caught our breath and righted ourselves, climbing back up onto the beds until we're facing each other.

"Oh hey, you've got a scar on your chin like I have," she says. She reaches out and runs her finger along the thing, a two-inch mark on the left side of my chin that runs vertically down underneath it. "Is that from hockey?"

"No, that's from my mom's mean old cat, Lenin. I tried to pet the damn thing when I was nine, and this is what I got."

"Lennon like the Beatles?"

"Like the Russian revolutionary. Mom was—is—a history nerd." She raises an eyebrow and tilts her head, trying to read my verb tense slip-up, but I don't give her a chance to ask. "What about yours?" I say quickly, to change the subject. "Did someone Tonya Harding you?"

"Nothing that glamorous. I fell off a platform when I was eleven. My father was giving his acceptance speech after his second election victory, and I got bored with all the thank-yous and God Bless Americas. My mind started to wander, I lost my balance, and down I went."

"Seriously?" I try to contain a little giggle. "*Please* tell me that's on YouTube somewhere."

"Thankfully no," she says. She looks down at her hands, which are folded neatly in her lap. She's quiet for a moment. "I'm very good about staying out of the shot."

"So matching scars," I say in an effort to cut the tension. "Any other injuries?"

"Of course. Skating is completely brutal on your body."

"Probably not as brutal as skating and having a big, burly German milkmaid of a girl come hurtling at you at Mach five. See my nose?" I face her straight on. "See how it slopes down and then, just after the bridge, sort of curves off to the right?"

"Holy crap, it's crooked like a mountain road," she says. She leans in and grabs my chin, turning my head to the left, then to the right. "I'm pretty sure any half-decent surgeon could fix that."

I pull away. "Never. It's a badge of honor. I took a puck to the face freshman year." I smile proudly and then tilt my head up so she can get a better view of the corresponding bump. "Bled like a fountain, but they had to drag me off the ice kicking and screaming. I still have the jersey in my closet. It looks like an autopsy. Beat that."

"Okay, how about this?" She stands up and drops her pants. I cover my face with my hands.

"Whoa, whoa, princess! I'm not into that!"

She slaps my hand away from my face and says, "Look."

On the side of her right thigh, just below her hip, is a blooming black and purple bruise so large I couldn't cover it with one hand. As it spreads out around her leg, it starts to turn red and blue, with a nasty red scrape slashing through the middle.

"Bar fight?" I ask.

"Triple lutz," she says. She takes my hand and rubs it over the bruise. "Can you feel that?"

The skin is hard, taut, and swollen, like her leg swallowed a softball. "Gross," I say, and jerk my hand away. "What, are you going to hatch baby spiders out of that thing?"

"Ew! Now that image is going to be with me forever!" She pulls up her pants and flops back down on the bed, but this time I notice she lands favoring her left side. "That is a hematoma. I've landed on my butt so hard so many times in that exact place, trying to get my triple back, that my leg has moved past a simple bruise and has started to collect blood and scar tissue underneath my skin. Cute, huh? That's going to look great in a bathing suit."

"Will it go away?"

"Yeah, once I stop biting it on the ice and jump like I used to," she mutters. She runs her hand absentmindedly over the bruise, now hidden by her sweats. Her brow furrows and her mouth moves ever so slightly, like she's giving a silent "I'm disappointed in you" speech to an invisible friend. I study her for a moment. She catches me staring and I quickly look away.

"Okay, okay. Listen to this." I lean my face in close to her ear. I open my mouth wide, then close it, open and close, like a fish gasping for breath, but the only sound is the cracking in my jaw. I don't know what it sounds like to her, but inside my head it's like someone's snapping No. 2 pencils in half over a firecracker.

"Ew, what's that from?"

"Seventh grade, middle school regionals, I took a shoulder right to the jaw. Dislocated, then wired shut for two weeks. Didn't break, but it's clicked like that ever since."

"Well, if you want to talk chronic injuries, how about this?" She throws her right leg onto my lap, peels off her sock, and then waggles her foot in front of my eyeballs. On the ball of her foot, just above her arch, is some kind of big, hard, scaly growth the size of a bouncy ball, one of the ones that cost *two* quarters, not one. I swat her foot away from my face.

"What in the hell is that thing?"

"That's my creature," she says with a wicked smile. "I think at this point it's a blister under a callous under a scar. I've had it pretty much my entire skating life. That's with me until I retire, my friend, and maybe even longer than that. Try strutting around in strappy platform sandals with that on your foot."

"That's worse than my grandma's bunions. You're gross. Have you named that thing?"

"Maybe I'll call it Devon." She giggles. "So do I win?"

"I'd say it's a draw. And you're still going to have to learn to take a hit if you want to last a day in my skates. I play full-contact figure skating, dude."

"Yeah, and you're padded up like a crash-test dummy. All that's separating me from injury is a pair of suntan tights and some rhinestoned Lycra. P.S.? Landing on a rhinestone is freaking painful."

"Hey, how do we handle the parentals?" I ask.

"What do you mean?"

"I mean, if your dad calls or something, what do I say? What do you call him? I mean, if anyone's going to be able to bust us, it's our parents."

"You don't need to worry about that," she says. Her face wrinkles into a frown. "I highly doubt my father will be calling."

Her tone tells me that this conversation is over. I guess if she's wrong, I'll just dodge the calls.

"Well, if *my* dad calls," I say, "just grunt about your knee and agree with whatever he says about the Phillies. And *don't* call him Pops."

"Uh, yeah," she says, looking at me sideways. "Not a problem."

"So . . ." I stare at her. A combination of excitement and nerves is bubbling in my chest. "Are we really doing this, then?"

She raises an eyebrow at me that is more of a challenge than any words she could have come back with. She may be prim and pretty, with a suitcase full of spandex and gold blades on her skates, but something about *this* Sloane means business in a way I'm not even sure I'm prepared for.

But I'm also not prepared for hockey camp, so at this point, I'll follow Sloane into the dark.

♡ ♡ ♡

The next morning I wake up in a pile of wrappers and crumbs. My mouth tastes like a three-day-old carnival. Through my sleepy haze I spot a half-empty Coke on the bedside table and reach for it. I take a swig, ignoring the syrupy flat flavor. At least it's better than the fiesta of potato chips and chocolate that's hanging out in my mouth. *Must. Find. Toothbrush.*

"Good morning, Sloane Devon, you ready to go glam?" Sloane Emily's voice echoes through the room from her position in the middle of the floor; she's wearing a hot-pink crop top and black stretchy pants, and is contorted into a pretzel on a hot-pink yoga mat.

I fling the comforter over my head and mumble, "How in the world are you awake right now?"

"Force of habit," she says, though her voice sounds strange, and when I peek out from under the covers, I see it's because she's on her stomach, her arms grabbing her legs over and behind her so that her body makes a circle. Just looking at it makes my stomach churn. "Years and years of five a.m. ice time sort of screws with your internal clock. You'll learn."

"Dear God, I've made a huge mistake." Coach Butler only runs Saturday morning practices as punishment if we're goofing off, and even then those usually don't start until nine a.m.

"Get up, sleepyhead!" she says, leaping up and bounding over to the bed. "You need to get showered and get Sloane Emily–fied. You can't wear that hoodie to figure skating camp. The jig will be up before you even walk through the door. I laid out some clothes for you and grouped the rest of my things in my suitcase by outfit to help you. Oh, and I took the liberty of swapping out our underwear, because while wearing your jeans is fine, wearing your skivvies is, well, skeevy."

"You're talking too much," I reply, burrowing further under the covers. I regret having given her the key to my room. "And too fast. One-word sentences until after I've had some coffee."

"Get up!" she cries, flinging the comforter off the bed. *She's just like Mom.* As soon as I think it, I feel a sharp pain in my gut that's enough to rouse me out of bed. I shoot Sloane a look, then shuffle off toward the shower. "I'll order some breakfast from downstairs. Eggs or pancakes?"

"Both," I say. I'm going to need some serious grease in my stomach to get through this.

Two hours, two fried eggs, four strips of bacon, a pile of home fries, and a short stack of pancakes later, and I'm wearing an outfit that would make my hockey team pee their pants laughing.

"Are you sure about this? I mean, no one there knows you, right? It's been three years since you competed. I could wear whatever I want."

"No one is going to believe for one hot second that I would wear *anything* in your suitcase, whether they know me or not." Sloane Emily winds a gauzy lavender scarf loosely around my neck, then steps back to give me room to check it out in the full-length mirror. I'm wearing black capri leggings (an item of clothing I didn't even know existed) underneath a gauzy gray miniskirt, topped with a cream-colored silk camisole. And when I complained about feeling naked, Sloane Emily gave me the "scarf," which appears to have the consistency and color of cotton candy and does nearly nothing to hide my chest, which is attempting to make a break for it.

"Okay, so you're a little chestier than I am, but that's not a big deal," she says, adjusting the scarf slightly over my boobs. "Once you're on the ice you'll be able to wear your own sports bras."

"You are definitely getting the good end of this deal," I say. Next to me, she's wearing my favorite pair of black Bermuda shorts with a white T-shirt and my yellow Jefferson High zip hoodie on top.

"Please, I look like a juvenile delinquent. The only thing this ensemble is missing is a can of spray paint," she says. "And wait until you see where you're staying. I'm pretty sure it's going to be nicer than the dorms at the University of Montreal. I mean, you'll probably have your own room. Now hurry up." She grins at me. "Your car is waiting downstairs."

François must have the morning off, which is a good thing just in case he's as observant as he is accommodating. He'd definitely notice something weird about Sloane Emily struggling under the weight of my gear bag while I stroll through the lobby with one rolling suitcase and a tiny (compared to my own) skate bag.

Sloane Emily was right: My car is waiting for me. Only it's not just a car. It's a limousine. I nearly drop her—I mean *my*—skates.

"Nice doing business with you, Sloane Jacobs," Sloane Emily says. She nods her head toward the limo to confirm that it is, in fact, for me. Why she'd turn this down in exchange for a city bus to a university dorm is beyond me. That girl must have something else going on. Whatever it is, I don't want to know about it. I'm happy doing her a favor by taking all this luxury off her hands.

"You too, Sloane Jacobs," I reply. We shake hands in that hokey, too-hard kind of way that looks like we're starring in a remake of *West Side Story* and negotiating a truce, not executing a plan that could get us thrown out of the country and grounded for the rest of our natural lives. But it's too late to back out now.

A chauffeur in a suit and jaunty little black hat hurries out of the driver's seat and around to the back door. He opens it, then steps aside and does that "This way, *mademoi-selle*" gesture I've only ever seen in the movies. Only this is real, and it's for *me*. I'm *that* Sloane Jacobs now. I give Sloane Emily one last wave, then climb into the car and end up bear-walking across the leather seat. By the time I've gotten settled, she's already heaved my hockey bag onto her shoulder and is making her way toward the bus stop.

Despite all our scheming, our pep talks, and one hard slap to the face, I'm not sure she'll last even one day in my shoes. I'm not sure I'll last that long in hers, either.

CHAPTER 7

SLOANE EMILY

A bus, dirty with road grit, pulls up and shudders to a stop. I climb aboard behind a tiny old lady dragging some kind of wire cart filled with cans of tomatoes. She taps her ratty old wallet on the fare box, then shuffles down the aisle. I drop in the two coins I've been clutching since Sloane counted out the bus fare for me this morning, then glance at the driver to see if there's anything else I'm supposed to do. He just scowls at me. I take that to mean I'm good to go. I grab a seat toward the front of the bus next to a tired-looking middle-aged woman in a rumpled business suit. She sniffs a couple of times, then gives me a dirty look and moves to a seat on the aisle. I don't blame her. Sloane Devon's hockey bag smells like sweat socks that have been marinated in pickle juice, then sun-dried in a swamp.

An old man starts to make his way down the aisle, then stops and stares at me long and hard. For a moment I think he's going to point a long, thin finger at me and shriek, "Imposter!" But then I see him look down at the seat next to me, where I've set one of my bags.

"Oh, sorry," I say, and pull the tote into my lap. I readjust, crossing my ankles and sitting up straight like I've been taught. I gaze around the bus to check out my fellow passengers. Across the aisle, a guy in a ball cap is fast asleep, leaning against the window, his mouth wide open. A few seats back, a teenage boy slouches down low in his seat, legs splayed out into the aisle. A woman in front of me has her head in her lap, her long brown hair cascading down around her knees.

I can't remember the last time I was on a bus, other than for a school function. It's exactly as gross as I'd always imagined.

With each bump down the street, I relax a bit. I lean back against the seat. I uncross my ankles and position my feet on the floor in a wide stance, letting my knees fall apart a little to make room for the tote. I can practically hear my mother hissing in my ear: "Sloane Emily Jacobs, sit up straight!"

But she's not here. I'm on a public bus in Montreal, on my way to play hockey for four weeks. I can sit however I want, and no one is going to tell me otherwise.

This is going to be the greatest summer ever.

Four stops later, the bus doors spring open and a tall boy who looks to be the human embodiment of a sheepdog gets on. His walk is confident, and he's smiling, as though mounting a cramped and smelly bus is the best thing to happen to him all week. He's got shaggy chestnut hair that, with some styling product and half an hour with a blow-dryer, could be sculpted into a decent-looking Bieber. It appears he's more in favor of the effortless-dude style that involves a hand towel and a stiff wind.

He ambles down the aisle and plops down next to me, in the seat the businesswoman with the sensitive nose vacated. I try to casually scope him out without actually turning my head: cute nose, perfectly upturned with an almost imperceptible sprinkle of freckles. Nice jaw. Long lashes.

He looks at the stinky duffel at my feet, then back at me. He breaks into a wide grin, and I notice a tiny gap between his front two teeth, creating a tiny archway into his mouth (ever since my own orthodontia adventure, I tend to pay a little too much attention to other people's teeth). His crooked smile falters a little, and it's at that moment that I realize I've gone from inconspicuous glancing to full-on staring.

"Hockey?" he says, gesturing to my bag.

"No, I uh—" I start, but then quickly slam my mouth shut, because I'm about to tell him that I figure skate. Jeez, very first test and I already fail. I hope Sloane Devon is doing better. I clear my throat and then continue, hoping he doesn't notice the moment of split personality. "Yeah, I play hockey."

"Nice," he says. His grin returns. "So based on the

luggage and the fact that you're on the eighty-six bus, I'm guessing you're on your way to Elite as well?"

I recognize the name of my destination, Junior Elite Hockey Camp and Training Center, from last night's briefing with Sloane Devon. "Yeah," I reply. *Excellent, a right answer.*

"Awesome! Me too." He raises his hand, and it takes me a couple of seconds before I realize he wants a high five. He puts a little heat behind it, and I rub my stinging palm on the leg of my jeans. Hmm. Sloane Devon warned me hockey players like to get physical. But maybe that's a good thing. It didn't even occur to me that in escaping my heinous, glittery summer I'd meet hockey hotties. "I'm Matt. Matt O'Neill. So, where are you from?"

"Sloane Jacobs," I reply. "Philadelphia." Two more right answers (though to be fair, the name one isn't going to be too difficult). I'm doing a happy dance in my head. I mentally keep a tally of my points. Maybe this won't be so hard after all.

"Shut up, same here!" he says. I nearly choke on my own tongue. "Where do you live?"

Oh crap. I can't screw this up now, I just got here! I feel the same metallic taste on my tongue that comes right before I attempt a triple-triple, which makes the hematoma on my leg throb a little. *What did she say again?* I rack my brain. *Something with . . . food? Meat? Oh, fish!*

"Fishtown," I say, letting out the breath I've been holding. I hope I sound as cheerful as I did when he first sat down.

"Sweet, I'm in Chestnut Hill," he says. He's looking at me as if this should mean something. I give him a weak smile. I've been to Philly exactly once, when my sixth-grade class visited the Liberty Bell and Independence Hall. Beyond that, it was usually nothing more than an Amtrak stop on the way to one of Mom's New York shopping trips. If I'm going to survive this conversation, I should probably just shut my mouth now. But Matt's having none of it. "Where do you go to school?"

"I'm at Jefferson," I reply. Thank goodness last night's sugar high doesn't seem to have damaged my memory. "You?"

"Riverside Prep," he says. He gives a sort of lopsided smile and shrugs. Damn, he's cute.

I recognize the name from the small circle of elite private schools in the mid-Atlantic region. He's cute, and clearly smart if he's at Riverside. I look over to see him smiling that easy smile at me, and my stomach does a mini somersault. I quickly focus on the strings on my oversized hoodie, wishing I were wearing something a little cuter, or at least something that *fit*. But I push the thought out of my mind. I don't need that kind of distraction this summer. Besides, a boy as cute as Matt probably has a million girlfriends, or a million girls who *want* to be his girlfriend. I've always avoided relationships, partly because between all my practices I'd never have time, and partly because high school boys are dogs who could use a healthy dose of Cesar Millan.

"We've probably seen each other at tournaments," Matt says. My hands go instantly cold. My stomach feels jumpy, like I'm about to go over the first hill of a roller coaster.

"Maybe," I say. The word comes out too sharply.

He throws an arm around the back of my seat so that he can turn and get a better look at me. "Did you play at the All-East Invitational?"

"Uh, no," I say. "I was sick."

"Too bad, that tournament was rad. What about the charity thing for Children's Hospital?"

"Nope," I say. I keep my eyes locked on my knees. I can only say no so many times before he gets suspicious. Can't he just stop asking?

"Did you guys make all-city champs last year?"

This one I don't even respond to, because there's definitely a right answer to it that I don't know. Instead, I choose to stare at my nails, which could really use a touch-up after last night's hotel hockey practice.

The bus shudders to a stop, the doors swish open, and another line of passengers files on. A petite blonde in a low-cut tank top skips by, and I watch Matt's eyes follow her down the aisle. At least the distraction gets him to shut up. *Saved by the blonde.*

For the rest of the ride, I mostly ignore Matt. He chatters here and there about Philly, asking me if I've been to some place called Geno's or if I know this guy or that coach. I try to give half answers or vague shrugs, but my lack of attention only seems to make him chattier.

While he talks, I mentally study, preparing myself for my arrival at Elite. When the bus finally stops at our dorms and Matt jumps up, I hustle to gather my bags and follow him. I know from reading the brochure last night that all the players will be in the same building, single-sex by floor. The doors to the dorms are flanked by red and white balloons. Inside, Matt bypasses the check-in table, but not before high-fiving the girl sitting behind it. She smiles at him as he heads straight for the elevators. He stops short and turns.

"It was nice meeting you, um—what was your name again?"

"Sloane," I say. I feel a little pinch in my gut.

"Right, Sloane." He smiles. "I'll see you around."

I give my name to the girl at the table, a fierce-looking blonde in a red T-shirt with ELITE emblazoned across her sizable chest.

"I'm Mackenzie," she says. She runs her finger down the list, then uncaps a yellow highlighter with her teeth and sweeps it across my name.

"Oh, you're from Philly too!" she says, a big smile on her face, and my stomach drops. *Not again!* "You must know Matt."

My stomach stops doing somersaults when I realize *she's* not from Philly. Thank God. "I just met him on the bus," I say, thankful that at least in this instance, I can tell the truth.

"So cute, right?" Mackenzie sets about gathering various

sheets of paper and envelopes and folders for me. "This is his second summer. He totally dominates. On the ice *and* off, if you know what I mean." She winks at me.

"Sure," I say. Ew. *Dominates?* What is this—a rodeo?

Mackenzie throws a glance at the elevators, as if Matt might reappear. Then she leans forward.

"You're new. That means it'll be your turn soon enough," she says. Double ew. I wonder when *her* turn was. I make a private vow: no more looking at or speaking to Matt this summer.

Ten minutes later, I'm standing outside a door marked with the number 214 on an ancient brass plate, holding my key, an orientation guide, a list of emergency contacts, and a camper directory in my hand. I fit the key into the lock and wiggle it a bit before it will turn. The lock clicks and the heavy door swings open into a linoleum-tiled common room. There's a love seat made of something green and flame-retardant and a wooden coffee table that looks like three generations of students have used it for a footstool.

I knew hockey camp would be a downgrade in the ac-commodations department, but I didn't quite expect *this.* For a moment, I imagine my room across town, with the fluffy queen beds and private bathrooms. Then I remind myself what I'm getting in exchange. Sure, this isn't as nice, but I won't have to spend my summer having strangers judge me, whisper about me, and laugh every time I screw up.

I'd sleep in a prison cell for that deal.

Off the main room are two doors. I go to the one on the left, closer to me, and push it open. I'm pleasantly surprised to find a sun-drenched room with a single bed and a giant bay window along the back wall. And the sheets look brand-new (at least, that's what I'm going to tell myself). I throw my bags on the bed and hurry over to the window, which overlooks a lush green park across the street. I slide the window open and poke my head out, taking a deep breath of fresh air.

I feel good. I know my name, this room seems cozy, the view is great, and no one here expects me to land an axel of any kind.

A door slams, jolting me out of my reverie. It startles me enough that I jump and smack my head on the window frame. I hear someone enter the room. A shadow falls over me, and the hairs on my arms stand up straight.

"Get out."

I turn around slowly and see a girl at least a head taller than me. In her Under Armour, she looks muscled enough to bench-press me, and maybe the other Sloane too. Two long blond braids hang down over her thick shoulders, the least cute pigtails I've ever seen on anyone. With her muscular arms and Heidi braids, she looks like the angry German milkmaid type Sloane warned me about.

I gulp. "Uh, I'm Sloane," I say, but she doesn't even blink. "I don't understand."

"I'm Melody, and this is my room," she says.

"Aren't the rooms the same?"

She finally blinks and lets out a tiny snort. "Yeah, same, except this is mine, and that"—she waves her hand over her shoulder—"is yours. Out, New Girl."

"Um, I was here first," I say, but I hear it come out more as a question than a declaration, and my voice sounds impossibly tiny and airy. Maybe it's that I'm wearing someone else's life that doesn't quite fit, but my usual composure has abandoned me. Any shred of it flees for good once Melody takes a giant step toward me, and I have to tell myself that it's just my imagination that she grows three feet taller.

"I've been coming here for three summers, and this has *always* been my room." If I weren't already up against the window, I'd take a step back. As it is, I consider leaping out the window. "But hey, if you want to *earn* the room, you're welcome to try."

In an instant, everything from a fistfight to some sort of terrifying hazing ritual flashes through my mind. And here I thought Tonya Harding was scary. I take my bags off the bed and try to look like I'm leaving because I can't be bothered and not because I'm worried I'm going to pee my pants.

I'm barely through the door before it slams hard behind me. I cross over to what is apparently my room. I nudge the door open with the rubber toe of Sloane Devon's sneakers. One step and a quick visual sweep of the room and I know right away why the room across the hall is worth fighting for.

This one is about half the size of the other one. I hold my

arms out: I can touch both walls at the same time. I squeeze by the twin bed and make my way to the window. It's almost too narrow for me to fit my head through, and thanks to the giant tree growing just inches away, not a sliver of light comes in.

I sigh and flop down on my bed. *I know my name. I know my name.* I repeat it over and over like a mantra, and when that doesn't ease the tension in my neck, I switch to *No triple axels. No triple axels.* Through the wall (which is way too close to my head) I hear a toilet flush so loudly it sounds like a small child could get sucked through it. Then a faucet turns on, loud as a fire hose. Apparently, my neighbor is the floor's community shower. Excellent. At least I won't have to walk very far to brush my teeth. And my roommate can protect me in a bar fight, assuming she didn't start it in the first place.

To take my mind off the hulking barbarian next door, I roll over and riffle through the bag on the floor until I find my phone. I slide my finger across the screen to check my messages and see a little red circle with a one in it to indicate a voice mail. It's from my mom. I tap the Play button and listen as her clipped, slightly breathless voice comes through the speaker.

"Just calling to make sure you've arrived in one piece. Let me know so I don't worry."

I check my missed calls to see if there's anything else, but there's nothing. Dad didn't call.

I dash off a quick text to my mother letting her know

I'm fine and shove my phone under one of the pillows out of sight.

"Don't turn the AC off, or it'll be a sauna in here!" Melody's gruff voice comes through the door. Then the door slams. Guess she's not interested in making a friend.

I fling my pillow over my face. Scream, nap, or suffocate — I can't decide which path to take.

No triple axels. No triple axels.

CHAPTER 8

Sloane Devon

I rock the limo ride *hard* for twenty minutes and am mid–drum solo when the car turns and bounces off the road onto a cobblestone circular driveway. I press my nose to the window. We've passed through a set of wrought-iron gates at the entrance to the camp compound. As we wind up the drive, the building comes into view beyond the ancient, stately trees. My mouth drops open and the window instantly fogs.

The pictures in the brochure did not do it justice. The Baliskaya Skating Institute, or BSI for short, looks like it came straight out of one of those boring nineteenth-century novels we're supposed to read in English class that I never actually do. Two stories of perfectly weathered limestone. A pitched roof with a long row of dormer windows. A glossy black front door with an oversized knocker in the shape of a mythical beast I don't recognize. Giant rosebushes, weighted down by the explosion of pink and red blooms.

A shiny silver Mercedes pulls away in front of us, allowing my limo (*my* limo?!) to pull right up to the entrance. I catch a glimpse of a blond head and a Louis Vuitton handbag—a real one, not one of the Chinatown fakes everyone at school totes around—disappearing through the door. I climb out of the limo while the driver unloads my bags. There are butterflies beating around in my stomach, and I'm not sure whether I'm scared or psyched or both. I've been to a hockey camp or two in my day, but they usually involve bunk beds and dorms that smell like sweat socks. Something tells me this will be different.

I tip the driver with the cash Sloane Emily gave me before we left, then drag my bags up to the front door. Did the other girl knock? I look around for a doorbell. Nada. What if I'm not supposed to barge in? Am I supposed to be summoned? Why isn't there a sign? I reach for the brass knocker but decide at the last second that, like most fancy things in ritzy houses, it's probably just for show. I take a deep breath, then grasp the knob, give it a turn, and push the door open.

I brace myself for the shrill sound of an alarm but am greeted instead by the sound of classical music floating softly through the wood-floored entryway. I take a tentative step inside and look around. I hear chattering and laughter coming from somewhere in the house, but the foyer is empty.

"Check in right here, dear," a soft voice tinkles. To my

left, in what might have once been a sitting room of some sort, is a check-in desk. A high mahogany counter runs across part of the room, and a thin older woman with a severe gray bun and wire-rimmed glasses sits behind it, a shiny silver laptop open in front of her. "Name?"

"Sloane Jacobs," I say, and for a split second, I feel like myself again.

The woman taps quickly into the laptop, then sets about arranging a stack of papers and folders. She barely looks at me as she explains that my room is down the hall and up the grand staircase (she literally uses the words "grand staircase"); gives me a schedule for the first few days, a map of the grounds, and a student handbook; and notes that I'm late and missed the morning orientation session.

"Late? How can I be late? She said I had to be here—"

"Who said, dear?"

I realize I can't tell her that I'm late because the real Sloane Jacobs—at least, the one these white leather skates belong to—didn't tell me there was a morning orientation session. Instead, I mumble an apology. The woman at the desk nods curtly, then points me toward the stairs—er, grand staircase—to my room.

"Where's my key?" I flip through the folder, looking for an envelope or one of those plastic key-cards like at a hotel.

"No keys, dear. The honor code is in the folder, so there's no need to lock the rooms. If you have anything particularly valuable, just bring it down here and I can put it in the safe."

No keys? We're not in Fishtown anymore, Zaps. Thinking of my sweet puppy, and my home, makes my heart hurt for a moment. I'm the second person to leave him. I hope he knows I'll be back.

I make my way to the grand staircase. Oh, and it is grand. Wide enough to drive a Buick up; carpeted in something red and thick enough to sleep on. The foyer and the staircase are filled with campers, which is where all the noise was coming from. I weave through the crowd of skinny, giraffe-shaped girls, feeling a bit like a bull in a china shop. I worry I'm going to brush shoulders with one of them and she'll go pinging off me, landing on something antique and priceless. I notice a few of them staring at me suspiciously as I pass, and I wonder if they're worrying about the same thing.

Midway up the stairs, I pause to hike up Sloane Emily's skate bag. The bottom swings a little more than I anticipated and knocks right into a petite, dark-haired Asian girl. I immediately lunge out to catch her, but she doesn't budge, not even a little bit.

"Watch where you flail, mm-kay?" She reaches up to smooth a stray hair that's escaped from her tight bun. I mumble an apology. Maybe these girls aren't as delicate as I thought.

At the top of the stairs, a discreet brass sign directs me to the left, toward the LADIES' QUARTERS. Another arrow points to the right and is labeled GENTLEMEN'S QUARTERS. I stifle a gag. Oh God, this place is totally Jane Austen. I *hated* those books.

My room, number 12, is all the way at the end of the hall. The glass doorknob is heavy and slick, but I get the door open on the first try, and what greets me inside is much closer to a hotel than any dormitory I've ever seen or imagined. Two queen beds on the left wall, each with a fluffy white comforter, face two huge antique-looking armoires on the right. An overstuffed love seat is nestled into a giant bay window on the far wall, and just off to the right, another door is slightly open, leading to my very own bathroom.

There's already a pink garment bag and a matching pink carry-on laid out on the bed closest to the window, and I notice a matching pink suitcase large enough to contain its owner on the floor next to the bed. My roommate must already be here, so I heave my bags onto the bed closer to the door and start to unpack.

I've barely started when I hear the door creak open. I turn to see a teeny, tiny girl twirling a pink rabbit's-foot keychain waltz in. And I do mean waltz. She sashays in like she owns the place and gives me a look like I *do not*.

"Ivy," she says, and since that's not my name, I'm guessing it must be hers. "You must be Sloane." I hear a very slight Southern twang in her voice. She doesn't offer her hand or even a second glance, just brushes past me and around to her side of the room. She climbs onto her bed, fluffs up a pillow, and snags a magazine off the bedside table. I guess that's all the greeting I get.

"Yup," I say. Since she won't look at me, I take the opportunity to size her up. She can't be more than five feet tall. Her hair, which may have once been brown but has now been highlighted within an inch of its life in about six different shades of blond that definitely do not occur in nature, is gathered back in a very high and tight ponytail. And there's a bow tied around it. A *bow*. A *pink* bow. This does not bode well.

She has narrow, almond-shaped eyes and a slightly downturned mouth. It's the kind of face that makes me wonder if being born with it made her a Mean Girl, or if years of scowling and frowning made her face develop that way. Whichever it is, she's itty-bitty and clad in fuchsia, so she's probably harmless. I decide it's best just to ignore her, which is perfect, since she seems to have no intention of interacting with me.

I continue to unpack, but all the lifting and hefting and stair-climbing have made my knee swell a bit, and by the time I'm done putting the rest of Sloane Emily's jeans (seriously, how many pairs of jeans can one girl need?) in the bottom drawer of my armoire, the zaps of pain are really starting to heat up. I find my ACE wrap and an instant ice pack, one I stole from my own gear bag before handing it over to Sloane Emily, and slam the pack on the desk to activate it. Then I flop down on my own bed and set about RICE-ing my knee (RICE, the athlete's best friend: Rest, Ice, Compression, Elevation).

I hear the magazine drop to the table and look over to see Ivy's narrowed eyes trained on me. "Oh my God, they gave me a cripple?" she mutters.

I glare at her. "You know I can hear you, right?" I continue wrapping my knee, then fasten the wrap with two metal teeth. "A little sympathy wouldn't be out of line."

"If you think I'm helping you hobble around here, you're mistaken," she snaps. "I'm not here to make friends."

"You can't be serious." At the utterance of reality TV's most famous line, I instinctively look around for the cameras. I'm already having fantasies of meeting Ivy on the ice—*my* ice. I'd wipe that sour little smirk off her face so fast she wouldn't have time to roll her eyes. I take some deep breaths to try to release the tension. I can't get into a fistfight on my first day. *I could wipe the ice with you any day with two bum legs.*

"Oh please. That may fly in whatever podunk Disney Channel movie of a rink you skate in, but around here you're nothing," Ivy says, and I realize that I must have threatened her out loud. "What, you thought you could flee to Canada and hide from your epic fail? Oh yes, I read all about you, and between choking at junior nationals and that bum knee, you're almost completely useless as a competitor. Why don't you just retire to the Ice Capades already?"

Her Southern accent is in its full glory now. She must forget to enunciate when she gets pissy. I'm ready to tell her she can take her attitude and shove it where the sun don't shine, but something she said gives me the pinprick of an idea.

If Sloane really *is* underrated—if people are expecting her to fail—then no one is going to expect much from me by way of ice ballet or fancy jumps. Low expectations are my friend. So I just shrug.

"My parents sent me, so here I am," I reply. Her eyes narrow, and I realize my "whatever" attitude enrages her even more than a good old-fashioned smack-down. I hold her gaze, like I'm challenging a bull. I may not be able to keep up on her ice, but I will *not* play some weak-willed little pushover off the ice.

"Pathetic," she says, and finally looks away. She grabs a pink and black scarf from the couch, winds it around her neck, and heads toward the door. She hesitates before pulling it open. "And I thought the saying was that the camera *adds* ten pounds. You ought to write those cameramen a nice little thank-you note."

My brain practically boils. While I struggle to find the perfect retort that doesn't include a primal scream, she smirks and saunters off. The door slams so hard behind her that an oil painting hanging over my head almost falls off the wall.

I bury my face in a large pillow and scream as loud as I can. My transformation into the other Sloane Jacobs must have already begun, because back in Philly Ivy would be picking her teeth out of the oriental rug. I think back to Coach Butler's warning about my temper and my future. Maybe four weeks here will actually have a better effect on me than four weeks playing hockey.

"You dead?"

I peek up from my pillow to see a shaved head and wide

smile. A good-looking African American guy has just poked his head through my door.

"Not yet," I mutter. I roll over, wincing from the pain shooting through my knee. I adjust the ice pack so it's back on my kneecap.

"Pardon the intrusion," he says blithely. He's got a set of well-defined biceps and muscular shoulders, which he clearly wants to show off in his tight, slightly see-through powder-blue V-neck. "I know boys are persona non grata in the ladies' quarters, but when I saw Ivy Loughner stomping out of here, I just had to come meet the poor soul who's stuck sharing a room with her. I'm Andy."

"Sloane Jacobs," I say. "How do you know Ivy?"

"Oh, I don't. *Thankfully.* I just saw her terrorizing some poor, quivering junior skater this morning. I believe she used the words 'talentless chief of the Lollipop Guild,'" he says. "I can't imagine what it's like sharing a living space with her."

I smile. "At least I know it's not personal. She's just an all-around terror, then?"

"Girl, it's *so* not personal. She should hook up with a Hoover, because that girl needs the BS sucked out of her."

The comment makes me laugh so hard I unleash my truly sexy pig-snort guffaw. "I could have used you five minutes ago."

"You can use me any time you like," he says with a wink.

Well, what do you know? I've made my very first friend at skate camp.

♡ ♡ ♡

The schedule in my glossy folder says "Opening Night Formal Dinner," so I dig around in Sloane Emily's wardrobe and find a pair of khaki pants and a mint-green button-down. Instead of my normal messy ponytail, I pull my hair back in a loose braid, and I even throw on some mascara and a sweep of some lip gloss that tastes like watermelon.

I've barely opened my door when I hear Andy. "Oh, honey, no."

"What?" I say, looking down to see if my pants are wrinkled or if I got toothpaste on my shirt.

"You're telling me you didn't pack a dress?" He doesn't wait for me to answer, just breezes past me and flings open the armoire. He flips through the hangers until he comes across a hot-pink, one-shoulder dress with a ruffle cascading from shoulder to waist.

"I'm not wearing that," I say. It's so bright I feel like I need to avert my eyes before it burns my retinas.

"Then why did you bring it?" he replies. Fair question. I forgot that all this is supposed to be mine. I fumble for a response that will get him off my back and that dress back in the closet. He shakes the dress at me. "*This* is formal. That"—he gestures to my outfit—"is Sunday school."

I look from the dress to Andy's stern face, then back to the dress. I could fight. I could tell him my mom packed it, that she's crazy controlling (and from the impression I got from Sloane Emily, I'd probably be right). But looking at Andy making yuck-faces at my outfit, I realize it's not worth it. I am Sloane Emily, and this is Sloane Emily's dress. I take the hanger from him while he turns around to face the corner. I swap out my bra for something strapless, then wriggle into the dress. I hope Sloane Emily appreciates my much less blinding and binding wardrobe.

"Ta-da," I say, holding out jazz hands.

"Perfect." He drags me over to the full-length mirror inside the door and yanks out my braid. He rearranges my hair into a loose side ponytail cascading down my exposed shoulder. Then he trots back to the armoire, riffles around for a second, and returns with a black sparkly headband and a pair of black open-toed kitten heels. When he's done with me, I've got to admit, I look damn good. I bet Dylan would eat his nasty Phillies hat if he could see me. I think for a moment about snapping a photo and texting it to him, just for the "Look at me now!" satisfaction, but I don't want to have to explain where I am. If he even cared to ask.

Andy slips his arm in mine. "Come on, Sloane Jacobs," he says. "Let's get down there before we miss all the fun."

The dining room looks like Hogwarts mated with one of those *Masterpiece Theatre* shows, with floor-to-ceiling windows, gleaming wood paneling, and glistening chandeliers. There are even white-coated servers scurrying around filling water glasses. The little card on top of my plate lists four courses, and my stomach starts growling.

When the first course lands in front of me, I'm ready to dig in. Unfortunately, one glance at my plate and I realize there will be no "digging in." The salad, if you can call it that, is made up of about six leaves of romaine lettuce, two fat cucumber slices, and an almost imperceptible drizzle of something that may or may not be a vinaigrette.

I lean over to Andy. "There's no salad on my salad."

"And you were expecting . . . ?" he asks. A quick glance at his face tells me that this is standard fare in the skating world—*this* skating world, anyway. Andy may be my friend, but he doesn't know the truth. And it needs to stay that way. I have *got* to stop shooting my mouth off, or it's going to get me in just as much trouble here as it does back home.

"Just surprised there isn't more celery. You know, it's like the *only* food that burns more calories to eat than it contains." I throw in a quick giggle to make my fashion-magazine-diet-tip thing land.

"That's a myth," Andy replies. I exhale; at least I haven't outed myself at the first meal. "After dinner we can hit the convenience store down the street. Only about a third of these skaters will actually survive on this food alone. The rest of us mere mortals scarf Snickers bars between meals."

I try to make my salad last as long as possible, but within three bites it's gone and a server whisks away the empty plate. Next up is a soup, which comes in a cup so small I wonder if they stole it from a child's tea set. I resist the urge to toss it back like a shot. When the main course finally arrives, I'm glad to see it's on a grown-up-sized plate, but my spirits drop when I see it's a boneless, skinless chicken breast, grilled and topped with a miniature pile of greens. Alongside it is a tiny scoop of what seems like no more than a dozen grains of brown rice and a heaping helping of steamed broccoli. All around me there are girls cutting their chicken into teeny, tiny pieces, every once in a while bringing one to their mouths and chewing about a thousand times before swallowing.

I want to scream. Or ask them for their leftovers.

Within minutes I'm swallowing my last bite of chicken, while some of the other skaters at my table are still on their first forkful of broccoli.

"This isn't a refugee camp, you know." The acid voice oozes into my ear, the accent thick and syrupy. I turn around and see Ivy, in head-to-toe pink, her dress a carbon copy of my own. When she recognizes it, she crosses her arms across the ruffle and glares at me. She turns to her friend, who looks like she'd like nothing more than to sew her lips to the ass of Ivy's dress. "Look, Sabrina. How cute. She thinks if she dresses like the best, she can *be* the best."

Sabrina giggles like she's watching an episode of *Saturday Night Live*, which is appropriate, since Ivy's act is just about as tired.

Ivy leans in close and whispers in my ear, "If you want to eat like a lumberjack, squeeze yourself into that dress, and walk around looking like a gummy bear, that's your prerogative, but I thought I'd just give you some friendly roomie advice: pink is *my* signature color."

I'm all for keeping a low profile, and I know I need to

keep my anger in check, but I'm not about to let this Manic Pixie Nightmare Girl push me around. I drop my fork on my plate, where it lands with a clatter.

"Listen, Steel Magnolia, you can take your Pepto-Bismol butt over there, or you'll be icing your knee right alongside me."

Sabrina's eyes get wide, and she steps back slightly, as if she's worried a fistfight might break out and she'll be caught smack in the middle.

"Don't mind the crip," Ivy says to Sabrina without turning away from me. Her gaze is steely. Finally, she pivots and takes Sabrina's arm, and the two of them stalk back to their table.

"She meant 'cripple,'" Andy says.

"I know what she meant," I reply through clenched teeth.

"Oh, so that puzzled look was—"

"Nothing," I mutter, because I'm pretty sure admitting that I was figuring out how to remove her arm from her body and beat her with it would get me labeled as Not Classy. The server sets dessert down in front of me, a clear glass dish with a scoop of sorbet topped with a mint leaf. I push it away. I'm too pissed to eat. I need to think. I need a plan.

"She's just trying to psych you out," Andy says, helping himself to my discarded dessert. "I think her motto is 'Those who can, do; those who can't, make the competition too scared to try.'"

"I think it's time for a little psychological warfare of my

own," I say. Prissy places like this are all about the pranks, and I am the *queen* of the prank at Jefferson. Just ask Libby Keegan, last season's rookie of the year, who skated champs with Icy Hot in her sports bra.

"Color me interested," he says. He leans in conspiratorially.

I turn and stare at him, then slowly break into a smile. "Thank you, Andy. You've just given me an idea."

♡ ♡ ♡

I lie in bed for what feels like hours, waiting until Ivy is snoring and I can be sure she won't wake up. I creep out of my room and down the hall, past the staircase and the sign directing me to the gentlemen's quarters. I get to room 22, Andy's room, turn the knob, and ease the door open in silence. Andy's in the bed closer to the door. Apparently his enthusiasm didn't keep him awake: he's sound asleep, and I have to shake him lightly to wake him. He rolls over and glares at me.

"You are *so* disturbing my beauty sleep," he whispers.

"It's game time," I tell him. His roommate is snoring like a buzz saw in the other bed, so I don't worry too much about waking him.

"You were serious?"

I nod. "I need your help. Scissors—you got 'em?"

We creep back down the hall and into my room, where Ivy is still dead to the world. I wave Andy into the bathroom and take the lid off the back of the toilet, where I stashed my supplies in a Ziploc bag. A pair of Sloane Emily's nude tights, a rubber band, and an envelope of raspberry Kool-Aid I picked up post-dinner at the convenience store down the street, while Andy loaded up on pints of ice cream and Snickers bars.

"Make sure she's still asleep," I whisper, and he nods.

I set to work cutting one of the feet out of the tights, then filling it with the Kool-Aid. Then I fit the tights over the showerhead and secure it with the rubber band. I wave Andy back in.

"I need you to spot me while I do this part." Andy stands behind me while I climb up on the ledge of the bathtub and unscrew the lightbulb from the fixture overhead. I wrap the bulb in paper towels and discard it in the trash can.

"You are so crazy," Andy whispers. I feel a sudden sense of unease. I'm not supposed to be the old Sloane here. I'm supposed to be pretty, poised, perfect Sloane Jacobs, not scrappy, scary Sloane Jacobs. I hesitate. I could disassemble the whole thing in seconds and just ignore Ivy for the next four weeks. That's what Sloane Emily would probably do.

Then I spot Ivy's mountain of makeup, lined up in perfect rows on the counter. She's kindly taken my toiletry bag (the pink floral fabric one on loan from Sloane Emily, full of tubes and pots I don't even know how to use) and dropped it on the floor. Next to the toilet.

"Remind me not to mess with you," Andy says, shaking his head.

"You won't forget," I reply with an evil grin.

♡ ♡ ♡

I'm woken by the loudest, longest, most shrill scream I've heard this side of a B-movie murder victim.

"Who? What? OH MY GOD!" Ivy's voice slices through the closed bathroom door, through the feather pillow over my head, and drives into my eardrum like a spike. Despite the pain from the decibel-shattering yelling, all I can do is smile.

I hear the bathroom door swing open, and I take a quick moment to compose myself and wipe the smile off my face. I peek out from underneath my pillow and see Ivy tearing out of the bathroom. Her rainbow of blond highlights is now varying shades of fuchsia—a color also running down her face, neck, and shoulders. She's clutching one of the fluffy white bath towels around her. I should say, one of the fluffy, previously white towels. Now it is streaked and stained in various hues of rose and blush.

"YOU! You did this!" she screeches, shaking a salmon-colored finger in my direction.

"Gosh, you were right, Ivy," I reply, all mock innocence. "Pink really *is* your signature color."

CHAPTER 9

SLOANE EMILY

My phone rings underneath my pillow, which has become my hiding place of choice. Sloane Devon's number flashes across the display. I tap the Answer button after seeing the time: 7:13 a.m. Two minutes before my alarm is set to go off.

"How's life among the rhinestone band?"

"No rhinestones yet," Sloane Devon says. I barely know her, but hearing her voice is oddly comforting. "But your roommate, Ivy Loughner, is a real peach."

"Oh, I've heard of her. She's apparently the General Patton of psychological warfare."

"Well, I'm waging my own battle. You'll never believe what I just did." She launches into the details of some prank that resulted in dyeing Ivy pink. I snort into my pillow. I saw Ivy once at an invitational about four years back. She was a tiny sprite of a twelve-year-old clad in a hot-pink unitard with a tulle flounce around her butt. She was giving her coach, a man of at least forty, a full-on dressing-down over the volume of her music. I can only imagine what living with her must be like.

I think again about how lucky I am: being a terrible hockey player is a hell of a lot better than killing myself to be an elite figure skater this summer. The Mack truck that's usually sitting right on top of my chest is gone.

"Your roommate is no treat either," I say. "She barely had to look at me to decide she hated me."

"She's probably just tough," Sloane Devon says. "A lot of hockey players I know are so crazy competitive that they come off as bitches. She's probably all about the game. If you really want respect you're going to have to show your stuff on the ice."

"You mean *your* stuff," I mutter.

"Hey, this was *your* idea, princess. You've gotta sleep in your bed, or whatever that saying is."

"Done and done." I yawn. I never knew pretending to be someone else could be so exhausting. Yesterday was all check-ins and training assignments, which are basically broken down by age. I'm with all the rest of the juniors and seniors, which means Melody.

Today will be our first day on the ice, and I'm dreading it.

This was already going to be tough without some competitive rage monster as a roommate trying to kill me on the ice. "How are you handling it? Showing my stuff, I mean?"

"Not that it's easy to follow in your tiny twinkle foot-steps, but I can handle it," Sloane Devon says smoothly. Of course, I'm pretty sure she hasn't started training yet either. I make a mental note to call her tomorrow and see how confident she is then.

"'Tiny twinkle footsteps'? We have the same shoe size," I counter.

"You know what I mean. You've spent years training to carry yourself like a cotton ball while I'm hulking around trying to knock everyone over. It's like you're a sports car and I'm a midsized SUV."

"I don't follow," I say, trying not to drift off in the middle of her metaphor.

"They're on the same chassis, but one has a bigger body," she says. There's a moment of silence where I try to untangle what she's saying. "You don't know what a chassis is, do you?"

"My head only has room for so much, and right now I'm working my ass off trying to hold on to facts about hockey and facts about you," I say.

"Well, it seems to be working. One day down, and no one suspects a thing."

"See? I knew we could do this." I allow myself to smile.

"Yeah, let's see how things go on the ice."

"Ice schmice," I reply.

We giggle for another minute, then hang up. I curl up in my tiny twin bed, pull the soft industrial comforter up to my chin, and squeeze Buddy Bear, who my brother gave me when my parents brought me home from the hospital. The fluffy brown bear has one mismatched white ear from our brief experiment with a family dog. Peppermint was a gorgeous, purebred golden retriever puppy that James and I had begged and begged for. When he arrived at our house with a red ribbon tied around his neck, he looked like he should be in a dog food commercial. A perfect specimen, my mom said. But then he ate the handle of Dad's briefcase and a pair of Mom's leather driving moccasins. When he went after the oriental rug in the foyer and the baseboards in the formal dining room, that was it. Back to the breeder he went.

But on his last night, I kidnapped him from his crate and kept him in my room, where he promptly ate one of the ears off Buddy Bear. The next day, I was so distraught, partly over the loss of Peppermint and partly over my poor maimed bear, that James hacked the ear off one of his old bears and stapled it to Buddy Bear. And that's how my fluffy brown bear ended up with one raggedy white ear.

I think about calling James. He'd love that for once in my life I went rogue, that I'm living another girl's life while she's on the other side of the city trying to live mine. And as a former high school hockey star, he'd *love* to see me attempt to play.

I reach under my pillow, where I left my iPhone, tapping my Favorites list on the glowing screen, but I stop before I get to his name. If I tell him what I've done, he'll love it, but he'll also want to know *why* I've done it. Why, after all these years of obedience and restraint, I finally decided to flip my parents and my skating career a big middle finger and skip off to fake it as a hockey player. And "I don't know" wouldn't satisfy him, especially since I *do* know, and he'd be able to tell right away. I'd have to tell him what I saw, what I continue to see every time I close my eyes and try to concentrate on a jump. What it means—what it could mean—if it ever got out. My family isn't perfect, but at least it's whole, and chances are it wouldn't stay that way for much longer if Mom knew what happened.

I climb out of bed and pull open the dresser. So far, the only downside of this whole experience (other than Melody) is the wardrobe. Four pairs of sweats, two pairs of jeans, a pair of cutoff khakis, and one knee-length denim skirt. That's what Sloane Devon has given me to work with for the next four weeks. At least I have pretty undies. And picking out what to wear won't be difficult. Looks like today it's sweats.

"Hiya. Are you Sloane?" A smiling pixie face peeks out from beneath a carpet of blond dreads at my door.

"That's me," I reply, spinning around. This is it: I'm Sloane Jacobs, hockey player, Philly resident, and ska enthusiast, who doesn't know a minority whip from a junior senator and who wouldn't be caught dead in my favorite red skating dress.

"I'm Cameron," she says. She steps farther into my room. "Cameron Rosenbaum. I'm your TP."

I run through my limited bank of hockey knowledge,

but I can't think of anything that computes. *TP . . . toilet paper? That can't be right.* My confusion must be written all over my face, because Cameron explains.

"Training partner," she says. "Buddy. Support system. We'll do workouts and drills and stuff together. The list was posted this morning. I saw it when I was out on my morning run."

"Oh right. Training partner. Yeah, I thought you said *BP* and I was like, 'What?'" I laugh, and Cameron does too, but from the look on her face, she doesn't quite buy it, and she may think I'm on drugs.

"Don't worry, you'll pick up all the lingo pretty quick," she says, before taking the half step required to get to my bed and flopping down next to Buddy Bear. "This is my second summer here."

"Seems like there are a lot of repeat customers," I say. I'm trying not to be too grossed out by the fact that her dreads are all over my pillow. Surely she washes those things, right? "My roommate's on her third."

"Who's your roommate?"

"Melody," I say, and Cameron chuckles.

"From the look on your face, I can see you've already met her."

Cameron laughs again. She's wearing bright red capri pants matched with a simple black cotton tank and black ballet flats. A thin silver chain winds around her neck, a tiny wishbone pendant hanging from it. She's even got tiny diamond studs in her ears, which makes it all the stranger that she has a creature dotted with smatterings of wooden beads growing out of her head and going down her back. Despite her questionable hair choices, I think I like her.

"I can't tell if she's mean or just scary," I say.

"She's just übercompetitive. Dead serious about hockey. She doesn't like rookies or wimps, and she hates new people. Just show her what you got and you'll be fine."

What I've got? Save for a decent triple lutz and a bruise on my butt, that would be a big fat nothing.

"That's what Sloane said," I mutter, and then my mouth goes immediately dry.

"What?" Cameron scrunches up her brow.

I realize my mistake too late and scramble to cover.

"I mean, I was just thinking the same thing," I say. *And I'm totally just a crazy person who talks about herself in the third person.* At least now I know why Melody seems to hate me so much already. Not only am I new, but I'm also a rookie *and* a wimp. I've hit the trifecta.

"Look, when you annihilate her on the ice once, she pretty much leaves you alone. That's what happened with me last summer."

"Uhhh . . . ," I say, but what I'm thinking is *Uhhhhn-likely.* I wonder what happens if *she* annihilates *you* on the ice? I'm going to need a strategy beyond faking a stomachache to skip practice. "So how did you finally get her?"

"I put her into the boards during a scrimmage last year," she says. "I had to do it when she wasn't looking, and I'm pretty sure hitting her hurt me as much as it did her. I swear that girl's filled with lead. But I think I cleaned her clock well enough to get her off my back. It's just an alpha thing. Get her on the ice, and you're golden off."

Then I'm screwed, unless it's legal in hockey to trip someone while executing a camel spin. But maybe . . .

"What's up?" Cameron sits up, prim ballet flats on the floor, and raises a perfectly plucked blond eyebrow at me.

"I just had an idea," I say. I may not be ready for Melody on the ice, but I can bring the ice to her. "Is there a freezer in this place?"

"There's an ice machine on the guys' floor. Two up."

"Even better."

I hop up and stride toward the door and gesture for Cameron to follow. I flip the top lock over the door, just in case, then creep into Melody's room and open the top drawer of what should have been my dresser. I start rifling through the contents.

"Where are her bras?" I shove aside a stack of matching gray boy shorts, looking for something even mildly lacy or racy.

"You mean these?" Cameron loops her finger through the strap of a white industrial-strength sports bra and dangles it in front of my face.

"No, like, the girly ones." I swat the bra out from under my nose.

"I'm sorry, I thought you met Melody." Cameron wrinkles her perky little upturned nose at me, and I see an almost invisible smattering of freckles dance across her skin.

"That's it?"

"Dude, she wears two of these bad boys at once. You wouldn't know it from her sweats-by-Nike fashion sense, but homegirl's got quite a rack."

In all my years of sleepovers and overnights at summer camp, I've never frozen a sports bra, particularly not one that looks like it was designed by the architect of the Golden Gate Bridge. But I guess this summer is going to be full of firsts: first time playing hockey (that isn't a pickup game against my brother), first time disobeying my parents, first time impersonating someone.

Cameron and I pull out all the bras we can find, six in total, and soak them in the bathroom sink. Then we climb the two flights of stairs to the boys' floor and creep into the little alcove that contains a vending machine filled with Gatorade and one of those old ice machines with the sliding door that could practically fit a person inside. Cameron holds the bag of soaking wet bras while I carefully lay them out over the mountain of ice. Hopefully no one wants a cold drink for the next couple of hours. I want these bad boys good and frozen by the time someone spots them.

"Now you're definitely going to have to tag her on the ice," Cameron says. "But this ought to earn you the respect of everyone *else* around here."

"We'll get to that," I reply. *I hope.* I place the last bra, a gray underwire number that has a bit of duct tape over a tear where the underwire is trying to escape. Hot stuff. I slide the door shut over my arrangement.

I duck out of the alcove, turn the corner, and run directly into what feels like a brick wall. Only the brick wall is wearing a soft henley and reaches out to grab me before I topple onto my butt. I look up to see big-eyed, sweepy-haired Matt looking down at me from underneath his shaggy bangs.

"Hey there, pretty lady, watch where you're going," he says, faking a Southern accent. His hands are still on my arms, and I feel a heat radiating down into my palms. He's the living, breathing embodiment of that effortlessly cool/possibly Swedish, possibly Californian/definitely studly-dude archetype from every teen television show ever. I totally see why Mackenzie was fawning all over him.

Then I remember what Mackenzie said. *You're new. You'll get your turn.*

I pull away from him quickly.

"Uh, yeah, sorry," I say. Over Matt's shoulder, I see an equally tall guy with a buzzed head, a pair of sunglasses perched on top, the collar of his polo shirt popped up to his ears.

"Sneaking up to the guys' floor?" the guy says, a smirk on his face.

"It's hardly sneaking," I say. "I just—I just got lost. But thanks. Didn't realize I was on the wrong floor. See you later." I grab Cameron's arm and practically haul her down the stairs.

"Holy God, he is SO. EFFING. HOT," Cameron groans, once we've reached our floor.

"Not you too," I mutter.

"Uh, yeah, every girl with a heartbeat thinks he's gorgeous," she says. Then she laughs. "And just about every girl with a heartbeat has been there. Some of them at the same time."

"What are you talking about?"

She leans in conspiratorially. "Last summer, he was supposedly dating Sarah Black, but then Coach Hannah found him making out with Holly Scott in a janitor's closet." Cameron shakes her head, looking amazed. I feel sort of queasy. Any kind thoughts I had of Matt fly out the window, and I vow then and there to stay away from him.

"Come on," I say. "Let's get breakfast."

After breakfast, I head back to my room to change into my practice clothes for the first scrimmage of the summer. Twice I turn quickly toward the garbage can, worried my nerves might make me heave, but my breakfast stays down.

I pull one of Sloane's jerseys out of a drawer, pull it over my head, and shove the drawer shut. It sticks about midway, and I have to give it more of a bump. It doesn't budge. I take a quick step back, ready to go at it with my hands, but then I picture Melody. She's on the ice, calling me a rookie and ordering me to sleep in the bathroom. I bend slightly at the knees, cock my hip back, and slam into the drawer. It closes with such force that the whole dresser tips back on two legs, banging into the wall before righting itself.

"Checkmate, Sloane." I giggle. I rub my hand over the site of impact on my hip. I'm going to have to practice that one a little more before I attempt it on an actual human. Luckily I've got this dresser all summer, and it doesn't appear to want to fight back.

CHAPTER 10

Sloane Devon

*H*oly. Crap.

I feel like some alien being reached into my body and drained all my energy. It's taking concentration and actual effort to blink properly. My hamstrings feel like they've calcified. I was under the impression that figure skating was just fancy ice ballet with a few jumps thrown in, but Oh. No.

We started our morning at six a.m. with a ninety-minute hot yoga class. I wobbled and stretched and saluted the sun or whatever with sweat pouring into my eyes the whole time. From there, we grabbed a quick breakfast (oatmeal, a banana, and some yogurt . . . I had two), then hit the pool for water aerobics. I had imagined little old ladies in floral swim caps walking slowly and carefully across the pool.

Did you know that you can use free weights in a pool? I didn't, but my biceps certainly do now. Our "break" involved reviewing tapes of Olympic routines and analyzing the point values, which involved *math*. In the *summer*.

Post-lunch, we finally hit the ice, and thankfully I was in a large group with all the other advanced skaters, meaning the fourteen-to-seventeen-year-olds. In a crowd of about thirty, I was able to hide in the back and wave my arms while practicing figures and spins. I wobbled and faked and hoped no one saw. There were plenty of weird looks and side-eyes, but no one asked me to leave, so I guess that's a plus.

By the time I get to my room, I'm ready to collapse. I swing the unlocked door open to find Ivy, Sabrina, and two more identical unnamed minions giving each other mani-pedis. Seeing four girls roll their eyes at me and sigh in stereo is enough to send me bolting from the room.

I wander downstairs and around the first floor until I find an empty sitting room. And even though the couch looks like it's just for show, when I flop down onto it I find the leather is buttery soft and the stuffing is good and fluffy.

Within minutes I'm asleep. In my dream, I'm on the ice back home in Philly, playing a team made up of only Ivy clones clad in hot-pink jerseys, all wearing the number 1. I've got the puck and I'm driving toward the goal.

"Why don't you just give up and join the Ice Capades?" twelve Ivys screech in unison. I feel the tingles starting in my shoulders, pricking around in my joints. Right when I rear back for a shot, I look down and see that instead of my perfectly broken-in hockey skates, I'm wearing stiff white leather figure skates.

"Crip!" the twelve Ivys shriek, and my toe pick digs into the ice. I'm hurtling forward, face and knees aimed straight for the ice.

I jerk awake, one hand on my throbbing knee, the other on my nose, which is thankfully still intact.

"She kicks when she sleeps. Kind of like my dog," an unfamiliar voice says.

"Don't be mean," Andy singsongs.

I peel my eyes open and see a tall girl with a mop of frizzy, carrot-colored hair and sparkling emerald eyes opposite me, splayed out on a leather wingback chair that matches the couch I'm still lying on. Her skin, where it isn't blanketed in freckles, is pale, nearly translucent. I recognize her from this morning's group skate. Andy is perched next to her.

"Hey." I sit up and try to shake off the sleep and the memory of the nightmare. I hope it's not a sign of things to come.

"Skating dream?" the girl asks. When I stare at her, she explains: "Your little feet were just flying on that couch."

"Yeah. More like skating nightmare."

She nods sympathetically. "I'm Beatrice Browne, but you can call me Bee."

"Sloane Jacobs," I say, straightening my throbbing knee gently.

"Nice to meet you, Sloane," she says. She lowers her voice. "Andy here says you're one of us."

"Meaning?"

"Junk food junkie," she says. Andy nods heartily. "Not gonna subsist on baked chicken and steamed veggies. Am I right?"

"That is correct," I reply, happy I've met another person here I don't have to lie to about my hockey player's appetite.

"Then let's go." She hops up from the chair and cocks her head toward the door.

"But dinner—"

"If you're interested in hanging around for variations on the theme of leafy green things, be my guest. But we're going out for burgers." At the mention of burgers, my body jolts awake, and suddenly my energy reserves skyrocket.

"Won't we get in trouble if we skip dinner?" I ask.

"Please, no one will miss us," Andy says. "BSI is like college. As long as you show up to class and do the work, no one cares what you do the rest of the time."

I haven't yet been off the BSI campus, and I'm glad for the chance to explore. A few blocks away from the campus are residential blocks filled with these crazy row houses: three floors with outdoor entrances and winding staircases climbing all over the façades like metallic ivy. I can only imagine what they're like shellacked with ice in the brutal Canadian winters.

Bee seems to know where she's going and leads the way, turning onto a busy commercial street. A white sign reads RUE ST. DENIS. The street is crammed with boutiques, salons, restaurants, and pubs, not to mention people. We pass a shop with a window full of pastries, and I stop to press my nose against the glass, trying not to drool.

"I know a *much* better place a couple blocks up," Bee says. She grabs the strap on my bag and pulls me up the street.

"Bee's a native," Andy says. We have to double-time it to keep up with her.

A few blocks later, we come to a narrow, two-story building covered in chipped red paint. A blue neon sign overhead labels it SHAY'S PUB. A chalkboard out front advertises two-for-one guacamole double cheeseburgers.

"Score," Bee says, fist-pumping and flinging the door open. "You guys are gonna love this."

Inside it's dark and wood-paneled, stale with generations of beer, old cigarettes, and meat smoke, grimy from the pressure of decades and hands. There's an old-fashioned jukebox in the corner, and faded photographs are plastered to the walls. It's legit crap. I'm already in love.

"Anyone up for beers?" Bee cocks her head toward the bar, where a young, hot bartender is pouring a pint for the one and only customer seated there, an overweight trucker type whose pants do not fully cover his rear end.

"Holy crack," Andy whispers to me.

I barely hear him. Bee is still watching me intently, waiting for me to respond. I figured a place like figure skating camp would get me away from the Dylan types always trying to pour drinks down my throat and reveling in the *Afterschool Special*–ness of my Just Say No stance.

My heart is pounding. I don't want to lose my new friends. I don't want to explain why I don't drink. And I don't want to accept the glass and then pour it into a plant somewhere when they're not looking.

Bee leans over and slings an arm around my shoulder. "Dude, I was totally kidding. *As if* I have a fake ID. Besides, beer tastes like cow piss. Coke?"

"Yeah," I manage to croak out, so overwhelmed with relief I nearly hug her.

"Me three!" Andy says.

Bee heads to the bar while Andy and I park at a nearby table that's made almost level by two sugar packets wedged under one of the legs. Bee returns with three Cokes. We sip quietly for a few minutes until a guy appears from the kitchen holding four plates piled high with french fries and cheeseburgers.

"Uh, there's only three of us," Andy says. He slides one plate in front of me and pushes the fourth into the middle of the table.

"Two for one! What, you think between the three of us strapping young athletes, we can't house that?" Bee plucks a fry off her plate and drags it through a river of ketchup. Yesterday, I would have laughed out loud if anyone dared to describe figure skaters as "strapping athletes," but after today's workout, I know it's the truth.

"Dibs," I call, but it comes out *"Dimmf."* My mouth is already stuffed with burger.

Bee leans in a little closer. "Did you guys notice the bartender?" she says between bites. "He's so hot."

Andy glances over my shoulder, and gasps. I turn around to get a look, but Andy grabs my arm.

"Don't be obvious!" he stage-whispers.

"Sorry, sorry!" I reply. I turn back to my burger.

"Today was totally lamesauce," Bee says, wiping a bit of guacamole from her mouth with the back of her hand. I love her already. "Workouts and figures? What are we, five?"

"BSI loves those fundamentals," Andy replies.

"Well, I don't. I'm hoping to finally land my triple-double by the end of this summer, and it's not going to happen if I have to spend my time jogging around the rink and practicing extensions."

"All the skill in the world won't win the Olympics," Andy says. "Just ask Evgeni Plushenko."

"Ugh, always the Lysacek apologist, aren't you?" Bee tosses a fry that bounces off Andy's forehead, leaving a little grease mark behind.

"Pretty wins gold, Bee," Andy says. He rubs at the grease spot with the corner of his napkin. "Besides, we'll be jumping soon. Jumping until our little ankles are snapping with joy. That's how they weed out the wimps."

I choke. Guacamole nearly shoots out my nose.

"You okay, Sloane?" Andy asks while Bee slaps me hard on the back.

"Wrong pipe," I say with a weak smile.

The jukebox clicks, an old-fashioned number with an arm that swaps out real vinyl records. A reed scratches, then the chiming guitar of "More Than a Feeling" fills the bar.

"I love this song!" Bee grabs her fork and starts lip-syncing the opening lines.

"I skated an expo routine to this last year," Andy says.

"I bet it was hot." Bee giggles between lyrics.

"Oh, it was. I'll show you!" Andy jumps up from his chair and lifts both arms and one leg over his head. Then he skips off toward the jukebox, jumping and spinning on the way. Bee and I applaud. Andy leaps back over to our table and grabs my hand.

"You ever skate pairs?"

Without a moment to think (or text Sloane Emily for the right answer), I decide to go with the truth. "Nope!"

"Then follow my lead, and for God's sake, point your toes!"

Andy pulls me out of my chair and to his chest. He dips me, then lifts me until my toes are just slightly off the floor. I do as I'm told and point my toes, kicking off my flip-flops in the process. Andy spins across the floor. Instinctively, I extend my arms like the girls in those YouTube videos Sloane Emily made me watch.

Andy sets me down, then executes a spinning jump, which I do my best to emulate, wobbling on the landing while he sticks it perfectly. He glides across the floor to me and puts his hands tight around my waist, and then I'm flipping. It's all I can do not to kick him in the head as he deposits me bum-first on his shoulders.

"For God's sake, cross your legs," he says. "This isn't burlesque."

Bee cheers. "Something tells me you've done this before."

"Illinois State junior pairs champion two years running!" Andy replies. He waves to the nonexistent crowd while I hold my breath, trying desperately not to plummet to the ground. With only a slight squeeze as a warning, Andy flips me backward over his shoulder and under his arm, and then I'm standing two-footed on the black-and-white-checkered floor of the bar. "I am an *excellent* partner."

He's not kidding. I barely did any work at all, and from the impressed look on Bee's face, Andy made me look pretty damn good. Maybe I should give this pairs thing a whirl. Safety in numbers.

We take our seats, laughing. Even though Andy did almost all the work, getting twirled like a deranged music-box figurine has made me thirsty. I pick up my glass and slurp the last of the Coke through the straw.

"Refills?" I ask. Andy and Bee push their glasses toward me.

I'm halfway to the bar when it happens. My foot lands on something mushy—probably the french fry Bee pegged at Andy—and goes out from underneath me. I barely manage to keep hold of the glasses as I'm falling, I'm falling, I'm—

I'm caught.

A pair of arms grip me tightly and haul me back to my feet. "Watch yourself," a gruff voice says into my ear. "The insurance doesn't cover drunken sorority girls."

"I'm not drunk," I say, shrugging him off once I'm sure I'm steady. I set the glasses down on the bar and spin around. "And I'm *not* in a sorority."

The words die off in a little gurgle. It's clear that *this* is the bartender Bee was talking about. He's about my height, maybe an inch or so taller. He's wearing a Montreal Canadiens tee advertising their 1979 Stanley Cup win. The logo stretches across his chest, distorting it slightly. His skin is dark, the color of coffee with milk, with matching deep brown eyes and dark hair, thick and longish, curling up around his ears and sharp jawline.

In a word? He's *HOT*.

He's also oddly familiar. There's something in his face that sets my mental Rolodex flipping at top speed. I notice a tiny cut across his left eyebrow, where the hair never grew back. His right ear bears a tiny spot from where he used to wear an earring. It all feels so familiar, but I can't place him.

"Sloane Jacobs?" His eyes widen and his voice softens. "Oh wow. It's you, right? What are you doing in Canada?"

Ding ding ding! Fernando Reyes, better known as Nando to his friends and teammates. All-state hockey all four years of high school, Philly high school player of the year, and my teammate during city peewee when I was nine and he was eleven. That's when he got that scar over his eye. In fact, I was the one who gave it to him — or at least, the puck I shot during a practice drill did.

Looking at him now, I'm surprised I didn't see it sooner. He's got the same eyes, the same sturdy build, the same dark, untamed hair. Only he's grown up some. Or a lot, actually. He went to high school across town, so I only ever kept up with him through the hockey grapevine. Last I remember he'd gotten some amazing scholarship to McGill, but his parents moved away soon after graduation, so I never heard much about him.

"Nando, hi," I say, suddenly very uncomfortable about my outfit. I wish I were wearing something a little less clingy. I cross my arms over my chest and try to smile like nothing is weird.

"I almost didn't recognize you," he says. He pulls me into a bear hug, one of those boy kinds complete with three heavy thumps on the back. "You've grown, like, a foot since peewee!"

"Yeah, you too," I say.

"You still playing hockey?"

"Yeah, um . . . pretty much." It's a weird answer, but thankfully he doesn't seem to notice.

"If you're in town for a while, you should come to my pickup game. It would be good to catch up." All of his irritation is gone. Now he beams at me. I practically melt into the floor.

"Absolutely," I say, completely ignoring Andy and Bee, and the fact that I'm not supposed to be hockey-playing Sloane this summer. All I can think about is spending more time with Nando.

I hear someone clear his throat, and Nando turns to see a burly guy at the bar, tapping the top of his empty pint glass.

"Listen, I gotta get back to work, but give me your number. I'd love to catch up, really," he says. I nod, and he pulls out his phone and types my number in. He gives me a sort of two-fingered Boy Scout salute, then heads back to the bar.

I walk back to the table empty-handed, completely forgetting about the refills. Andy and Bee don't even notice.

"Please tell me you just gave your number to the studly bartender," Andy says.

"Yeah, uh, I know him from home," I say. "When we were little." I instantly regret saying it. If for some reason Andy and Nando ever speak, it might come up that Nando's from Philly and that I'm a big fat liar. I quickly shove four fries into my mouth so I can avoid answering any other questions.

This living-another-life thing is harder than I thought. Everywhere I look there's some kind of truth landmine waiting to explode and expose me.

Although in Nando's case . . . it just might be worth it.

CHAPTER 11

SLOANE EMILY

I'm at junior nationals, behind the judges' table, waiting on the blue carpet to take the ice. All the girls are thirteen and fourteen, but I'm sixteen-year-old me wearing fourteen-year-old me's powder-pink skating dress from my long program. I tower over the other girls. I'm worried I'll trample them.

Then I'm on the ice. I'm spinning, skating, taking the long arc around the end of the rink, picking up speed, ready for a triple. If I land it, first place is in the bag.

Just before I leap, I glance up into the stands like I always do, and there are my parents, just like they always are. To Dad's right, Mom's wearing one of her impeccably tailored dresses, the powder-blue one that makes her black Irish eyes sparkle. But to his left, it's not James, who would always try to rearrange his schedule to make my competitions. Instead, it's a tall redhead in a gray pencil skirt and cream silk shirt, unbuttoned scandalously low. I don't recognize her at first, because she's so out of place, sort *of like when you see your biology teacher at the gym and can't quite place her.*

Then I realize: It's Amy, my father's press secretary. My eyes are on her as I leap, and they're on her as I crash down on the ice. My eyes are on her while the crowd gasps. And my eyes are on her when she reaches over and kisses my father hard on the lips.

I wake with a start, blinking, trying to remember why I'm in this tiny room. I spot the hockey stick leaning into the corner. It all comes back. I find Buddy Bear wedged between my bed and the wall and clutch him tightly, focusing on my breathing.

When I was little and would wake up from a nightmare after having accidentally watched a Stephen King movie on TV, my mom would make me some "coffee" in my pink Disney princess mug. Really it was just a glass of milk into which she'd toss a splash of decaf from her own coffee mug, but it made me feel grown up and never failed to calm me down. I eventually outgrew my nightmares, and thus my need for late-night comforting. But for the last few months, the nightmares have returned—this nightmare in particular. At home, I've taken to sneaking downstairs, my fuzzy socks sliding along the marble tile in the kitchen, to make my own coffee milk. These days it's heavier on the french vanilla, with only a dash of skim milk. Doesn't do much for my sleep patterns, but the warm, vanilla-flavored caffeine somehow soothes me.

But in this tiny cell of a room, there's no Keurig and no marble, and Sloane Devon has my fuzzy socks on the other side of town. *So what would Sloane Devon do?*

I creep out of bed and throw on some baggy flannel pajama pants. It's warm in my room, so I leave the hoodie on the back of my desk chair and venture out in just the old white tank top I was sleeping in. On my way across the common area, I hold my breath, worried the door will squeak, worried the sound of my breath will be enough to wake Melody. The only thing worse than a nightmare would be the wrath incurred by waking my sleeping giant of a roommate.

I tiptoe down the hall and get in the elevator. The button for the basement, where I remember a tiny kitchenette from when Cameron and I went exploring earlier, is cracked and worn, and no matter how many times I punch it, it doesn't light up. The elevator shudders to a start, though.

After what feels like minutes in the glacially slow elevator, the doors slide open to reveal the brown linoleum of the basement. Across the room, some old hockey game is crackling across the TV screen at low volume, but I don't see anyone. Someone must have left it on. I'm happy to have a little sound—there's nothing worse than the tense silence of a lonely basement.

I go toward the back corner, where an ancient kitchenette houses a fridge, a microwave, and a sink, and—thank God—a coffeemaker waits. I may actually be able to get a taste of home. But when I grab the pot to fill it with water, I notice the bottom of the glass is crusted with dried, crystallized dregs from whenever someone made coffee last (perhaps last summer, from the looks of the pot).

"Argh!" I sling the pot back into the coffeemaker. I feel completely pathetic. After going to such great lengths to run away from home, I'm standing in a dirty basement trying to find it again.

"Anything I can help with?"

The deep voice comes seemingly out of nowhere, and the shock sends me into a spinning jump that ends with me nearly sitting on the counter. Coupled with my insane acrobatics is a loud, girly yelp that sounds like I've just witnessed someone dropping a box of kittens on the floor. So much for my übertough hockey-girl façade.

"Wow, that was graceful."

Matt O'Neill's shaggy head peeks up from the back of a ratty dorm couch. His normally crazy hair has gone full-on mad scientist. A major cowlick is backlit by the glow of the TV screen. Or maybe it's the light coming off his mile-wide brilliant white smile. I half expect him to hold up a tube of Colgate and start giving me a peppy pitch about tartar control.

I immediately cross my arms over my chest to cover the fact that I stupidly skipped the bra in my ninja-like stealth to get down here, and it is *cold*. But with my hands under my armpits, I can't adjust my ponytail, or check to make sure the drool crust isn't still on my cheek.

"What are you doing down here?" I ask, trying to sound as if I don't really care to know.

Matt points a remote at the TV, pausing the action. "Watching some old hockey film I brought. Getting myself psyched up for tomorrow," he says. I notice the stack of blank DVD cases on the coffee table.

Tomorrow we'll be divided up into teams for the first time, where we'll play a full regulation game. I've been dreading it, and also crossing my fingers that Melody ends up on my team. She hasn't really been able to come after me during drills, but I know once we hit open ice during game play, it's only a matter of time.

"Oh, cool," I say, still backed up against the counter.

"Wanna join me?" Matt pats the cushion next to him—too close.

"No thanks," I say quickly.

"C'mon, I don't bite," he replies. I bet there are at least five girls upstairs who would gladly take him up on his offer, whether he bites or not. I stay planted. Matt doesn't look deterred.

"Where were you earlier? We had open ice, and a bunch of us got sucked into a wicked game of keep away. You should have come by."

"I was in my room, getting everything organized. You know, laundry," I reply. It's true. Thanks to a whole week of brutal workouts in full gear, my room smelled like an old meat locker.

"You know, when you said you were from Philly, I kind of thought you'd be a little more . . . adventurous," Matt says, raising an eyebrow.

"Hey, I'm adventurous," I say, but from the way my shoulders are hunched and my arms are gripping my body like a straitjacket, I can't imagine I'm giving off much of that vibe.

"Then you and I have very different definitions of adventure," he says.

I'm tempted to say: *Does switching places with a girl you just met count as adventure?* But Matt points the remote back at the screen, and the tiny men on the ice start zipping around again, the announcer screaming something about a power play, whatever that is.

I loosen my kung fu grip. Is Matt right? Since I got here, I've been desperate not to screw up. I'm trying to follow the rules and do what I'm told.

I'm *me*.

And I didn't come here—become Sloane Devon—to be *me*. I came here to get away from all that. A laundry list of un-Sloane-Emily-like things go running through my head, each more insane than the next. Flip him off. Fling the dirty coffeepot at him. Flash him. I nearly dissolve into giggles when I think of walking over and punching Matt in the face—something I would *never* do, and something Sloane Devon would probably never do either, if she saw how cute he is.

Then I spot the fire alarm.

I drop my arms and stride toward the couch. I circle around the side and walk right into his view, past the hockey game, and over to the opposite wall, where a clear plastic box covers the red handle. I cup my fingers under the cover and flip it off, then I turn and make sure he's watching.

And he is. He's paused the game again and is staring right at me with a mix of amusement and bewilderment. I keep my eyes locked on his.

"You want adventure?" I say.

"You wouldn't," Matt says.

"Is that a dare?"

He laughs. "Double dare. With a cherry on top."

What would Sloane Devon do?

I turn around and flip the switch.

The cacophony is instantaneous. The siren blares at a rate of a honk per second, loud and scratchy, like it's being pushed through a muddy funnel before coming out of the speakers. Emergency strobe lights flash from the corners of the room. Instantly, I regret what I did. What if I'm caught? What if I'm *arrested*?

"What the hell?" Matt covers his ears, but the grin on his face is unmistakable. He says something else, but I can't hear it between the screech of the sirens and the press of my palms over my ears. I shake my head, and he nods toward the door with the glowing red SORTIE printed on it. We run.

Outside on the sidewalk, our fellow campers are starting to stream bleary-eyed out of the exits, some of them barefoot, some of the guys still shirtless. The coaches are waving everyone across the street and out of the path of the fire truck. Already, we hear it screaming off in the distance. Crap, I forgot the actual fire brigade would be coming. I give Matt a scared look, but he holds a finger over his lips and shushes. He won't tell.

I shiver, wishing I'd grabbed my hoodie. Of course, I didn't realize I'd be resorting to petty crime. I just thought I was getting a cup of coffee. Matt puts one of his arms around my shoulders and pulls me close. But I don't want him to get the wrong idea, so I inch away.

"Oh my God, look!" Cameron comes swimming through the crowd on the sidewalk and pops out next to Matt. She points. Melody is stumbling out of the building, her braids fuzzy and falling down. Her eyes are narrowed, her eyebrows nearly meeting in an angry V on her forehead. And like me, she too is clearly braless, caught off guard by the alarm. Her arms are crossed so hard over her chest I worry she's going to lose blood flow to her lower half. Yet despite all her clutching and juggling as she scurries across the street, she's not able to contain her ample—well, you know. I *almost* feel sorry for her, but then I see her hip-check a junior camper nearly into the curb.

"Guess her assets are still frozen, as they say," I whisper, and Cameron and I dissolve into giggles.

Matt looks from Melody to Cameron and me, and back to Melody. "That was you? *You* froze the Tundra's bras? A couple of guys found them. I hear they kept one and are planning on running it up the flagpole!"

"*The Tundra?*" Cameron and I repeat back in near unison. And then we're past giggles into a full-on laughter fit.

The coaches are now making their way through the crowds, counting and randomly interrogating people about the cause of the alarm. I can't stop laughing. Coach Hannah has a clipboard and is checking off names as she moves through the crowd.

"We need to get out of here before you give yourself up," Matt says. He raises his hand, catching Coach Hannah's eye. She nods and marks us both off on her list, then moves on to a crowd of seniors under a tree playing hacky sack in their pajamas.

"Now's our chance," Matt says. He grabs my hand and pulls me away from the edge of the group and around the side of the building before any of the coaches can spot us. We run until we're at the bike racks in the back of the building, and he fishes a key out of the pocket of his sweats.

"Seriously, a getaway bike?" I stare at the shiny mountain bike, all glossy red paint and chrome, that he's unlocking from the rack. "You have a spare for me?"

"Nope. Just the one. My parents shipped it up for me so I'd be able to explore the city." He shrugs, and I note a slightly sheepish expression on his face. He wheels the bike back, climbs on, then pats the handlebars.

"Um, no way. I'm not riding on the handlebars! That's dangerous!"

"Ah, so brave when you're doing a pull-and-run, but too careful to ride on my handlebars?" Matt shakes his head. "Come on, most girls just hop right on." He gives me a mischievous look, and I don't know what offends me more: the idea that I'm one in a long line of girls to hop onto his handlebars, or the idea that I'm not as brave as the rest of them.

"I'm not like most girls," I say, crossing my arms again.

Something flickers in Matt's eyes. "I know," he says. "You're better."

Then he puts his hands around my waist and lifts me, so I'm able to deposit my rear end directly onto the bars. I'm glad my back is to him so he can't see my terrified expression as he pedals away, though he can probably see the way I'm white-knuckling the handlebars.

He pedals through the streets of Montreal, past blocks of row houses with crazy staircases coming off them like scaffolding. Matt makes a hard right, causing me to nearly pee my pants in fright, and soon we're on a bustling street full of pubs, shops, bistros, and what look like bodegas but have neon signs in the windows spelling out DEPANNEUR. Convenience store. I hear Madame LeGarde's voice in my ears drilling me in my after-school French lessons.

Ahead of us, the green light starts flashing. "What does that mean?" I call over my shoulder.

"It's like the green arrow back in the States. Means we have the right of way to turn," he says, and when we hit a pothole, his lips brush against my neck ever so slightly. A zap of electricity runs from the spot down to my belly button.

I, Sloane Emily Jacobs, am sitting in my pajamas on the handlebars of a boy's bike, being whisked around a foreign city at midnight.

I can't even *imagine* what my mom would say. The thought makes me grin.

We bike for blocks, until we're out of the more

neighborhood-y areas and into downtown Montreal. It's late, so all the office buildings are dark, but the hotels are bustling with tourists wandering, photographing old churches wedged between new glass high-rises. It's a typical urban downtown, except there's art and sculpture *everywhere*. As we ride, Matt periodically taps my shoulder and points here or there, at sights for me to see, and I'm reminded that he's been here before.

I turn to catch a glimpse of a statue of an angel with a gaping hole in its midsection, but Matt is pedaling us so fast I have to turn my head over my shoulder to get a good look. And as I do, this time it's *my* lips that nearly brush his cheek. I spin my head forward so fast I almost give myself whiplash. My heart pounds. Did he notice? And then I feel his warm breath close to my ear again. My heart slows down to a near stop while I wait for him to speak.

"We can probably head back now." It's loud on the bike, the sounds of traffic and the rushing of wind, but all I can hear is his voice, and all I can feel is his breathing. I just nod, and Matt circles around the next block to start us on the journey back.

When we climb off the bike at the dorm, I'm struck by how quiet it is. The sirens must have been turned off a while ago, and now that we're standing still, the silence is nearly deafening. He locks up his bike, and I follow him back into the dorm. His hand brushes mine as we walk, but I jerk it away, crossing my arms again. I forgot about my undergarment issue.

We step into the elevator, and he turns to me. I can feel his breath on my neck again, and I suppress a shiver.

"So that was fun," he says. He pauses. He seems like he's about to say something else.

One of many, I remind myself. *Focus on skating.*

"Yeah," I say stiffly. "Sure."

The elevator door dings open on my floor, and I bolt off as if the doors might slam on me at any second. Matt gets off the elevator right behind me.

"Where are you going?" I ask.

"Taking the stairs," he says. He points to the end of the hall. "Seems dumb to ride up another two floors."

"Oh. Okay," I reply. I feel a tightness in my stomach. I walk the ten steps down the hall to my door and take out my key. The hair on the back of my neck stands up as I listen to Matt's footsteps. He doesn't even pause.

"Night, Sloane," he calls over his shoulder.

"Night," I reply. But the door to the stairwell has already swung shut behind him.

CHAPTER 12

Sloane Devon

I'm growing my very own creature.

I sit on the edge of my bed and peel off my sweaty sock to examine my new friend, who's joined me after a week of grueling figure skating sessions. He's about the size of a pea, bubbly and blistery, with a hard red callous starting to form over the top. If he gets any bigger, I'll have to name him and invite him to the family.

I'm nurturing my creature through hours of hot, sweaty sessions on the ice with my feet crammed into tight leather skates. Though these skates have "Size 7.5" stamped into the tongue in gold, the same size as my own hockey skates, it must be some crazy European size or a conspiracy by the figure skating industry to ruin the feet of America's sweethearts.

I pull my foot into my lap to examine the creature's progress. Our room phone rings, and I nearly tumble to the floor in a pretzel knot of arms and legs.

I pull myself to my knees and snag the phone from its resting place on the table between my bed and Ivy's.

"'Ello?" I'm slightly breathless.

"Sloane, honey, I was hoping I'd catch you. I've tried your cell several times this last week but haven't heard back." The voice on the other end of the phone is deep and brisk. Something in my brain goes *ping* — I've heard the voice before. I'm so busy trying to place it that I just mumble a hello, and the man charges on. "Sloane, I know things have been strained lately, and that's my fault. I should have spoken to you about what you saw. You know I love you and your brother more than anything, and I do love your mother, but — "

A gasp catches in my throat, and I nearly choke on my tongue. It's Sloane Emily's *dad*, and he doesn't know I'm not her. And worse, he's rambling on in that clipped tone about something to do with an "indiscretion." Oh God, I have to make him stop. I have to make him stop talking and get Sloane Emily to call him and finish whatever this is he's starting.

I cough hard and sputter, and the effect is good. He stops midsentence, a long silence on the other end of the phone.

"Sloane? Are you okay?"

What to do, what to do? If I pretend I'm Ivy, then he'll be all freaked out and embarrassed about spilling secrets to a stranger. But if I try to be Sloane Emily, he's going to know from the sound of my voice that I'm not her. I have to say *something*.

I cough again, then clear my throat and drop my voice a

bit until I'm confident it sounds convincingly gravelly. "Uh, Dad, I'm uh, not feeling so great. I think I picked up a cold from the rink. I'll have to call you back."

There's another long silence, and I worry the jig is up. I hear him sigh loud and long. "Please do, Sloane. I'd really like to discuss this."

"Yeah, will do." I cough again, then hang up the phone before he can say anything else. *Holy crap, that was a close one.* I go to the wardrobe and flip through the hangers until I get to the cardigan in the back with the deep pockets, where I've been storing my phone to keep it away from Ivy's clutching little hands.

Your dad called. I answered. Covered by saying I'm getting sick. Call him back. NOW.

I press Send. I have no idea what that was all about, but from the sound of it, maybe perfect Sloane Emily doesn't have the perfect family I thought she had. I push the thought out of my head. I have enough of my own problems here at the Ice Hotel. Last night over a stash of gummy bears and some videos of Andy's old pairs routines, I'd hatched a devious plan. I'm risking too much skating alone. It's too easy to spot my weaknesses. So today, I have a meeting with Juliet Rowe, BSI's camp director, to talk to her about switching to pairs. I have no idea if it's even going to be allowed, but I have to try. This last week of trying to hide while skating all by myself has been *waaaaaay* too hard.

I'd rather be knocking Andy over than letting him carry me across the ice.

I shut the phone and put it back in the cardigan pocket. I glance in the mirror and catch sight of myself as Sloane Emily in a pair of black capris, a white cami, and a pale pink cardigan with little yellow flowers embroidered on it. I may look a little bit like a kindergarten teacher, but at least I don't look like myself—the girl whose mom is in rehab, who dated a loser like Dylan for close to a year, who can't keep her fists to herself.

I smile at myself in the mirror.

I slip on a pair of flip-flops and hurry downstairs. Juliet's office is in the front foyer area, just behind the desk where I checked in the first day. I arrive at the front desk and am directed through a set of mahogany french doors. Juliet is sitting behind an enormous desk that looks large enough to ford a river on, and it only looks larger in front of her delicate butterfly frame. According to Sloane Emily's brochure, Juliet used to train Olympians. Looking at her sitting there twirling a powder-blue kerchief between her fingers, I gulp. She's the tiniest woman who's ever scared me.

"Miss Jacobs, please sit down." She gestures to one of the overstuffed leather chairs across from her desk. I plant myself in it, and unlike the couch upstairs, this one is exactly as hard and uncomfortable as it looks. I fidget as the brass buttons dig into my butt. I see Juliet watching me and wrinkling her nose. "What can I do for you today?"

"I wanted to talk to you about switching to pairs for the summer," I say. Best just to dive right in, and also I want to end this conversation as quickly as possible and get out of here. I'm not positive, but I worry that Juliet has the power to smell hockey on me.

"Well, that is very unorthodox," she says. Her accent is odd, a mix of American English and a twinge of Canadian, with some French and possibly Russian undertones.

"I know, but I was just hoping to try something new, after, well . . ." I'm not quite sure what I was going to say, but it seemed like a good idea to come up with an excuse. Under Juliet's steely gaze, my mind goes blank.

"Yes, I know about your history," she says. There's a long pause, and I wonder if she wants me to talk about it. From what I gathered from Ivy and Sloane Emily, something happened a few years ago that took Sloane out of competition, and it's been a while since she's skated. Apparently this summer is supposed to be some kind of comeback, but it looks like that won't be happening. "Normally it would be impossible, as we invite a certain number of singles skaters and a certain number of pairs skaters to the program. You are very lucky that Miranda Bates broke her ankle before arrival."

I want to laugh. No one's ever been so blunt as to say that someone else's misfortune is my gain, but the look on Juliet's face tells me she's deadly serious.

"We do need one more girl for pairs," she says, then sniffs. Oh God, she can smell the hockey. I knew it. "I guess that will be you."

I let out an enormous sigh and thank her, but Juliet has

already turned her attention back to her computer. I guess our appointment is over. Thank God.

I leave the chair, most likely bearing the imprint of brass buttons on my bum, and rush out the door before she changes her mind or banishes me from camp altogether.

In the outer office, I find Andy practically jumping up and down. "Well?"

"Done and done!"

"Yes!" he says. "I hear some girl snapped her tibia, so I figured it would work out. We are *so* partnering up for the end-of-season exhibition."

I gulp. For the last week, all anyone can talk about is the stupid exhibition that's not exactly an exhibition, since we'll be judged and there will be winners (and losers). The pairs kids have been scrambling to buddy up. No one wants to be left out or stuck with a dud partner. The singles skaters have all been not-too-subtly dropping hints about their chosen music to make sure no one else picks the same thing. It's all very passive-aggressive ice-skaterly.

"You and me," I say, hoping he can't tell that the idea of the exhibition makes me want to upchuck my lunch. Poor Andy. When he lifts me, I'm about as graceful as one of those hippos from *Fantasia*, if those hippos were missing four toes and deaf. He's not going to buy my faux skating pedigree for long. Soon it'll be put-up-or-shut-up time.

"Of *course* you switched to pairs." The syrupy voice makes the hair on my arms stand up. "Isn't that just *adorable*."

"Nice dye job, Ivy," I say as I turn around. It took her two days and a three-hour hair appointment to return her hair to its bleached-blond glory. I reach up and point to a patch near her forehead. "Looks like they missed a spot."

She swats my hand away. "Don't think this is over, Sloane Jacobs," she says. "It's *so not over.*"

"Sure thing, Ivy," I say sweetly. Another benefit of the partner thing: it will bump me out of Ivy's group and into the pairs group, which means larger lessons since there are twice as many of us. More people to hide behind. I'll still have to do singles for the end-of-season competition, just like everyone else, but at least it will only be the short program. That means I'm spared—and am sparing the audience—two minutes of horror.

It also means I won't even have to have a one-on-one session with a coach, since all our one-on-ones will be *two*-on-ones—with Andy running interference, even if he doesn't realize it.

Ivy turns on her heel and marches away. Andy is doubled over laughing. "What do you think she'll do to you?"

"I'm not worried," I reply. "Now let's go practice."

♡ ♡ ♡

Another day of practice has left my body a wreck. My hamstrings have practically calcified from all the leg extensions, leaving me feeling a little like the Tin Man as I walk back to my room. All this standing up straight has done a number on my neck and shoulders, not to mention the strain on my core. My abs feel like Muhammad Ali has been using them as a heavy bag all day.

I hobble into my room and gaze at my bed. It looks just as fluffy and soft as it did in the brochure Sloane Emily showed me, and I can't wait to fall into it.

My phone buzzes inside my bag. I dig it out and see a text message from a number I don't recognize.

Playing a pickup game today. Wanna join up like old times?—Nando

I breathe in, reading the text over again, and find my neck loosening up. I put my phone on the floor, bend over to stretch my legs, and read it a third time. *Old times.* I stand up with another deep, yoga-style breath, and find my abs don't hurt quite as badly as they did just a few minutes ago. I read the text one more time and smile.

Suddenly, I'm no longer feeling sore at all.

One Google search, two buses, and a twenty-minute walk later, I'm standing on a concrete landing looking down at an ice rink. Only this one isn't perfectly crystal and smooth. There aren't a half-dozen skinny princesses spinning around making figure eights on the ice. There isn't classical music tinkling softly out of the overhead sound system. This isn't BSI.

This is the Rue de St. Laurent Patinoire Communauté. And with rented hockey skates over my shoulder and an armful of smelly rented gear, I'm ready to hit the ice with the dozen guys down there working on slap shots and checks to the tune of something loud and metal that is too loud and metal for the crappy sound system to handle.

"So, you think your peewee skills are still sharp?" Nando is already geared up and heading toward the rink, a hockey stick in one hand and a crate of yellow and red pinnies in the other. The sight of him—dark hair curling out from underneath his black helmet, brown eyes shining behind the mask—almost makes me drop my helmet.

"Without a doubt," I reply.

"Then get changed. You can be on my team." He grabs a red pinny from the crate in his hand and tosses it at me. I have to stop myself from skipping to the locker room. While I'm changing, I wonder if Sloane Emily is out some-where in the city doing axels in secret. She's probably busy icing down every bruise on her body. My body is barely hanging on trying to figure skate. There's no *way* she's sur-viving hockey camp.

I'm the only girl on the ice, but that's not unusual. I played coed hockey until I got to high school, which more often than not meant guys plus Sloane. Nando does some quick introductions, and the guys greet me with either a nod or a gruff *"Salut."* Within minutes we're all in pinnies and the puck is dropped.

Nando mentioned it was just a pickup game, but these guys know their stuff. I try to look for the weak link in the yellow team to prey on and steal the puck, but I can't find one. And from the way everyone swarms me when Nando passes me the puck, it's clear they all assume our weak link is *me*.

I haven't played in a week and I'm rusty. It takes me a few minutes to settle back into skates without a stacked heel. One good charge that sends me tumbling straight over backward is enough to remind me not to stand up so straight.

Nando comes skating up quick and hockey-stops right next to my head. "You okay?"

"Fine," I mutter, thankful I've got a helmet on to hide the blush that's creeping into my cheeks. I hate that I just bit it in front of Nando. This is my game. I'm back on my ice. I should not be falling over like a peewee hockey kid. I climb back onto my skates, nod at him to show I'm not dead, and take my position.

Once I'm settled in, it comes back, just like riding a bike — or a really kickass motorcycle. And I find that some of the new spin techniques I've picked up from group sessions are even coming in handy. I'm able to steal the puck from a yellow skater named Mathieu by executing a near-perfect camel spin while sweeping my stick underneath his. Even though his face mask is on, I can see his mouth hanging wide open.

I'm able to offer a lot of assists, mostly to Nando, who is an ace at positioning himself perfectly for the shot. After only ten minutes have ticked off the clock, the red team is up 2–0. We take a timeout. I've almost completely forgotten about life at BSI and the creature growing on my foot. Even rented skates can't hold me back. This is exactly what I needed: down and dirty community hockey. No lights, no coaches, no scouts, just play.

I'm back.

The buzzer sounds and we take the ice again. The yellow team must have had a hell of a powwow, because within three minutes they've scored twice. We're tied 2–2. On the next play, red number 8, whose name I didn't catch, snatches the puck and drives it toward the yellow goal, where I'm skating backward ready to assist. A yellow player charges him, and 8 passes the puck to me with barely a glance. I scan the ice quickly to see what my next move should be, but everyone is covered or out of position. It's just me, the goalie, and the net.

"Shoot!" Nando's voice bounces off the ice and around the boards. Out of the corner of my eye, I see Mathieu skating hard, gunning for me. It's now or never. I plant my blades and raise my stick. I'm going to score. I'm going to take the lead back. For a split second I take my eye off the goal and see Nando watching me, trying to fend off a yellow player who's all over him.

My heart pounds. My shoulder comes up and I'm ready. . . .

The tingles start, first as tiny little pinpricks in my joint, then as a swarm of bees flying down my arm into my fingertips. Within seconds the yellow player is on top of me, stealing the puck, skating away. No one expected it. I was lined up for the perfect shot, and I just let him skate up and take it. The buzzer sounds, the scoreboard flips, and the yellow team cheers. 3–2. They've won.

I swallow hard and slap the ice with my stick so I don't

start crying. There's no crying in hockey, especially not in front of a bunch of dudes. We line up for good game, and the guys thank me for stopping in. They're all really nice, which only makes me feel worse. If they'd just rag on me for missing that shot, I'd feel okay, but the "good tries" and the "nice games" just seem like pity.

Can't figure skate, can't play hockey. God, maybe I should take up curling. I'm in the right country for it.

Back in the empty girls' locker room, I take a quick shower and change back into street clothes. I need to return this gear and start the trek back to BSI before someone notices I've gone absentee.

In the lobby, I return the gear and skates and turn to head back toward my bus, but Nando is waiting out front for me. He's got his gear bag slung over his shoulder, a tight, faded blue T-shirt showing the remaining drips from his post-game shower.

"Good game," he says.

"Not really," I reply.

"So you missed one shot. You can't make 'em all."

"I didn't make any," I say a little too forcefully.

"Yeah, but you had some great assists. Those two goals we scored were thanks to you."

"Assists don't bring the scouts," I say, then slam my mouth shut. Too much.

He frowns and shakes his head. "Scouts aren't everything."

"Says the guy who got scouted," I reply.

"Why don't we go get some food?" he suggests.

"I wish I could." Dammit. I can't believe I have to ditch Nando to go back to the land of the ice queens. "Next time."

He's obviously disappointed, but he smiles. "At least let me give you a ride," he says.

One look at those rosebushes in front of BSI and he won't believe for a second that it's a hockey camp.

"I'm actually, um, taking a class," I say, latching on to the lie, another one I'll have to remember for later. BSI definitely looks like some chichi private school. "For college credit, you know. Figured while I'm here, two birds, one stone. Whatever. You can drop me off there."

I follow him out to his car, and as I walk I notice a twinge in my knee. The adrenaline must have been enough during the game, but now that I'm back on dry ground, I can feel the stiffness coming on fast.

I limp after him to a beat-up old Mini Cooper, an original, that looks like a tuna can on wheels. He opens the hatch in the back and tosses his gear bag in. He has to slam the door hard—twice—to get it to latch.

When Nando turns the key the car sputters for a second, then roars to life, and we're headed off. After I give him the address it's quiet for a while, and I stare out the window watching the city roll by, happy I don't have to give directions because I don't totally know how to get back.

"So how's your mom?" The question shocks me like a punch to the gut.

"You remember my mom?" I ask carefully.

"Sure, she used to come to all our games in that red Mama Jacobs T-shirt." When he smiles, the corners of his eyes crinkle.

For as long as I've played, my mom has had one of those shirts made in whatever team color I happened to be wearing that season. She cheers louder than all the other moms, and most of the dads. She did mention figure skating lessons once, when I was first learning to skate. But when I stamped my foot and shook my head and said "No way, José," she got on board the hockey train right away. Dad was the hockey fan, but he worked long hours, so it was Mom who carted me to practices all over the city. She learned enough about the game to cheer along with the other parents and even yell at the refs a time or two. But she stopped coming to my games in the last year or so, when things started getting bad for her—for us.

"She's fine," I say quickly. "How's college?"

"Fine," he says, just as quickly. He obviously doesn't want to talk about it, and I don't want to push.

The throbbing in my knee is getting worse. I really should just get the surgery the orthopedist has been recommending for over a year now, but I didn't want to take the time off when he first told me. And now with Mom in rehab, it really doesn't seem like the right time. Not to mention the fact that every spare cent is going into covering her legal problems and her treatment. Even with insurance, surgery would be a hefty chunk of change I'm fairly certain we don't have.

A couple of ibuprofen and some ice and I should be fine for tomorrow's workout. I just need to stop thinking about it.

"You looked really good out there tonight," I say in an effort to take my mind off my knee. "You always were a great team leader. Even as a peewee."

"Thanks," he says. His gorgeous smile is back. "You were really great too."

"I was okay," I say.

"Sloane, you're too hard on yourself," he says. "I can see you getting all worked up out there. You need to calm down."

"Easy for you to say," I reply. He's the one with the scholarship.

"It's not," he says. "I know just what it's like to be burned out, ya know? The pressure can really mess with you."

I stare at him, wondering whether he'll say more. But just then he slows the car, and we pull up to BSI.

"Nice place," he says, peering out the windshield and up the hill at the main building.

"Yeah, not too shabby," I say. I climb out of his tiny car as quickly as I can before he asks too many questions. As I unfold myself from the seat, my knee nearly groans in anger, and I stumble onto the sidewalk.

"You okay?" Nando ducks so he can see me through the passenger-side window. I don't respond; I'm too busy gritting my teeth against the pain. In a flash, he's out of the car and next to me. "Let me help you."

"No, no," I say. "I'm fine. I just need to stand here for a minute."

"Let me at least help you to the door." He gives me the single most genuine smile I've ever seen. My chest aches. I don't want to say good night to him. It's like saying good-bye to home all over again.

So I nod, and he scoops me up into his arms. I wind my arms around his neck, and he marches up the long circular drive to the front door.

"You're the densest skinny girl I've ever met," he says when we get to the patio in front of the door. "What are you filled with, lead?"

"Muscle," I reply. He gently sets me down on my feet.

"I bet," he says. He stands there for a second, looking around, then puts his hands in his pockets and sort of shrugs. "So . . ."

"Uh, um, thanks," I say. He's nearly my height, and so we're almost eye to eye, nose to nose.

"You're welcome." His voice is almost a whisper. He smiles at me, a crooked half smile, but he doesn't lean in. Which is good. I think. I let out a deep breath. This is Nando, a guy who knew me back when we were still too scared to watch parts of *The Goonies*. Nando, who knows my game, my mom; who could expose me to everyone. I shouldn't kiss him. I *shouldn't* kiss him. But that look, and he's so close, and—

The front door swings open and Ivy nearly knocks me over. She stops short when she sees me standing there. She glares at Nando, then at me, then at Nando again. I step back and put some distance between us. Nando mutters a quick "bye" and practically sprints back to his car.

"Mmmmm, very scandalous, senator's daughter." Ivy raises one defiant eyebrow at me.

"I don't know what you're talking about," I reply. I head inside, desperately trying to conceal my limp.

Wherever Ivy was headed when she ran into us clearly isn't as important to her as torturing me, since she follows me back to the room.

"Hooking up with a *townie*," Ivy says, and I can hear the satisfaction ringing through her voice. "That's the kind of behavior that can get you kicked out of camp, you know."

I spin around. "What do you want, Ivy?"

"Whatever do you mean?" The Southern venom drips from every word. She's practically batting her eyes at me like Scarlett O'Hara, and frankly, I don't give a damn. I'd been hoping my prank would be enough to scare her—let her know I mean business—so that she'd leave me alone. Apparently I've misjudged her.

"Cut the crap, Ivy, and just tell me what I have to do to shut you up."

She marches right over to me and crosses her arms, like she's been waiting for this moment since the second we met.

"I want you to stay out of my way," she says.

"I'm not even in your category anymore," I say. "I switched to pairs. What more do you want?"

"I want to end this summer on top, the talk of BSI. I

want all eyes on me, so that when I start this competitive season, it's *me* everyone's talking about, and not *you*."

I can't believe this. I can't believe she's admitting that she's scared of me. I can't believe she's asking me—well, Sloane Emily—to throw the competition. I can't believe she's saying all this *out loud*. And I can't believe she's just given me the perfect out to be a semiterrible skater all summer. I don't even hesitate.

"Deal," I say. I stick out my hand to shake on it, but she waggles her fingers at me.

"Manicure," she says, then winks and sashays out of the room.

CHAPTER 13

SLOANE EMILY

I lean into the mirror, checking my teeth to make sure I brushed well. As I'm checking the spot in the back where my wisdom teeth used to be, I feel a bump from behind. I tip forward and smack my forehead on the mirror.

"Ow!" I cry. I turn to see Melody lining up at the sink next to me. She's been "accidentally" bumping into me all week. Both my shoulders are bruised and sore, thanks to the fact that every time I see Melody anywhere—on the ice, in the hallway, at meals in the cafeteria—she steers right into the side of me, banging into my shoulder and knocking me off balance. I've dropped a pair of skates, an armful of pucks, and three bottles of cranberry juice thanks to her attacks. "Would you watch it?"

"Oh, I'm so sorry," she sneers. "You just always seem to be in my way."

This has been her excuse on the ice, too, even when I'm

on *her team.* At first I thought it was just her hating me because I was a newbie rookie, but it's worse than that.

If only Cameron had been able to contain her jokes about Melody and her frozen assets. But no. Two days after the fire alarm, Melody walked up behind Cameron making an "It's a bit nipply in here, isn't it?" joke, and things have been bad ever since.

I rinse and spit, stopping myself just short of spitting *on* her, then head back to my room. Unfortunately, my brain is entirely too restless to sleep. I pull out my phone. Since my international data roaming is turned off for the summer, I can't scroll through Facebook or play late-night games of Words with Friends. All I can do is read through my old texts. A few from Mom asking how things are going, all met with a bland *fine* or *it's great.* There's one from James letting me know that Haiti is awesome and that he's already planning a return trip during spring break next year. I almost wish I could have been home to see Dad's face when James told him *that.*

And then there's the newest one, from Sloane Devon, telling me to call my dad. It's been two days, but I can't bring myself to call him back. I'm worried about what he'll say—or what he won't say. I haven't decided whether I want him to bring it up or apologize or pretend it never happened. I mostly don't want to think about it at all, so I've been avoiding the call.

Lying in my extralong twin bed, bruised and sore all over, the sound of a toilet whooshing on the other side of my wall and the laundry list of misery that is my life running through my head, I realize I feel just as trapped as I felt when I was back in DC, training for junior nationals and hoping against hope that I'd break my ankle. It's the exact feeling I was trying to escape when I looked Sloane Devon in the eye back at the hotel and asked her to trade lives for the summer. I came here to escape that. I came here to be someone else.

I need a plan.

When my alarm goes off at seven, that's exactly what I have. A plan. For Melody, anyway. In the breakfast line I load a plate with bacon, eggs, wheat toast, and a bowl of oatmeal. I'm going to need some serious fuel.

I spot Cameron already at our usual table in the back and weave my way through the crowd. Her blond dreads are pulled up into a knot on top of her head, and she's wearing her favorite powder-blue Lululemon zip hoodie. I drop my tray and plop down into my seat.

Cameron eyes my plate over a bite of her favorite breakfast, sesame bagel with lox and capers, a Montreal standard. "You planning to trek to Toronto on foot with that?"

"Today's the day," I say.

"You're finally going to get her?"

"I haven't exactly been slacking," I shoot back.

She shrugs. "You won't last with that she-hulk out to get you. You have to step up and do something about it."

I stir the brown sugar into my oatmeal and take a huge bite. I take time to swallow and go over my story one more time. "You know I'm not much of a physical player, right? I mean, I'm not much of a defender, and I don't really go for the hits."

"Sure, I guess," Cameron says. We've only had a couple game-play drills, but it appears my hiding technique has been working—and in this case will work to my advantage.

"Well, I came here to work on my aggression. You know, step up my game," I say. I lift my eyes from my plate. Cameron is fiddling with a dread that's escaped from the knot, and she looks curious but not suspicious. "I need your help."

"Sure thing," Cameron replies. She pops the last bite of bagel into her mouth and chews hard. "Aggression is *not* a problem for me."

It's true. In just two days, I've seen adorable, sweet, preppy Cameron lay out enough skaters to make up an entire team. She's like a tiny human wrecking ball, and opposing teams just crumble around her. She even took Melody down during a defensive drill yesterday afternoon.

"We have our first scrimmage this morning," I say. I've been dreading it since I first saw the schedule. I know the rules of hockey. I can technically ice-skate, and I've been managing okay in the drills. But lining up against a bunch of girls who've played since they could walk, one of whom is the size of the Jolly Green Giant and *hates* me, is possibly worse than flashing a boob on national television in the middle of my long program. "I'm going to get her, but I need you to help. I'll never even get close to her if she's got her eyes on me."

"You're the boss, applesauce," Cameron says. She winks. "I'll distract her, and then you can come in and crush her."

"Something like that," I reply. I swallow a last dry glob of oatmeal. It takes its sweet time getting down my throat. In my head I replay the YouTube videos I watched last night on my laptop. I practiced on my dresser this morning until it practically grew a mouth and begged for mercy.

All I need now is not to be afraid.

I manage to keep my resolve up all morning as I fumble my way through drills and the moment of truth finally arrives. Coach Hannah, a McGill hockey player and former Elite camper who's serving as one of our den mothers for the summer, counts us off into two teams. Melody is on black; I'm on white. It's not hard to arrange. Most of my fellow campers shuffle around in the hopes of ending up on the same team as Melody, so it's easy to jump into the white team line of fire.

"All right, ladies. For the last two weeks you've been playing in your positions, trying to show off. But enough showboating. Today I want to see you out of your comfort zones. Try out some different positions. If you usually play offense, try defense. And everyone should take a turn in the goal. Nothing to prove today, just have some fun," Coach Hannah says, then blows two quick blasts into her whistle to indicate we need to move our butts.

We don our practice jerseys and hit the ice. I'm placed at right defense, opposite Melody, who clearly has ignored Coach Hannah's instructions to step out of her comfort zone. Melody lives at defense. It's as comfortable for her as the unflattering oversized T-shirt she sleeps in. When I volunteer to guard Melody, Amanda Gallatin gasps. No one guards Melody, and certainly no one *volunteers* to try.

"Just trying something new," I say, and attempt an aw-shucks shrug. It comes out looking a little bit like a neck spasm. I swallow hard. I still feel that last bite of oatmeal sitting somewhere in my throat, making me feel like I'm going to gag.

But I have to do this. For me. For the *new* me.

"All right, skaters, let's do this," Coach Hannah says, pulling the striped ref shirt over her head. "Play clean. Play smart. Show me what ya got."

Cameron lines up at center ice against Rosie Eastman, a cute brunette from Michigan with two long pigtails streaming out below her helmet. Coach Hannah raises the puck, blows the whistle, and then drops it.

Chaos ensues, or at least that's what it looks like to me. Coach Hannah skates off to the sidelines, out of the line of fire, while Cameron and Rosie bat at the puck, trying to swipe it free. Cameron wins, and the puck sails over to another white player whose name I can't remember. She drives toward the goal, but a whoosh of black comes flying in from the right. Within seconds, the white player is on her butt and Melody is off in the opposite direction. She jukes around Cameron, who tries to steal the puck, spins off another white skater, and then shoots. The light flashes, the buzzer sounds, and the scoreboard overhead clicks to show 1–0.

"If you're going to volunteer to defend against Melody, you could at least try." The white player who got leveled by Melody skates by, her dark eyes narrowed. "Just because she's a human Mack truck doesn't give you a free pass to just stand there."

I can't even respond. My heart is pounding—everything happened too fast. I shake my head and give another shot at swallowing the lump in my throat. I need to wake up. I came here to play. I'm *going* to play.

Rosie and Cameron are center ice again. Coach Hannah has the puck. The whistle blows, the tussling begins, but this time I keep my eyes on Melody. Where she goes, I go. I may not be super familiar with the intricacies of hockey, but I'm a pretty good skater. Fast, too. Most people don't realize how much speed is necessary to get those jumps off the ground. So when I put a little effort into my skating, I've got no problem whatsoever keeping up.

I can tell Melody is surprised. She's only seen me in drills at this point, never in a game-play scenario. She keeps changing directions, juking left and right, sprinting and stopping, her braids flying, and the whole time I'm right with her.

Cameron is nearing the opposing goal. She passes the puck to Jen, another white player, who lines up for the shot. Melody goes after her immediately, but I hold back. When Jen sees Melody coming at her full-force, she passes the puck quickly back to Cameron. Melody turns and goes for Cameron, positioning herself perfectly between my friend and the boards. This is my moment, I know it.

My heart is pounding practically out of my jersey. I skate as hard as I can, head down, shoulder forward. It takes only three strides, and I'm on her. She's watching Cameron and the puck, so she doesn't see me, my hip and shoulder aimed right at her chest.

The crash is riotous. It sounds like a thousand Sloanes have taken a million Melodys right into the wall. She grunts loudly. Her hockey stick clatters to the ice, and she goes down backward. I manage to right myself and sweep a circle around her. She looks up, and I just grin down at her like I've landed a triple-triple while she's still lacing her skates. From the expression on her face, I got her. I know it, and she knows it.

"Nice defense, Sloane," Coach Hannah calls across the ice. "You saved Cameron's shot."

I didn't even notice the light flashing or the buzzer, but I do see the scoreboard flip: 1–1.

Melody grabs her stick and climbs to her feet. Now she's towering over me. She looks down, eyes narrowed. But after a second, her face softens just a little, just a teeny tiny bit, so that only I can see it because we're helmet-to-helmet. Then she nods, almost imperceptibly, and skates away.

I nearly pee my pants.

The rest of the game plays out without too much drama, and we lose 4–2. But I don't care. Melody played hard. She took me down a couple times, but only when I was in her way. She wasn't gunning for me, not anymore.

And the best part? I survived my first hockey game

without looking like a total spaz. Sure, I managed to handle the puck only once (Cameron passed it to me, and I passed it quickly on to Jen), but I didn't do anything stupid like shoot for the wrong goal or pick up the puck and attempt to throw it in.

The rest of the afternoon is filled with drills and strategy talks, and I find myself paying really close attention. High off my own personal miracle on ice, I wonder what could happen if I really *try* to get good at this. Maybe team sports are the way to go. Less pressure, less judging, and no one here has cried yet.

By the time I get back to my room after dinner, I'm exhausted. I take the longest, hottest shower of my life. I pull on a pair of Sloane Devon's comfy sweats and a soft, washed-just-the-right-number-of-times T-shirt. Maybe there's something to this whole dressing-like-a-thirteen-year-old-boy thing.

Then I climb onto my bed. I check my phone, but there are no messages or texts. All I see is the old text from Sloane Devon at the top of the list, telling me to call Dad *ASAP*.

I've worked one miracle today. Maybe it's time for another one.

If I've learned anything from the near-constant whooshing of the toilet, it's that these cinder-block walls with their hollow insides are annoyingly thin. So I tuck my phone into the deep pocket of my sweat pants, slip on a pair of flip-flops, and tiptoe out into the common room.

"Nice take-out." Melody is sitting in the common room.

Considering that she's barely spoken a word to me since we moved in, I didn't expect her to say anything, much less pay me a compliment of sorts.

"Thanks," I say.

"Watch your ass," she says, but there's a hint of a smile on her face. She doesn't look exactly *friendly*, but she doesn't look like she's preparing to roast me on a spit either. Oh, she's going to get me, but I think maybe only on the ice. And that I can live with. At least down there I'm wearing pads and a helmet.

I nod at her, then slide out the door to the hallway.

I head all the way outside and around the back of the building. I don't want anyone overhearing me. Satisfied that no one is around, I lean against the bike rack and click my dad's cell number in my favorites menu. It only rings twice before he answers.

"Sloane?"

"Hi, Dad."

"How's camp?" There's some static, or maybe it's wind, but his voice sounds strange, maybe a little strained.

"Oh, you know, the usual," I reply, and I have to stop myself from nearly laughing at the absurdity of the statement. "Lots of skating."

"I'm glad you're having a good time," he says. "Sounds like your cold is gone too."

"What?" I say.

"Your cold. Two days ago, when I called, you were hacking into the phone."

Oh my God. Sloane Devon must have actually spoken to him. "Oh, right," I squeak. "All gone!"

"Listen, I'm glad you called. I've been wanting to talk with you."

"What about?" There's a long silence on the other end of the line. I hear him clear his throat a few times. "Dad, it's late and I'm exhausted. If you're not going to talk, I'm going to bed."

I shock myself a little with the statement. I've never spoken to either of my parents so plainly before. Maybe I really am exhausted, or maybe I'm just high from my win on the ice. Whatever it is, it obviously shocks my father too.

"I don't like your tone, Sloane," he says. His voice no longer sounds strained. Now it's clipped and angry, like when he's on *Meet the Press* getting grilled about something he doesn't want to discuss.

"That makes two of us, Dad," I shoot back. "Listen, I know it's an election year. I'll be a good daughter. You don't have to worry about me. I know you're busy, with everything—and *everyone*—else you have to worry about."

I hear him suck in a hard breath. He sputters for a few seconds.

"That is completely out of line," he says. "You are completely out of line."

"I'll see you back in DC," I say, then jam my finger down on the red End Call button. I grasp my phone tight in my hand. My heart is pounding so fast that I just want to throw the phone as hard and as far as I can. The urge is so strong that I actually raise my arm over my head, aiming for the parking lot next door.

"Am I interrupting something?"

I turn around and see Matt, the keys to his bike lock in his hand. He's wearing a black zip hoodie over a pair of loose, worn-in jeans, and his hair is wet and curled up around his jaw, fresh from the shower. Oh my God, he's so hot. *Oh my God, stop it.* Oh my God, how long has he been standing there?

"Bad phone call," I reply. *More. I need more. Think.* "Just a friend having guy troubles."

He seems to buy it, thankfully. I'd be toast if he overheard anything about DC, or worse, the campaign. I tell myself to be more careful next time. But there won't be a next time. I don't plan to call my father again this summer. I loosen my grip on my phone and slide it back into my pocket.

He shoots me a patented Matt O'Neill half grin and shrugs. "Guys," he says. "Nothing but trouble."

"You would know," I say, before I can stop myself.

His smile falters. "Listen, I'm not sure what you've heard about me—"

I cut him off. "I haven't heard anything."

"I think you have," he says. He steps closer, and I catch a whiff of his smell: mint and clover and something smoky. I try not to sway on my feet. "I know I have a bit of a reputation, but I don't want you to think—"

"Is it true?" Again, I cut him off.

"Is what true?"

"The story about the girl and the janitor's closet?" I see the recognition flash across his face in waves, first shock, then anger, then something else. Embarrassment? Shame? I can't tell in the dim light.

"Yeah, it's true," he says. He opens his mouth to continue, but I stop him.

"That's all I need to know," I say. I start back into the dorm. I hear him call to me from the bike rack.

"Sloane, wait, let me explain," he says, but I don't need an explanation.

Not from him. And definitely not from my dad.

CHAPTER 14

Sloane Devon

*P*airs sucks.

I was under the impression it would be half as hard. I thought my incompetence would stick out half as much. But it turns out pairs just sucks times two. It *double* sucks.

Even though we're going to be exhibition partners, in class Andy is in the good group, whereas I am in the sucky group. And in most of the classes I'm paired with Roman Andrews, a lanky, pizza-faced blond guy from Kansas whose long program costume is an exact replica of Captain Kirk's uniform. He started sweating the moment our names appeared next to each other on the training lists.

Then there are our coaches, Katinka and Sergei Bolosovic, former Russian national champions turned husband-and-wife coaching duo. Sergei doesn't speak much English, so his coaching is mostly relegated to raised eyebrows, grunts, and strategic eye rolls. Katinka does her best to be supportive, but every piece of advice she offers sounds like it's coming straight from the Cold War.

I can skate and spin, and I've been practicing all those arm-swishing movements in my room whenever Ivy's not around to give me the evil eye. But when it comes to letting someone lift me over his head? That I'm not so good at. I have trouble putting my trust in a pair of arms that have roughly the density of a cooked piece of linguine.

"Sloane! You must go with dee lift!" Katinka skates over to center ice, where I'm flat on my butt, my legs out in front of me in a V shape. Roman is towering over me, sighing.

"You keep saying that, but I still don't know what that means." I mean to say it under my breath, but Katinka hears me.

"I know dis ees first time you do pairs. Ees not easy, I know dis. But you must try." Katinka offers me about one-eighth of a smile, which in Russia is practically a hug. "When Roman lifts, you must lift. Breathe in with dee lift, yes?"

"Yes," I say. I stand up on my skates and turn, eye to eye with Roman. Looking at his lanky arms and narrow hips, I'm thinking the lifting problem might not be only with me.

"Roman, you lift." Katinka nods and crosses her arms behind her back. I'd feel more comfortable if she prepped herself to catch me, because it looks like the last thing Roman lifted over his head was his Han Solo action figure as he positioned it above his bed. No joke, the kid brought his dolls to summer camp.

"I'll do my best," Roman says, with another gargantuan sigh.

Katinka counts off, and Roman and I take off side by side. The move, which three couples before us all completed without incident, calls for me to drop back a stride. Then Roman is supposed to grab my right hand, pull me toward him, then wrap his hands around my waist and use the momentum to lift me straight up. It's an "elementary lift," as Katinka keeps saying, in that Roman uses both hands and I'm not upside down or anything, thank God. He isn't even supposed to hold me up very long. It's supposed to be a fluid lift, my arms artfully over my head. Afterward, he's supposed to deposit me gracefully back onto the ice.

So far he's deposited me onto my butt. Three times. Thanks a lot, Roman.

At the required speed, I drop back. Roman grabs my hand with his sweaty palm, and pulls me in. His hands are around my waist. I breathe in and try to go with the lift, like Katinka says, but as I feel my skates leave the ground, I hear Roman let out a grunt the likes of which I haven't heard outside of a Wimbledon tennis match. It does not inspire confidence. And so I do what comes naturally. I try to catch myself. I grab onto his hands, which are holding on to my waist so tight I think his bony little fingers are going to leave bruises. I feel his arms buckle, his grip slip.

I yelp, and then I flail, as if I'm trying to hoist myself back up into the air like you would if you were falling out of a piggyback ride. This causes Roman to just sort of let go.

And then I'm tumbling again. I swing my legs to get them down before my butt, but it's not the ice they make contact with. It's Roman, or, to be more accurate, Roman's groin.

The impact is so hard, my knee actually hurts. Katinka yips, the other skaters gasp, and I think I actually hear Sergei say "Oh my God."

The only person who doesn't make a sound is Roman. He's on his knees, doubled over, staring at some invisible point on the ice, his face red and getting redder. He looks like a pressure cooker about to blow with the loudest, longest stream of profanities.

"Roman, I'm so sorry," I say. Even though it was mostly his fault. I went with the lift. Where was he going?

Roman looks up and focuses his angry stare on me. His beady little eyes narrow. "You," he finally says. "You are the *worst* partner *ever*. No one could partner you. *No one!*"

Sergei and Katinka speed over to him. Sergei helps Roman to his skates and starts leading him off the ice. But before he goes, he looks over his shoulder and shouts, "No one!"

Jeez. Drama queen much, Roman?

"I think I need a new partner," I say to Katinka, who offers me what I think is a sympathetic nod. That or she's considering shipping me off to a gulag.

"We will find you someone more . . . substantial," she says.

"Yeah, okay," I say. "Preferably someone who can at least bench the equivalent of my weight?"

"Muscles ees not dee issue. You need partner who control you, because you no trust. You must *trust*," Katinka says.

Across the ice, the three other male skaters seem to almost shrink behind their partners. Their body language screams, *Not me! Oh please God, not me!*

"Maybe Andy could join this group?" I give Katinka my most pathetic face, in hopes that she'll take pity on me. "I think we might be a good match."

"Andy ees very good skater." She looks at me hard, as if trying to determine whether I'll bring Andy down with me. That one-eighth of a smile reappears, one penciled-in eyebrow arched high. "Yes, I think you are right. Tomorrow we meet during free time. You need work." I hope she means "you need *to* work," but I think she means I need some serious skater renovation. With only two weeks until the final exhibition, I'm pretty sure she's right.

At least Ivy will be happy. I'm not giving her a run for her money—or spandex—out here. It'll be the Cinderella story of the summer if I manage not to maim my partner.

After practice I lie in bed, flat on my back, my arms and legs splayed out around me. It turns out falling on your butt over and over again is pretty stinking exhausting. When I agreed to the swap, I figured I'd be giving my body a bit of a rest from the body war that is hockey. I assumed that my knee might even get a little time to heal over these four weeks. Wrong, wrong, double wrong.

I hear a drum solo coming from inside the wardrobe—my

ringtone. I groan, thinking that my phone might as well be all the way back in Philly. There's no way I'm getting up and going all the way over there.

Who could be calling me, anyway? Dad hasn't bothered to check in with me since I left, and so I haven't bothered to call him either.

Mom always used to make me call her and let her know where I was. That was the rule. In exchange for never having a real curfew, I had to agree to call her anytime I "changed location," as she said. Even at her worst, she'd always answer the phone when I called and always expected me to check in. But ever since she's gone away, I haven't spoken to her at all. No phones in the first thirty days. Them's the rules.

The drums reach a fever pitch, and I know the call will go to voice mail soon. What if it *is* Dad? What if it's an emergency?

The drum solo starts over, and now I know I have only a few seconds left. "Aw, hell," I mutter, then leap out of the bed with the last ounce of energy I have. I fling open the wardrobe door, reach into the pocket, pull out the phone, and click the Answer button without even checking the number.

"Hello?"

"Sloane?" It's not my dad, although it's definitely a guy's voice.

"Who is this?"

"It's Nando."

It takes me a good solid five seconds before it all clicks together. Nando, of course. Nando with his dark eyes and that confident-but-not-cocky swagger and lips close to mine and—

"Oh, Nando! Hi! How are you?" It comes out a little more enthusiastically than I'd hoped. I wish I could swallow back the words. I sound like a greeter at Walmart.

"I'm great," he says. I can hear the smile in his deep voice. "I just wanted to see if you could get away. No hockey this time. Maybe food. We can hang out?"

"That sounds great," I reply. I collapse onto the bed, my phone pressed against my ear, equal parts exhaustion and excitement. Nando. Studly, sweet, kickass Nando. This totally makes up for my hippo-on-skates performance in practice today.

But then I remember that before I finally left the rink in shame, Katinka told me that if I didn't start improving, she'd schedule me for evening sessions on the ice. My stomach drops. Katinka didn't say it, but I'm pretty sure this is the equivalent of after-school tutoring for the kid who can't pass the algebra test. I don't care if figure skating isn't my thing, I can't turn in another performance like today's. No one will believe I'm Sloane Emily if I spend 90 percent of my time flat on my butt. And worse than that, I'll be a loser. I'll be the worst. I'll be the bottom rung—if I'm not already; word of my attack on Roman today has probably gotten out. I can't take that.

If I'm going to make it through this summer without

totally humiliating myself, I can't spend my nights with Nando, even if he does have a badass slap shot.

"I can pick you up in an hour?"

"I'm really sorry," I say. "It *does* sound great, but I can't." I can feel the excitement ebbing away, the exhaustion taking over. "I'm sort of behind. I need to focus."

"You're behind? Not from what I could see at the game the other day," he says. Oh right, I'm supposed to be at hockey camp. Crap.

"Well, you remember what it was like," I explain. "Before you got scouted? It's just a lot of pressure."

"Yeah, I remember." Something changes in his voice. "Listen, maybe another time. You gotta relax every now and then, or trust me, the pressure is going to get to you."

"Totally," I say. "I'll call you soon, okay?"

"Sounds good," he says. "Night, Sloane."

I click the button, roll over, and fling my phone underneath the bed. I feel a twinge in my shoulder at the motion. I bury my face in the covers and moan. But I know what I've got to do. If I can get my act together by Friday, maybe Katinka will let me out of my detention—er, extra training.

It takes me fifteen minutes to lace up my sneakers. That's how tired I am. It takes me another ten to make it down the stairs and to the east wing of the building, where all the practice studios are. By the time I get there, I feel a second wind coming on. I choose a studio all the way at the end of the hall, in hopes that it's the last one anyone will walk into.

The room is about the size of a master bedroom. The

front and back walls are mirrored. There's a desk in the corner with an iMac and a full stereo. I pull up YouTube and click through to some how-to videos Sloane showed me. They're hosted by a smiling Nancy Kerrigan in crisp black leggings and a fitted fleece, gliding effortlessly across the ice demonstrating salchows and camel spins. I press Play, then step back and do the moves along with her on my sneakers. And when the video is over, I do it again.

As I work my way through a series of videos on choreography, I start to think about those brisk fall nights back home in our backyard. Okay, "backyard" might be a charitable description of the twenty square feet of broken concrete that make up our fenced-in patio. But it was my own little practice room under the moon. I'd take a ball and my stick out there and practice slap shots over and over against the brick wall until my neighbor, Mrs. Fernandez, would poke her curler-covered head out the upstairs window next door and beg me to cut it out. When I'd finally call it a night, Mom would be "asleep" on the couch, the glow of some Lifetime movie cast over her face, an empty wineglass on the floor next to her. When I was younger I'd nudge her awake and help her up the stairs to bed, but in recent years I just left her there. It was getting harder and harder to wake her.

On the glowing screen in the practice room, Kristi Yamaguchi is skipping and spinning across the ice in a black and gold dress at the 1992 Olympics. She goes up for a split jump. The crowd roars, and I drop my arms. I just stand there, watching her while she moves into the slow section. The commentator is talking about how, if she can just land this one jump, she'll surely win the gold medal.

She skates backward, winding up for the jump, and I hold my breath. She goes up, wobbles, and falls out of the jump. Her hand goes down on the ice.

She gets back up and finishes her program, an almost-convincing smile on her face. I let out a long sigh. The biggest name in figure skating ate it in front of millions of viewers.

Then she picked herself up and finished. And she scored a gold medal.

Maybe I should pick myself up too.

CHAPTER 15

Sloane Emily

My nails are a disaster.

And it's not just my nails. My cuticles are ragged, I've got callouses forming on my palms, and the french tips I had done at my favorite salon in Arlington before I left are turning about six shades of gray. It's all from having my hands crammed in Sloane Devon's grubby gloves for five hours a day. I don't know when the last time she cleaned those things was, but based on the smell, I'd say it was around the time Miley Cyrus was still Hannah Montana.

Luckily, today I plan to do something about it. I used my laptop to Yelp a salon for the perfect manicure and found one on Rue St. Denis only a few blocks away.

Today is our free morning workout. It's a time for us to work out any stiffness or sore muscles or practice a new skill we learned in class. I plan to work out my cuticles, thank you very much.

I gather my phone, keys, and purse and head out the door. Halfway down the hall I realize I should probably ask Cameron if she wants to come along. I pivot-turn and walk back down the hall, past my room and the bathroom. Cameron has the room on the *other* side of the bathroom, only hers is a single, meaning she gets her very own sitting room and no Melody.

I knock on the heavy wooden door.

"Coming!"

The door swings open and Cameron is there, only instead of one of her adorable outfits, she's got on a pair of yoga pants, a tank, and a red practice jersey.

"Are you seriously working out right now?" I eye her ensemble.

"And you're not?" She stares back at Sloane Devon's ratty jeans, which I've rolled and cuffed into a reasonable approximation of a trendy boyfriend capri, and a red Jefferson High hockey tee. I cut the collar out so it hangs off one shoulder. I'm sure she won't mind—they probably give these things out like candy.

"Uh, no," I say. I hold out my hands. "I was thinking it was time for a manicure. I thought you might want to join me."

"Sloane, didn't you see the notice?"

"What notice?"

She grabs my hand and drags me down the hall to the elevator and jabs at a neon-yellow flyer tacked onto the corkboard next to the Up and Down buttons.

BOSTON UNIVERSITY SCOUT ON CAMPUS TODAY
OPEN ICE 10 A.M.–2 P.M.
SIGN UP AT THE OFFICE FOR AN INTERVIEW

"Their women's team scout is here today. How did you not know?"

Uh, probably because I spent my morning hiding in my room letting a deep conditioner do its magic on my hair.

The reality hits me hard, though. A scout? Here? Oh crap.

"Manicures tomorrow," she says. She leads me back down the hall and stops in front of my door. "There's a hole in the schedule just after lunch; we can be out and back before anyone notices we're gone. There's a place close by that has the *best* organic products, and your nails *have* been looking seriously torn up. But now? We skate. Go get changed. I'll finish getting geared up and meet you back here in ten."

As soon as her door is closed, I turn on my heel and bolt to my room. Inside, I whip out my phone and dash off a text to Sloane. I hope she's not in class or something, because I need serious advice. Like, now.

Scouts are here! What do I do?

It takes about point two seconds for my phone to buzz a response. There's just one word in the little blue bubble on the screen.

Hide.

I grab a tote, stuff my phone and wallet inside, and then run to the elevator. I have to get out of here before I see a coach, or worse, the scout. It's one thing to lie to the staff; it's another to possibly jeopardize Sloane Devon's entire future. At one point she mentioned needing a hockey scholarship for college, and I do *not* want to be responsible for screwing that up. If anyone asks me later where I was, I'll just claim I never saw the notice. I reach up and snatch it off the bulletin board for good measure.

There. Plausible deniability.

The elevator doors slide open and I jab the Lobby button. The elevator glides down the shaft and the doors slide open. I take one step out into the lobby and see Coach Amber walk through the door with a tall, thin guy in a red polo, the words BOSTON UNIVERSITY stitched across the heart in white.

Oh God. The scout. Amber spots me and starts to wave me over, but I quickly avert my eyes and pretend I don't notice. I leap back into the elevator and jab the button for the basement. I can sneak out the back.

The elevator doors open again, and I take a giant leap out onto the linoleum tile. Ten more steps to the other side of the room and I'm out the back door and home free.

"Sloane!"

Crap. Matt.

Not just Matt—the entire guys' advanced team. They're piled on couches and chairs, and when they ran out of seating they spilled out onto the floor. There are giant, sweaty boys as far as the eye can see. They're watching some grainy old game that looks like it's from the Olympics.

"Oh, hi, Matt!" I say, trying not to break stride. "I was just on my way out."

"Come watch tape with us!" he says.

Eleven heads pivot back to the screen. Matt jumps up from his spot on the couch and jogs over to me. He sticks his hands in his pockets and tosses his bangs out of his eyes. I notice he looks nervous.

"Listen, about last night . . . I just want to be friends, okay?"

It strikes me as an odd change of tactic, but I'm anxious to get out of here. "Fine," I say. "That's fine. Friends."

"Awesome," he says, smiling broadly. "So I was thinking we could go out for a bite. As friends."

If I say no, he'll just try to convince me. And I need to get out of here.

"Yeah, sure," I say quickly.

"Great," he says. He reaches over and adjusts my purse strap, which is about to fall off my shoulder. "Meet you in the lobby, two o'clock? Come hungry."

"That sounds perfect," I say. "I'll be back."

I bolt for the door, trying to process the fact that I just agreed to spend time with the playboy of Elite. At least meeting Matt at two means I can disappear during all the open-ice time and then peace out again right when the scout is leaving. It's perfect.

I push through the back door, emerging just in front of the bike racks. I stride up the little stone path that leads around to the street and start to breathe easy. I made it.

"Sloane!" Coach Hannah. She's coming at me from the front of the building. "I'm glad I ran into you. I didn't see your name on the interview list, and I figured since you're going into your senior year, you definitely wouldn't want to miss out on a chance to talk to the scout."

"Right." *Damn damn damn!* "I was planning to sign up. I just wanted to run an errand really quick. I can sign up when I get back."

"Well, his schedule is filling up fast. Most of the later slots are taken. But I saw the list—he's got an opening right now. Do you want to jump on that?"

"Oh, uh, great, well—" I try to grasp for an excuse, but from Coach Hannah's stern expression, I know if I ditch, she'll realize something is up. I take a deep breath. "Let's go, then!"

"Great!" she says. "He's down at the rink. I was just heading over there. I can walk with you."

I follow her down the sidewalk to the arena next door, feeling like I'm heading to my execution. She chatters on about meeting the McGill scout for the first time and all the visits she made and how hard it was to decide which school to pick. I hear her say something about "the Harvard of Canada," but I'm barely listening.

Sure, from across a room you could mistake Sloane Devon and me for each other, but if this scout wants to conduct some kind of interview, he'll remember my face. And then he'll remember that it's *not* the same face as the girl who could potentially show up on campus in a year.

And if he meets me and hates me, Sloane Devon isn't going to make a visit at all—because she won't be going to college there. Either way, I lose, and she loses.

Hannah leads me into the front doors and down the steps. "He's over there." She points across the stands to the other side of the ice, where the scout is sitting next to Coach Amber. They're talking, and Amber is pointing to a skater on the ice who's making shot after shot. It's Melody.

"I can go myself!" I practically screech. I have to formulate a plan between here and there, and if that plan involves running for my life, I don't want Hannah at my side to hold me back. She gives me a strange look, but just nods and turns to head toward the locker room.

Think, think. I have probably three minutes before I'm in front of the scout. Three minutes to figure out what the hell I'm going to do. I get to the bottom of the steps and turn to wind around the far end of the rink (sure, it's three times as long, but this gives me more time to think). I'm just barely at ice level when I trip over something large that clatters beneath my feet. It's a hockey helmet with a thick wire face mask. It won't completely hide my face, but it's better than nothing.

I grab it and jam it onto my head. It's tight, but it fits, and it only smells like a dead fish a little bit.

I climb the steps, and within seconds I'm mask to face with Coach Amber and the scout.

She gives me a look that says, "Who let you out of the

asylum?" but instead just introduces me to Joe Rutherford, representative from the Boston University ice hockey team.

"Nice to meet you," I say, shaking his hand.

"Nice helmet," he says.

"Oh, thanks," I say, and giggle like I'm always wandering around in jeans and a face mask. "I was thinking about getting one like this, but I wanted to really test the fit, you know? Gotta protect the old noggin. So I'm just wearing it around. Safety first!"

I say this like it makes absolute total sense, and Mr. Rutherford just laughs. He *laughs*. Like this is all quirky, but normal.

"Sloane, I read your file. You come highly recommended by Coach Butler. He and I are old friends, you know."

"Oh?" The name rings a bell. Sloane Devon's coach back home, I think, but I can't be sure. Best to stay vague.

"Heard you're a serious offensive threat. Got a slap shot like he's never seen."

"Well, I'm flattered," I say.

"Also heard you've got a bit of an anger problem?"

"I, uh—"

Amber jumps in. "We haven't seen that at all here," she says. "Sloane has been a great team player. Never hogging the puck, always congratulating her teammates."

It's true. I don't hog the puck, mostly because I'm doing my best to keep from ever touching it. And the constant praise of my teammates helps takes the focus off my own playing. But I can see Mr. Rutherford is still looking at me for an explanation, and I have to give him one that'll make him think Sloane Devon isn't any kind of loose cannon or psycho on the ice. I have to reassure him. For her.

"I've always played hard, and there have been times in the past where my passion has gotten the best of me," I say. "But those have all been learning moments for me. I'd say I've learned to become an aggressive yet controlled player."

He smiles and nods and I relax a little. Maybe I did learn something from my father. I can spin with the best of 'em.

"That's really good to hear, Sloane," Mr. Rutherford says. He shakes my hand again. "I'm looking forward to seeing you on the ice."

"Definitely!" I say. My heart sinks. Great—I'm going to *have* to skate for him. Sloane Devon's entire future rests on my performance. I hope she knows how lucky she is to have someone as dedicated as me living her life. She had better be hustling just as hard across town. "Let me go get changed."

I race back to my room and swap out my jeans and T-shirt for practice gear. I take out Sloane's black varsity jersey, her name sewn on the back in thick yellow letters. I'm going to need it to get into character. I dash off a quick text to Sloane Devon before returning to the arena.

Scout here. Am skating. Will try not to suck.

A half hour later, I'm suited up and taking my first step onto the ice. I look up and see Mr. Rutherford, still parked next to Amber. Hannah has joined them, and the two coaches give me covert thumbs-ups from the stands. Like that will help me.

I shake out my left foot, then my right, then my left arm, then my right, just like I do before my long program. *Gotta shake out the jitters*, Henry always used to say. Thinking about his voice makes me miss my home rink back in DC, where I could do *my* skating for an audience of zero. How the heck did I end up at hockey camp?

I shouldn't be here.

But here I am. Mackenzie, the skater from check-in, is down here. There's another skater I don't recognize sitting in the goal. And Melody, of course. She skates up and skids to a stop intimidatingly close to me. Our helmets are nearly touching.

"Couch A says she wants us to do a little one-on-one for the scout," Melody says. "BU is my first choice, so don't make me look bad or I'll make you pay."

I don't want to know what that means. "Back atcha," I mutter, but she's already adjusting her helmet and slapping the ice to get psyched up. I mentally curse the skating gods, hockey and otherwise, for putting me with Melody on what is already the worst ice experience of my life, other than my epic fail at junior nationals.

"All right, let's have Mackenzie on defense. Melody and Sloane, I want to see some teamwork from you on offense," Coach Amber shouts across the ice. Melody slaps her stick hard on the surface, and the ice splinters a little beneath her. I'm sure she's none too happy to have to work with me.

But she looks over and nods. I nod back, hoping this means she won't kill me.

Mackenzie skates off to center ice and faces us, her back to the goal. Coach Amber slides a shiny black puck across the ice. I stop it with my stick. Melody and I line up for our attempt. Mackenzie starts skating backward, her eyes locked on us. I start to charge, then quickly pass the puck to Melody. Mackenzie apparently anticipated that her efforts were better spent on Melody, because she's already halfway to her, and Melody has no choice but to pass back to me. Mackenzie's not quick enough, and I shoot. The puck skids past the goalkeeper and hits the net.

Oh my God. I actually scored.

We line up again. This time Melody starts with the puck. Mackenzie goes for her right away, but Melody executes a spinning juke, shoots, and scores.

For the third attempt, I start with the puck. Mackenzie has learned her lesson and doesn't commit to either of us right away. I drive forward a few strides, then pass to Melody. Mackenzie charges her. There's no time for Melody to take a clear shot. She passes back to me. I take a few more strides toward the goal, heart pounding, just managing to keep the puck in control. Mackenzie heads toward the goal to defend. Her eyes are locked on me, and I realize that the best chance to score is to pass to Melody.

With Mackenzie's eyes glued to me, and her body turned to defend against my attack, I slap the puck left to Melody. She doesn't even stop it, just winds up and connects with the whizzing puck. It shifts direction and heads straight for the goal. Mackenzie wasn't expecting it, and we score.

"Nice!" Melody shouts, and I can't tell if she's congratulating herself or congratulating me. I see both Mr. Rutherford and Coach Hannah clapping in the stands.

"One more," Coach Amber calls, and we line it up again.

This time Mackenzie is all over Melody right from the start. I take a deep breath and skate. I drive straight for the goal, but in a flash, Mackenzie is on me. She was faking me out, just waiting for me to let my guard down. I look to pass, but I'd have to shoot the puck straight through Mackenzie. I move to her right at the last moment. She goes in to stop me.

And then something amazing happens. I pick up my left foot and spin fast on my right. I make it around her in one beautiful rotation, and then I'm off. She sprints after me. But just before she can get her leg in front of me, I execute a split jump and leap past her, giving the puck an extra push to go with me. *Swish, swish, swish,* and then I'm at the goal. I haul back in what I hope is a good approximation of all the YouTube videos I watched, and shoot. I score.

I hear applause and even a long whistle from the stands. Amber, Hannah, and Mr. Rutherford are on their feet. Inside my head, an entire marching band is playing a *Jock Jams* soundtrack. Holy crap, did I just do that? Melody skates over and gives me a high five.

"Nice moves, Jacobs," she says, grinning. I realize I don't think I've ever seen her smile.

"Thanks!" I say, and my smile beams out like a spotlight across the ice.

"Calm down, it was one shot, rook." Okay, so same old Melody.

The rest of the practice goes fine. Nothing spectacular. We switch up positions. When I'm on defense, I only keep Melody from scoring once, but I hope Mr. Rutherford chalks that up to Sloane Devon's experience as a predominantly offensive player and the fact that Melody is damn good. When Melody is on D, we score about three-quarters of the time. Each shot gets Melody more and more riled until I'm afraid she's going to lay me out from behind. I'm actually semi-disappointed that she doesn't.

When we're done, Mr. Rutherford shakes my hand and tells me he'll be in touch, which I take as a decent sign.

As I make my way back to my room to shower, I'm all smiles, until I step off the elevator and see a tall guy folded up on the floor in front of my door. It's Matt, his back to the door, his legs bent and still taking up most of the hallway. I glance at the clock by the elevator: 4:00.

"I'm sorry," I say. But Matt just shakes his head.

"Sloane, look, I know what you think about me. But people make mistakes. And people change." He actually looks wounded. "Blowing me off was not cool. You said we could be friends."

"I know. I'm so sorry," I say again.

"So you said." He stands up and walks away from me, heading toward the stairs at the end of the hall. He stops and looks back to me. "I want to tell you that you're wrong about me. Because you are."

Before I can speak, he turns on his heel and heads straight for the stairs.

CHAPTER 16

Sloane Devon

"Thirty-three . . . thirty-four . . . thirty-five."

My fingers sink into the plush white carpeting. I huff and puff out the count, trying to ignore the burn that's starting in my biceps.

"Thirty-six . . . thirty-seven."

"Give it a rest, GI Jane," Ivy says from the bed, where she's lazily filing her nails (probably into razor-sharp points).

"Shut. Up." I suck air as I snap back at her.

"Sleep. I need it." She tosses her file onto the nightstand and fluffs her pillow. Her pink cami and matching booty shorts are so tiny and so bright, they're practically offensive.

"Almost. Done," I say. I shake a bead of sweat off my forehead before it rolls into my eye. "Forty-two. Forty-three."

With the Pilates and the yoga and the morning runs around the grounds and the water aerobics, plus all the skating, I'm working out just as hard as I ever did back home. But it doesn't matter how long I can hold warrior pose if I can't still crank out fifty push-ups. Coach Butler will have me doing morning workouts for sure if I come home and can only get through twenty.

If I'm still playing when I get back, that is. None of it will matter when Coach Butler gets a crappy report from that scout. I texted Sloane Emily to find out what happened, but she never wrote back, which must mean it didn't go well. How *could* it? The girl only learned to play hockey two weeks ago.

I increase my speed and pound out the last few. When I hit fifty, I drop flat on the ground, my nose buried in the rug.

"Finally. Gold star for you." Ivy yanks the chain on the lamp by her bed, plunging the room into darkness, never mind the fact that I still have to shower and change into my pajamas.

I roll over onto my back and breathe quietly in the dark. I haven't done fifty push-ups since I left Philly over two weeks ago. I used to be able to get at least seventy-five no problem, but tonight was tough. I'm out of practice. I wonder what else is getting rusty while I perform camel spins and arabesques.

When my breathing returns to normal, I creep into the bathroom and close the door as quietly as I can before flipping on the light. I spot myself in the mirror. I'm wearing one of Sloane's black leotards with the puckering in the chest and a pair of pink knit leggings rolled at the waist. My long black hair is gathered in a messy bun, but a sheer pink scarf tied around my head mostly hides the frizzies. I don't look like someone who spends her evening doing fifty push-ups.

I yank the scarf off, strip out of the rest of my borrowed clothes, and climb into a steamy hot shower. I let the water run down my face in fat streams, and my mind goes where it always goes as soon as I get in the shower: to the game. This time it's the scrimmage with Nando and his buddies. I was okay. Not my best, but definitely not my worst. Not until that missed shot, that is. With my eyes closed, the steam closing in, I start to feel the tingles again. The humiliation climbs up my spine like a persistent inchworm of misery.

So maybe it's not such a bad thing that Sloane Emily was the one skating for the scout. It's not like I could have made a shot. I couldn't even make a shot while playing a pickup game in front of an old friend and a bunch of weekend warriors.

I spin the faucet and the water stops all at once. It's totally silent except for the sound of a million missed shots all in my head. And suddenly all I want is to make a shot. Just one. I need to hear the puck connect with the net so that maybe the sound of a million defeats will go away.

I creep back into the bedroom and feel my way to the

wardrobe. I find my cell phone in the back and use its il-luminated face as a flashlight, digging around until I find a pair of black sweatpants—flared-leg fleece things with PRINCETON printed down the leg in bright orange, but still, sweatpants—and a plain white tee. I wiggle into them, then pad toward the door, throwing Sloane Emily's skates over my shoulder.

The practice rink is inside a barn, outside the main build-ing and down a little grassy hill on the back of the property. For most of our classes and lessons we're down the block at a large, professional-looking arena. The practice rink is smaller, about half the size of a regular rink, and mostly used for one-on-one lessons and voluntary extra practice.

Inside, I fumble for the switch on the wall that illumi-nates the ice. The rink is very plain: a concrete perimeter and a two-foot-high wooden barrier encircle the ice. They must have Zambonied it before the end of the day, because it's smooth as glass.

I lace up Sloane's skates, then step over the barrier, test-ing the ice. It's perfect. I push off with my left foot, my right leg straight, my left extending behind me in a perfect arabesque. But after only one stride, I drop my butt and bend my knees. My arms go to my sides, and I push out hard with my left foot. I shoot forward, then push with my right. Left, right, left, right, my arms rising and falling just like I learned in my very first speed skating lesson when I was a kid. When I approach the end of the rink, I cross my right foot over and push deep with my left. In only two strides I've made the turn and am flying back down the straightaway. Midway through, I flip around so I'm skating backward, crossing over into the opposite turn. Then I'm cutting across center ice in a quick two-step. Then I'm back in the other direction. Step, step, step, slide. Step, step, step, slide. It's harder in these ridiculous skates with their ridiculous heel, but I've used them enough that I know how to make it work.

Soon I'm holding a phantom hockey stick, taking an invisible puck up and down the ice. As I drive to the end of the rink, I imagine a roaring crowd, the way it was before. I wind up, I eye the imaginary goalie, I shoot, I score. No tingles. Just cheers.

I skid to a stop and spin fast, holding the imaginary hockey stick high over my head.

"Nice moves, ice princess."

The voice comes out of nowhere and sends me spinning right onto my butt. I look up and around and spot Andy leaning in the doorway. His arms are crossed, and though I can't quite see him that well in the dim light, I can imagine his left eyebrow is arched high.

"How long have you been there?" I have to work to control my breathing.

"Long enough to see you win the invisible Stanley Cup," he says. He walks to the edge of the ice, and I see he has his skates slung over one shoulder. "And I thought I was the only one doing secret midnight workouts. You got something you want to tell me?"

My heart is pounding. I climb to my feet and start gliding, my legs out straight. "What do you mean?"

"Girl, don't mess with me. I know you're hiding something." He takes one tentative step out on the ice in his sneakers, and once he's confident of his footing, he strides over to center ice. "You do all right, but your posture is garbage, you eat like a trucker, you can't execute a simple lift, and you dyed Ivy pink. But obviously you *can* skate. After seeing this little display, I'm inclined to think maybe you're not the pretty princess you're pretending to be."

I rack my brain for an excuse. Maybe I can tell him I had a traumatic brain injury that caused amnesia as the result of a plane crash, and so I forgot how to skate.

As if he can read my mind, Andy holds up a hand. "Don't even think about trying to lie to me," he says.

Just like that, I know I have to tell him the truth.

"You figured right," I reply. I feel like Zdeno Chara, the biggest, scariest Boston Bruin, has just climbed off my shoulders. I breathe deep and don't feel afraid. He knows. I don't have to hide. "Please don't tell anyone."

A wicked grin spreads across Andy's face. He reaches out and pulls me into a crazy bear hug. When he steps back, his eyes are sparkling. We're not just friends anymore. We're conspirators.

"Your secret's safe with me, so long as you fill me in on all the dirt." He cocks his head toward the bench on the far side of the ice. I follow him over and we plop down. I scissor my skates along the ice, forward, back, forward, back, a nervous habit I've had since I first started playing. I hardly know where to begin.

"My name *is* Sloane Jacobs," I say. Might as well start with the basics. "Only, I'm not the Sloane Jacobs who's supposed to be here. I'm the Sloane Jacobs who's from northeast Philly, who's supposed to be across the city playing hockey for four weeks. Or trying to, anyway. But instead, I decided to switch places with the other Sloane. And now I'm spending my summer as a figure skater."

Andy stares at me hard for what feels like an eternity. I can practically see the wheels turning in his brain, and I know I've done a crap job of explaining. He finally takes a deep breath and puts his hand on my knee to stop my stationary skating. "So you're saying there's another girl, also named Sloane Jacobs, who is a figure skater and is supposed to be spending her summer here, but you guys pulled some kind of *Parent Trap* situation that has her being you playing hockey, and you being her trying to figure skate?"

"What do you mean, *trying*?" I punch him softly on the shoulder and try to feign being insulted.

Andy gives me another big, rocking hug, then sits back. "Sloane Jacobs, I think you're my hero."

"Thanks," I reply. I hadn't realized until I began speaking how much I've been aching to tell someone, anyone, my secret. "We met the night before I got here. Ran into each other—literally—at the hotel. And we decided to switch. It was her idea."

"C'mon, there's gotta be more to this story than that," he says. "Why were you so desperate to change places?"

"I don't really want to talk about it. Not right now, anyway," I say. "I hope that's okay."

"All in your own time, I guess." He kicks off his shoes and pushes them under the bench, then starts lacing up his skates. "Come on. Stand up. We have some work to do."

"What do you mean?" I'm still shocked that he hasn't written me off for being a big fat liar. Or at least a muscled one.

"These first two weeks have been cake," he says. He ties the last knot and jumps up onto the ice. "But things are going to get real hard, real fast. And you're going to need some help if you're going to keep this insane plan a secret. Now get up off that bench and come skate with me."

"But I was just blowing off steam out here, I wasn't—"

"Up. Now." Andy stamps his foot down into the ice and little shards shoot up around his foot. He points a finger down at a spot in front of him and glares at me until I relent. "I saw you in class yesterday trying to do that baby lift with Roman. Pathetic. We're going to master it, right here, right now."

"But, Andy, I'm tired, and—"

"You whine like that to your hockey coach?"

I imagine Coach Butler's reaction if I told him I was too tired. It would probably involve a red face and some flying spittle. I shake my head.

"All right, then. Let's do it."

For the next fifteen minutes, we work the move over and over until I worry Andy's arms are going to fall off. I can't seem to get all the way into the air.

"This sucks! Seriously, who learns to figure skate in a few weeks? What was I thinking?" I kick the ice hard, leaving a golf-ball-sized divot on the smooth surface.

"Your problem is that you're too tense. Too wound up. You're not letting go, not going with the lift."

"People keep telling me to go with the lift, and I *still* don't know what it means." I cross my arms and tap my toe pick on the ice.

"It means you need to imagine that you're lifting *yourself* off the ice. You need to breathe in with the motion and trust your partner to do the rest. If you're constantly trying to catch yourself, you're definitely going to fall."

"I'm going to fall because I'm a freaking hockey player in a tutu."

"I don't see a tutu, do you?" Andy gives me a friendly death glare. "Cut the crap and focus. You can do this. Don't make me go all *Dangerous Minds* on you."

"You're going to have to if you expect to get this butt in the air," I mutter.

"Eyes on me, tough girl." Andy puts a finger under my chin and pulls my gaze right to him. "You can do this. Most people fail because they're afraid to attempt the jump. But you're not afraid, are you?"

I look into Andy's dark brown eyes. They're focused right on me, unblinking. I think about the scout and the fact that I've probably tanked my whole future. I think about my mom, and how in one day she nearly died and then disappeared from my life. I think about hockey, and how much I love it, and how much I hate that I can't do it anymore.

"I'm afraid of a lot of things," I say, "but this isn't one of them."

"Damn right," he says.

Without a word, he pushes off down the ice. I follow him. At first we're side by side; then I drop back. Andy grabs my hand and pulls me in fast. It only takes a split second for me to be at his side again. I bend my knees and take a deep breath. As I do, I feel myself rise off the ice. I close my eyes. *Go with it.* Andy's hands are around my waist, and I let go of his grip and raise my hands high. When I open my eyes, I see that I'm over his head, speeding across the ice.

"Go with it," I hear him say below me.

"What?" And then I'm spinning back over his shoulder, the same move we did back at the pub. I trust him, and within seconds I'm back on my skates, gliding next to him. Andy grabs my hands and spins me around in a ring-around-the-rosie move. We spin to a stop and he gives me a hard high five.

"You did it!" he practically shouts. "If you keep this up, you're gonna give Ivy a run for her money."

I laugh. "Yeah, about that," I say. "It's possible that I told her I'd throw the final expo. Which probably wasn't such a bad thing, since I have zero chance of not looking like a fool out there."

"Screw that, and screw her," Andy says. He bends down and tightens the lace on his left skate. "What we're going to do is work on one jump. One double axel. It won't be easy, but you're going to get it, because you're not afraid, right?"

I sigh. "Right."

"I'm sorry, but that doesn't sound like that badass hockey player that you are," Andy barks. "Because the badass hockey player could land a double axel no problem, *right?*"

"Right!" I shout, my voice echoing off the ice and around the barn. I feel energized. I feel psyched. I feel *tingles,* only this time they're in my feet and they're making me want to leap into the air.

CHAPTER 17

SLOANE EMILY

The elevator door slides open, and the smell of fried food, melted cheese, and musty basement washes over me like a tsunami.

I stop outside the elevator doors, confused. "Your text said Coach Hannah wanted to see me down here . . . ?"

Matt is standing behind the couch, in front of the coffee table. I can make out a spread on the table behind him, and from the smell, it's some kind of heart-attack-themed picnic.

"Um, I might have told you a bit of a lie," he says. He steps aside so I can see the take-out containers, bags, and bottles on the table. He gives a little vaudeville-style "Ta-da."

"What's all this?"

"This is a culinary blend of cultures. First, we have cheesesteaks. I found this place that's almost just like Geno's back home. For dessert, we have French macaroons in blueberry, raspberry, and vanilla and a few slices of apple pie from the good old U.S. of A. And to drink, your choice of a fine sparkling cider"—he shows off the bottle like it's a ten-year-old bottle of champagne—"or Yoo-hoo, the American classic."

I still haven't moved an inch. "You got all this . . . for me?"

"But that's not all!" he says in his best game-show-host voice. "I also rented *Slap Shot* for our viewing pleasure. Or yours. I understand if you don't want me to stay. . . ."

"But . . ." I can hardly form a sentence. "Why?"

Matt shrugs. "You've been avoiding a date. Even a friendly one. So I decided to ambush you." He spreads his hands. "Remember, I play hockey. Ambushing people is kind of my thing."

"I don't get it." I shake my head. "I blow you off, and you bring me a picnic?"

"Sure did."

"Why?" I ask again.

"I'm going to change your mind about me," he says, watching me steadily. "I like you, Sloane."

I'm tempted to ask "Why?" again, but I refrain.

"I did some crappy things in the past," he admits. "But like I said, people change. I changed."

Looking at his smile and his floppy hair and the table full of food, I want to believe him more than I've wanted anything in a long time.

I cross the room and pick up a bottle of Yoo-hoo, which is sweating from the humidity in the basement.

"Swear on Yoo-hoo?" I ask. I present the bottle to him. He places one hand over the yellow label and solemnly holds up his other hand.

"I swear," he says. "I am no longer the cad I was. You can trust me. I hope you'll trust me."

"We'll see," I say.

He takes the bottle and cracks open the lid. "Now we toast."

We take turns swigging from the bottle. Somewhere in DC, my mother must be cringing: her spidey senses no doubt inform her that I'm not using a glass.

We chow down on the spread. We're so busy scarfing the food that we don't even bother putting on the movie. We just laugh and chat. I can't believe how comfortable I am stuffing my face in front of the cutest boy I've ever seen in my life.

When we're done, Matt leans back against the couch, both hands on his stomach. "I think I'm going to have a heart attack."

I'm lying with my head on the arm of the couch, my feet in Matt's lap. "It's possible I'm having a heart attack right now," I reply.

"You know what we need?"

"Tums?"

"A walk."

"Are you kidding? The only way I'm moving is if you put me in a wagon and pull me down the street."

"I'm serious," he says. Matt shoves my feet off his lap

and stands up. He offers me his hand, which completely envelops mine. He pulls me up. "Let's go."

We make quick work of the cleanup, head out the back door, and set off down the street.

"Where are we going?" I ask.

"Well, we got to *taste* a little of Montreal," he says. "Now I'm going to *show* you a little of Montreal."

The night is perfect: warm, with a slight breeze. Matt leads me down a residential street lined with the same kind of two-story row houses I saw on that first night we explored together, the night I pulled the fire alarm.

Matt tells me about how he first came to Elite two summers ago. One of his dad's old high school teammates had just been hired as a coach, and Matt was invited up. I hadn't realized that all the players were invited or recommended. No one applies to Elite. It's all about word of mouth and who you know. Which means Sloane Devon must be a pretty darn good player.

So why was she so eager to escape?

Matt leads me through a small green park in the middle of the city to a set of shiny glass doors that rise into the street seemingly out of nowhere.

"Where are we going?" I look around for some kind of subway sign, but I don't see one.

"Underground," he says, as if that's as normal a destination as a movie theater or coffee shop. "I'm taking you to meet the mole king. I'm pretty sure you'd make a perfect sacrifice."

"Excuse me?"

Matt laughs. "Trust me, okay?"

He holds open the door for me and I pass through it without pausing. We're at the top of a staircase, and as soon as we're inside I realize it's a bustling place. A pack of businessmen hauling rolling suitcases breeze past me, followed by a group of ladies laden with shopping bags. I dive into the crowd and head down the stairs.

"Wait up!" he says, taking the stairs two at a time until he's beat me to the bottom.

"This doesn't look like any subway station I've ever seen," I say. The place looks more like a club or a museum. Next to us is a wall of heavy metal panels carved with rows and rows of symbols, all backlit so they glow like ancient runes.

"Well, this takes you *to* a subway station, but actually it's just a series of underground tunnels," Matt says. "So which way?"

I choose left, and we end up in front of a big glass case. Inside is a street map on a platform. Above it is a video projection that shows a building growing up and changing. A plaque on the wall says it's a depiction of the first settlement in Montreal. We watch the building grow and then disappear, then grow and disappear again.

Next to the glass case is another set of doors, with THE WESTIN etched into them. It's the hotel where I stayed the first night in Montreal—the hotel where I first met the other Sloane and this crazy summer began.

"These doors go directly to the hotel?" I ask.

Matt nods. "There are dozens of tunnels running underneath the city so you can go from place to place without going outside."

"But why?"

"Because it's lovely here in the summer, but in the winter, it's a frozen tundra," he says. "I came up here for a tournament once in January and thought my eyeballs were going to freeze and fall out of my head."

Instead of going up to the hotel, we retrace our steps to the wall of runes. This time we continue past it. Only a few steps later, we come across a simple metal chair set into the wall and bolted to the ground. A spotlight shines down on it.

"What's this?"

"It's a chair," he replies.

"Ha, ha," I deadpan.

"I don't know what it is," he says. "Art, I guess. There's no sign. Just a chair."

We wander down the tunnel a little farther. We come to a few steps illuminated with faint blue light. Soon we're in another tunnel, where we're greeted by a wooden cart overflowing with brightly colored bouquets.

"Choose one," Matt says. When I hesitate, he insists, "Come on. I'm making up for lost time. Now pick."

I choose a small bouquet of pale pink peonies. Matt pays the vendor with a collection of brightly colored bills and coins of various sizes. I bury my nose in the bouquet and take a deep breath. My mother grows peonies in our backyard. And for a second I ache for home—not the way it's been lately, with my mom all pinched and angry and my father avoiding us, but the way it was when I was a kid.

We stroll through the tunnels a little more, stopping to look at maps and pieces of art. We toss coins into the guitar case of a folk musician and the hat of a blues guy going to town on a harmonica.

After about an hour, we're up the stairs and back where we started, in the little park surrounded by skyscrapers.

"Where to now?" I ask. I check my phone and am shocked to see that it's almost ten-thirty.

Matt smiles. "I think we have time to see one more thing before we head back."

We get to the end of the street and turn right, facing an enormously steep hill. I have to lean into it to make it up without huffing and puffing. At the top, we round the corner and enter a huge cobblestone plaza that features an enormous fountain, all lit up and gushing water. Despite the hour, people are milling about, tossing coins into the fountain or sprawled on the stone ledges that surround it.

Beyond the fountain, a cathedral of carved gray stone, soaring spires, arched windows, and Gothic-looking carvings rises into the night sky. Starkly illuminated from below, it has an almost movielike quality as if it's being projected on a big screen rather than standing right here in front of us.

"Holy crap," I say, letting out a long breath.

"'Holy' is right, at least," Matt says. "It's the Notre-Dame Basilica. Pretty cool, huh?"

"It's perfect," I say, my head tilted straight back so I can look up at the lighted spires.

Matt finds my hand and squeezes. "You're perfect," he says quietly.

Just like that, my neck and cheeks start burning. "Hardly perfect," I joke. "Have you seen this scar?"

I point to the whitish-pink slash that starts on my chin and runs underneath for about two inches. Matt leans in and runs his finger along the length of it.

"Well, then you're perfectly imperfect," he says, and flashes that million-dollar smile at me. My stomach does a triple lutz, and I'm almost relieved when he pulls away. Almost.

He digs around in his pocket and produces a heavy brass-colored coin. There's a picture of a duck on one side. "It's a loonie. Make a wish."

"This is a whole dollar," I say. "Shouldn't I be wishing with a penny or something?"

"Your wishes are worth it," he says. He leads me to the edge of the fountain. I close my eyes, and wishes start whizzing around in my head.

I wish I could land a triple-triple. I wish I could score a game-winning goal. I wish I had Melody's room. I wish that everything would turn out okay. I wish my dad would . . . well, I don't know what I wish my dad would do, but not this. I wish I hadn't eaten those chili cheese fries. I wish I weren't wearing Sloane's jeans with the back pocket falling off them. I wish —

I wish he would kiss me.

With that last wish, all the other voices in my head stop. I squeeze the coin hard in my hand, leaving an imprint of the edges in my palm. Then I take a deep breath, hold it for a second, and toss the coin. It disappears into the water.

"What did you wish for?" Matt asks. He's watching me closely.

I shake my head. "Seriously? You know better than that."

"Damn. Now I'll just have to guess." Matt raises my chin with one finger, and I almost pull away. I can hardly breathe; I'm sure my whole face is on fire.

But I don't pull away, and he doesn't either. He looks at me hard for confirmation, and I finally give a tiny nod. Then, stooping low, he kisses me. It starts out soft, but within seconds it's deeper. His hand slides to my cheek; his other hand slips behind my neck. He kisses me so hard he practically lifts me off my feet.

When he finally pulls away, I'm so dizzy I'm worried my legs will give way.

"Did your wish come true?" He smiles down at me.

"I'll never tell," I whisper, but my smile gives it all away.

CHAPTER 18

Sloane Devon

As I soak my aching feet in the bathtub, I mentally run through the short program Andy and I have worked out. Despite all my begging and pleading for some Journey, instead we're skating to "Hedwig's Theme" from the Harry Potter movies. All things considered, it could be much worse. At least it's not the theme from *Titanic*. But if I don't get my single axel down by tomorrow, we might as well be *on* the *Titanic*.

Luckily, I've got the rest of the routine down pat. With Andy's help, I've managed to master the spins and the lifts. I don't know if it was the pep talk or Andy's biceps, but either way, I'm now totally comfortable in the air. Turns out I already had all the skills for the footwork; I just needed to adjust my posture and center of gravity—another tip from Andy. Maybe I won't ruin Sloane Emily's rep after all.

The door slams hard, jolting me out of my reverie and

sending me tumbling off the bathtub ledge into the water. I jump up quickly, but it's too late. My bum is completely soaked.

"Ivy, could you *please* not slam the door?" I pull a fluffy white towel off the bar and try to soak up some of the water, but it's no use. These pants are a lost cause. I step out of the bathroom and see Ivy fling a box onto my bed with such force that it immediately bounces off and onto the floor.

"Special delivery," she drawls. She plucks her pink-flowered robe from the back of her chair and brushes past me into the bathroom.

"Oh, you go ahead, I was done in there," I say. Her response is yet another slammed door.

Suppressing a sigh, I pick up the box from the floor. The mailing label says "Sloane Jacobs."

"Care package! Score!" I mutter. Ivy already has the shower going full blast, so there's no chance she can hear me. Then I spot the return address—Washington, DC—and remember that this care package isn't for me.

I know I should stuff it under the bed and save it for Sloane Emily. But what if there's something perishable in there, like cookies or brownies? Even the idea makes my mouth water. I've been spending my cash on snacks to supplement the fat-free, calorie-free, taste-free meals here, but if I keep making trips to the convenience store down the street, I'm going to be out of money by the end of the week. And unlike Sloane Emily, I don't have a steady stream of cash flowing from the Bank of Daddy.

If there *are* brownies in there, it would be rude to let them get stale. And they might bring bugs, or mice. And as much as the thought of Ivy finding a mouse in her bed thrills me, I really should just open the box and eat the brownies.

It's the right thing to do.

I scan the room and spot Ivy's nail file on the bedside table. I snatch it and use it to slice through the thick brown packing tape that's sealing the box. I open the flaps and slide the packing peanuts aside. The first item is a sleek white bakery box. I crack it open and am greeted with — yes! — the sweet, chocolaty smell of brownies. I break off the corner of one and let it melt on my tongue. This was *totally* the right thing to do.

Underneath the brownies I find a bag of mini Reese's Cups, a gold box of some very expensive-looking chocolates, and another box of brownies. Below that is a giant purple patent-leather toiletry bag stuffed with a treasure trove of pots and jars and bottles. It's like someone vomited a Sephora inside. Wedged underneath the purple bag is a crisp white envelope with "Sloane" scrawled in thick black ink, and underneath, in smaller print, "Don't tell Mom." Where the return address should be, there's a fancy-looking gold seal of an eagle, and underneath it says "Senator Robert Jacobs."

Opening the brownies was one thing, but opening her mail is quite another, especially after I accidentally picked up that weird phone call. So I take out my phone and text Sloane that she got a letter from her dad (she doesn't need to know about the brownies just yet). It only takes a few seconds for the reply to come in.

Throw it away.

Uh, okay. I walk toward the trash, then think about her dad's voice saying he was sorry. Sorry for what? There was an urgency in his tone that I used to hear in my mother's voice, back when she'd sober up for a few days and apologize for all the times she'd passed out and missed this game or that event.

I put the letter in the pocket of a coat in the closet. She may not want it now, but she might want it later. If she wants to throw it away, she can do it herself.

I close the wardrobe door just as the bathroom door flings open. Ivy saunters out in her robe, a pink towel wrapped around her head like a turban. Even though the dorm provides amazing fluffy towels *and* sends someone to pick them up every day and swap them for clean ones, Ivy refuses to use anything but the ones she brought from home. After a few days of finding patches of pink skin behind her ears and on her neck, she's finally back to her normal color. Only her cuticles, still dyed a salmon color, betray evidence of my awesome prank. Sadly, the rest of her has returned to its normal color.

Ivy sniffs at the brownies and the mountain of candy on my bed. "Calories, calories."

"Shut up, shut up," I parrot under my breath in an evil-stepsister voice. The only thing that's keeping me from smothering Ivy in her sleep is that I'm convinced she would haunt me if I did. I quickly swap my wet pants for a dry pair of jeans, slip on a pair of ridiculous bejeweled black flip-flops (Seriously, flip-flops with rhinestones on them? Who does that?), grab my bag, and head straight out the door.

Outside, I plop down on the front steps and flip open my crappy old phone. I scroll through my call log just to be sure I haven't missed anything from my dad (fat chance) or even my mom (morbidly obese chance). Instead, all I see is the call from Nando.

Without thinking, I press Send and raise the phone to my ear. I hear the electronic ringing, and before I can formulate any kind of explanation, true or otherwise, he answers.

Oh, I'm supposed to talk now. Crap.

"Uh, h-hi, it's um, Sloane," I stammer.

"Hey! What's up, Sloane?" I can practically hear the smile in his voice, and the sound of it makes chills dance up my spine.

"Oh, not much," I say, then pause. Why did I call him? I'm supposed to be avoiding distractions, not seeking them out. How else am I going to get good at this figure skating thing? I think back to my butt-crack-of-dawn practice with Andy this morning, when we finally got our side-by-side spins in perfect sync. "Actually—nothing. Which is why I called. I was thinking we could hang out if you're free."

"Yeah, absolutely," he says. "I actually just finished my shift, so I can swing by and pick you up right now if you're ready."

"I'll be waiting out front," I reply. I snap the phone shut and allow the world's biggest smile to spread across my face. I cheese out all by myself like I'm in the evening-wear round at Miss Teen USA. I even give a little beauty-queen wave to the rosebushes to my left and right.

Nando rolls up within minutes. He's got on a perfectly worn navy-blue V-neck tee, which accentuates his dark complexion. His brown eyes sparkle, and I have to grip the sides of the seat so I don't feel like I'm melting into the floorboards. I remember the lift I did with Andy this morning, where he spins me under his arm and up until I'm flying on his shoulder. *I so deserve this distraction.*

"Where to, lady?"

"You tell me. This is your turf," I reply.

"You like junk food?"

"Love it." A few minutes later, the car shudders to a stop in front of a two-story building painted bright yellow with a purple roof and orange awnings.

"Did you bring me to clown college?"

"Better." He laughs. I climb out and immediately smell that perfect mixture of salt and grease.

"What's better than clown college?"

"French fries, gravy, and cheese curds," he says. He locks the door and steps up onto the sidewalk. I walk around the car until I'm right next to him, looking up at the monstrosity in front of me. LA BANQUISE is painted on the front window in a jaunty white font.

"You lost me at the word 'curds.'"

"It's the national drunk food of Montreal," he says. "You'll love it."

The inside is just as crazy and clown-collegiate as the outside. The chairs are all mismatched shapes in a Crayola box of colors. The tables have all been attacked with the same palette, probably by many different artists, from the looks of the scribbles and doodles painted on their tops. In the corner is a bustling steel kitchen full of waiters and cooks slinging plates piled high with fries into the pass-through. Only they're not just french fries. Each plate is covered in a variety of sauces and condiments and vegetables and other things I can smell but can't quite place. The menu is scrawled on the wall, but it's all in French, so I have no idea what any of it is. All I know is one plate is covered in peas, and peas have no place near french fries.

Nando high-fives a skinny waiter with a scraggly beard, then leads us to a table in the back against the brick wall. Someone has painted our table to look like a slightly insane version of Monet's *Water Lilies*.

The same scrawny waiter, his jeans falling off his bony hips, a ratty T-shirt with the words RADIO RADIO printed on the front, meanders over. *"Alors, qu'est-ce que vous voudrais?"*

Before I can even ask what in the what he's talking about, Nando takes charge.

"Nous aurons une classique, s'il vous plaît," Nando says, then nods to me. *"C'est sa première fois."*

I can't help it. My mouth falls open, and I stare at him with abandon. I've never heard a teenage guy speak French before, much less a *hot* teenage guy who is also an awesome hockey player and who wants to take me out for (possibly disgusting) food.

The waiter sees me staring, chuckles to himself, and wanders away to put in our order. At least, I think Nando ordered. Maybe he just made a crass joke or told the waiter about how he plans to ax-murder me later after he stuffs me full of french fries and peas.

"You speak French," I say.

"It's the official language of Montreal," he says. He unwraps his silverware and spreads his napkin in his lap. "Didn't you notice all the signage?"

"Yeah, but I just didn't expect it," I say. "You haven't lived here *that* long."

"You pick it up quick," he tells me.

"That is so cool." I wish I could speak another language. After three years of high school Spanish and an entire life of living in Philly, pretty much all I know is how to order dinner at my favorite Mexican restaurant. I can also ask where the bathroom is, though I probably wouldn't be able to understand the directions.

Before I can embarrass myself further with my pathetic monolingualism, a plate appears before us. It sort of looks like something that's already been eaten. There are definitely french fries, but the brown sauce and white goo covering the rest looks a bit digested. If it weren't for the unbelievably good smell coming off the plate, there's no way I'd eat it.

"This is poutine, the classic," he says, pushing the plate a little closer to me. He picks my fork up off the table and hands it to me. "And yes, we eat it with a fork."

"Such a native," I say. "Quick! Say 'what aboot it?'"

"You knock it off," he says, taking his own fork and stabbing a fry.

"Oh, oh, what are you gonna do aboooooot it? You're all Canadian now. I bet you're too nice to do anything." I'm laughing so hard I worry that gravy is going to come out my nose. Nando starts laughing too.

When the plate is empty save for a river of gravy, I'm ready to admit that poutine isn't gross. It's pretty stinking good, in fact. If I hadn't eaten those brownies before I got here, I might order another plate. But not the one with peas. That's still wrong.

Nando throws down some Monopoly money and slides back from the table. Normally I'd try to split the bill, but I'm already running low on cash. I feel weird about not offering, but it would be worse if he agreed and then I had nothing to contribute.

"I have a little more time, if you want to hang out some more," I say quickly, then catch myself before I start to sound desperate. I must be high on carbs and cheese, two items that are hard to come by back at the dorm.

"Perfect," he says, offering me a hand up from my chair. "Then we have time for a walk."

The next block over from La Banquise is the entrance to a gorgeous green park lined with lush, towering trees.

Nando, still holding my hand, leads me down the path toward a small pond. At the edge, there's a large weeping willow. He parts the branches and ushers me inside. We settle down at the base of the trunk, shoulder to shoulder.

"This is my favorite spot in the whole city," he says. "It was one of the first places I discovered when I moved here. I always come here when I need to get away."

I look over at him. The setting sun is peeking through the branches, throwing a scattering of light across his dark skin. I lean closer to him. There's a heat radiating from him, an energy that I never felt when I was near Dylan. For the first time I realize I was never actually *near* Dylan. He was always around but never close.

We're so quiet that the crickets start singing around us. Through the branches I can see a family of ducks paddling slowly through the water. A woman jogs by along the path, a happy black Lab trotting next to her. I feel miles away from figure skating, miles away from hockey, miles away from everything. I feel so relaxed I could cry.

But I don't, partly because I *never* cry, and partly because I know Nando is watching me. I feel his shoulder press into mine. He scootches over a little until we're hip to hip. I lean my head back against the tree trunk and sigh.

"What's up?" His voice is just barely above a whisper tickling my ear.

"I'm just . . . happy," I say. It sounds stupid and insufficient, but it's all that comes out. I haven't been able to say I was happy in a long time.

"I like that about you," he says. "I think I need it."

I look at him. "You're not happy?"

"Not lately," he says. I wait for him to go on. He sighs. "Look, Sloane, there's something I should probably tell you."

My stomach tightens. The thought flashes through my head: *He's got a girlfriend.* "What is it?" I ask.

"I'm not in school anymore," he blurts out, all in a rush. Immediately, he seems to relax, as if he's been holding it in for who knows how long. "I haven't been in school for a while, actually. I quit hockey, and since hockey paid my tuition, I had to sort of . . . drop out."

This is not the confession I expected. "What happened?" I ask. "Did you get injured?"

"Not exactly," he says. He pulls a blade of grass out of the ground and starts tearing it into tiny pieces. When there's nothing left, he flicks the tiniest piece into the wind and stares at the horizon.

"Nando, what's going on?" I nudge him with my shoulder. "How could you have quit hockey? You're amazing at it."

"Yeah, until I wasn't anymore," he says abruptly. He runs a hand through his hair. "When I got here my freshman year, everything was so intense. The coach kept telling me how much I meant to the team. Practices leading up to the first game were insane. Everyone was so focused, and I felt just . . . out of it. Like, suddenly I couldn't remember why I started playing or why I loved hockey or any of it." He shakes his head. "It's hard to explain."

"Try," I say quietly.

"I just . . . lost it. I played like total crap. I don't know what happened, but I couldn't get myself in the right place. I missed passes, missed shots, kept getting checked. The other teams figured out that I was outmatched and totally routed me. Preyed on me like the runt of the litter."

I stay quiet. There's a weird squirmy feeling in my stomach. The story sounds a little too familiar.

"Practices got tougher, and I didn't. Coach tried screaming at me; then he tried benching me. Midway through the season I was totally miserable. I was barely making it through classes. I figured it was only a matter of time before they pulled my scholarship, so I quit." He exhales. "I told my parents I was injured but that I was staying up here to be involved with the team until I could play again," he says. "But really I've been working in the bar, saving up some cash so I can take some classes again on my own. Hopefully figure out what to do now that hockey is over."

I realize, suddenly, that this is my chance to tell him the truth. He'll understand. He'll totally get it. And it's not like he's going to rat me out. I open my mouth to pour it all out, to tell him that my confidence is shot too. That I want to quit, that I'm not sure I can keep playing, and also that I'm not sure who I am without hockey. That right now, I'm hiding from the game completely.

"That's why I like being with you," he says. He places his hand on top of mine. The zap of electricity that runs between us causes my heart to pound. "You remind me of the time when I loved to play. Watching you, and how much you love the game, inspires me. I'm starting to think maybe I could—I don't know—get it back, somehow."

I slam my mouth shut. Looking into his eyes, I see the eleven-year-old kid who loved to play hockey. And I know he's trying desperately to find that again—in me.

I can't tell him the truth. I can't break him like that.

So I force a smile onto my face. "You'll get it back," I say. "I promise."

CHAPTER 19

SLOANE EMILY

I never thought I'd be so excited to see a plate of cafeteria-grade spaghetti and meatballs. I stab my fork into the mound of pasta, twist for maximum spaghetti delivery, and stab a red hunk of meatball, too. Even though it's the size of six bites, I cram the entire forkful into my mouth. And it is just as glorious as I imagined.

I started off the day joining the black team, my scrimmage team for the rest of the summer, for a five-mile run. Then we had three straight hours of on-skates drills. After lunch, we played a full-length regulation scrimmage, which we capped with a half-hour endurance skate in what Coach Hannah laughably referred to as a "cooldown." I burned off enough calories for an entire hockey team, plus their coaches, and now I'm *starving*. As soon as I got off the ice, I crammed Sloane Devon's gear into her bag and made a beeline for the cafeteria.

Did not pass Go, did not collect two hundred showers.

"Damn, you smell." Cameron, freshly showered and clad in a powder-blue tracksuit, drops into the seat next to me with a plate of spaghetti nearly as big as mine.

"I do not!" I stab another meatball.

"Yes, you do. You smell like your moldy old gear bag," she says. "Seriously, wash that thing or replace it."

I reach down and grab a handful of my T-shirt, bringing it up to my nose. Okay, yeah. So maybe I'm not exactly fresh as a daisy.

I can't believe how much has changed in the past two weeks. When I first met Sloane Devon, I was horrified by the smell of her gear bag. And now I hardly notice.

"Hey." Matt's massive frame overtakes me. "How was the scrimmage? Did you own the white team's face?"

I drop my shirt and smooth out the wrinkles, hoping he can't smell eau de garbage can. His sweaty head tells me that he skipped a shower too, so hopefully he's suffering from the same olfactory immunity I am.

"I was okay," I reply. Matt takes the seat beside me.

"She was the queen of assists," Cameron cuts in. She runs a crust of french bread through her marinara. "I'd say at least two of our four goals were thanks to her."

My dear-God-please-don't-give-me-the-puck strategy is working like gangbusters. And one of those assists was directly to Melody, my teammate on black. I've found that helping her be the star on the ice actually gets her off my back even more than checking her into the boards, so that's two for the price of one.

Matt chatters on about his own scrimmage and how he scored the winning point for the blue team today. I'm watching his mouth move, but I'm only half listening. All I can think about is the kiss last night. Each time I relive it in my mind, I feel a chill start at my lower back and race up my spine until the hairs on the back of my neck stand on end and I'm grinning like a fool. And now he's sitting next to me, despite the fact that I'm unshowered and totally disgusting.

Matt ends a story about a red team player who was nearly ejected today for trying to start a fight. He shovels a giant bite of salad into his mouth, and I jump at the chance.

"Wannawatchamovietonight?" I say it so fast it all comes out as one long, newly invented word (country of origin: Swoonistan; meaning: "to swoon so hard as to be rendered incapable of enunciation").

"I totally would," Matt says, "but I've got a strategy session with the blue team tonight. We're going to hit a pub up the road and talk about how we're going to crush the red team tomorrow."

To save a little face after getting brutally rebuffed by the hottest guy I've ever seen, much less kissed, I turn to Cameron.

"What about you? Lifetime movie marathon?"

Matt groans, and so does Cameron.

"I *so* want to, but I have to work on my summer reading tonight or I'm never going to finish. Whoever decided that *Les Misérables* was a great summer read can bite me."

"Can't you just watch the movie?" Matt is apparently not as stellar a student as he is a hockey player.

"Not if I want an A on my paper," Cameron says. She pops the last bite of meatball into her mouth, then gathers up her plate and silverware. "Mrs. Best, aka the Beast, has, like, a sixth sense for people who didn't read the book. She'll string me up by my toes and force me to recite *Beowulf* in Middle English."

"Good luck," I reply, although I sort of loved *Les Misérables*, the book *and* the musical. I did a long program two years ago to a symphonic arrangement of "I Dreamed a Dream."

Matt hoovers the last of his spaghetti and jumps up after her. "I gotta get going. I'm supposed to meet the guys in the lobby at seven." He bends down, then stiffens and stands upright again.

"What's wrong?" I ask.

"Well, I was gonna kiss you, but, um . . . I wasn't sure if, you know, with all the people, so I . . . well, now I feel royally stupid. This was easier the other—"

I stand up, rise to my toes, and plant a soft peck on his lips. Then it's my turn to go stiff. I drop back down in my chair so hard I have to keep from wincing. *I can't believe I just did that. In front of everyone! Who am I?*

A smile spreads across Matt's face. "I'll see you tomorrow?"

"Absolutely," I say, trying to suppress a massive grin. My cheeks are already aching.

He waves and saunters out of the room.

Who am I? I'm Sloane Jacobs.

"Holy crap, you tamed the white whale!" Cameron is staring at me openmouthed from across the table. Several other skaters are blatantly staring at me, and two girls in the corner are whispering behind their hands. "How did you do it?"

"He said he's changed," I reply. And as I look at Cameron's disbelieving face, my own belief wavers for a moment. Do people really change?

Cameron just shrugs and gathers her things. "Nicely done, Captain Ahab." She stands up. "I'm off to study. I'll catch you later."

Left alone with my plate, I chow down on the rest of my spaghetti and manage to scarf seconds, too.

Back upstairs, I consider checking in across the hall to see what Melody is up to, but then I remember that while she high-fived me for the assist, the force of said high five took me off my skates. I don't think we're ready to be besties yet. So instead, I take out my phone and text the only other person I know in Canada.

Wanna hang? Long time no see. —your doppel-ganger

She texts me back to meet her on the McGill University quad. According to Google, it's a fifteen-minute walk, and I take my time strolling through the streets. Even though school is out for the summer, when I get to McGill, the area is crowded with people having picnics, playing Frisbee in the fading light, and wandering along the paths and through the quad.

I spot Sloane Devon on a bench and trot over to meet her. I haven't seen her since that day two weeks ago when we switched places. She was already wearing my clothes, but she definitely still looked like herself.

But now she looks different, like the mint-green cami and black capris she has on actually belong to her. She's braided her long dark hair so it hangs over her left shoulder. She's wearing my favorite black ballet flats with the white flowers embroidered on the toes. Suddenly I wish I'd attempted to pick out an actual outfit instead of throwing on a pair of cropped sweats and a GET IN THE GOAL tank top.

"Holy crap, you look like a hobo," she says. I can't tell if she's teasing me or not. "You're in public, for God's sake."

"Oh, shut up," I say. "I'm embracing my inner jock."

"Hey, I *never* looked like that," she says. I see her catch sight of her reflection in the plate-glass window. "Did I?"

I notice her use of the past tense, but ignore it. "Good to see you."

"You too," she says. "Care to wander?"

"Yes, please," I say. "My quads are burning from scrimmage."

"I thought you said hockey was easy. 'All padded up like a crash-test dummy' were the words I think you used." She smirks.

"I admit I *might* have been wrong," I reply. And then, because I can't help it: "What about you? Is morphing into an ice princess as easy as you expected?"

She just shakes her head and smiles at me. "Let's walk," she says.

CHAPTER 20

Sloane Devon

We make our way along the paths, past the windows of the McGill bookstore. They're crammed with mannequins clad in red and white apparel: scarves, T-shirts, hoodies, sweatpants, all bearing the school's logo and name. A headless bust in the corner sports a MCGILL HOCKEY T-shirt. I feel an odd sort of fluttering in my shoulders, like I'm missing something. Or someone.

"So how's camp?" Sloane asks.

"Oh, you know. Just perfecting my double axel, working my way up to a triple," I reply.

She actually stumbles. "You pulled off a double in two weeks?" She practically screeches at me.

I burst into laughter. "I can barely hang on to a single," I say. "But I'm getting there. This guy named Andy's helping me."

"Who's Andy?" she asks. For the next few blocks, I fill

her in on Andy and his theatrics. I worry she's actually going to fall into the street when I tell her that he knows about our switch, and I have to swear up and down that he's cool and won't tell. When I tell her how he helped me dye my roommate pink, she seems slightly mollified, especially since she has heard of Ivy, the holy terror of the skate world.

"So how did the whole scout thing go?" I ask. I've been dreading getting the full report. If she bombed it, I really have dug my own grave with this stunt. I haven't yet decided whether that would be a blessing or not. "I never got a recap."

"It didn't suck," she says carefully. "Or more accurately, *I* didn't suck. I mean, I don't think I totally screwed up your future." I know she means to be reassuring, but I feel sort of nauseated.

"Like I give a crap about my future," I say. *When in doubt, act like it doesn't matter.* I try to laugh, but Sloane Emily gives me the side-eye.

"I'm serious," she says. "It turns out I'm a good team player. I'm good with assists."

"When Coach Butler gets that report, he'll *know* something's up. I never share the puck."

"People change."

"Maybe," I say.

"You changed," she says, and then nudges me with a shoulder. "At least, your wardrobe did."

"A temporary glitch, I promise you," I say. But my

stomach knots up. When I get back to Philly, will everything just go back to the way it was? Hanging out with
Dylan and his stupid friends, getting the tingles, getting
benched? I think of Mom, too, and whether she'll be the
same. And if she isn't—if she really does get sober—will
she change in other ways too? Will she still come to my
games and cheer me on in her Mama Jacobs T-shirt?
Will we still go on crazy, impulsive adventures where we
come home with a vintage sewing machine or a new dog?
I don't know what part of her is the alcohol and what part
of her is, well, *her*. I don't even know if I believe people *can*
change.

Then again, it sure seems like Sloane Emily's different.
When I first met her, she was wearing something with sequins on it, I think. There was definitely pink involved.
I remember that her hair was all shiny and straight and
smelled like the flower arrangements at my great-aunt Ele-
ta's funeral.

I wonder what *that* girl would say to the girl who's sitting across from me now. I'm pretty sure she'd lose her
mind over Sloane's still-wet-from-the-shower frizzy hair or
her mismatched clothes.

We wander for a little bit longer. Sloane Emily tells me
about some guy at her camp, Matt. I don't know him, but I
can certainly picture him: an oafish, rich-kid hockey dude.
Sloane Emily tells me he comes from Chestnut Hill. I saw
their hockey team at a tournament once. It was like an army
of blond guys named Sven, all in perfectly worn-in rugby

shirts with Ray-Bans on top of their heads. He's probably Sloane Emily's dream guy.

Nando's face pops into my head, but I will his image away. I don't want to talk about him — I'm not sure what I would say.

We end up in front of a giant stone wall in the shape of a crest. It's filled with red and white flowers to mimic the McGill shield. Sloane Emily takes a seat on the edge. I sit down next to her and pull my knees to my chest.

"Oh, I have something for you," she says, then reaches into her bag. She pulls out a stack of envelopes, maybe four or five held together by a paper clip, and holds them out to me. I take them carefully, like they're something poisonous that might bite.

The letters are addressed to me, care of Elite Hockey Camp. The return address is preprinted on the envelope in a soft blue ink. "Hope Springs Rehabilitation Center," it says. There's a little illustration of a babbling brook across the logo. Underneath the address, in black ink scrawled in familiar handwriting, is my mother's name, Elena Jacobs. I blink at the words over and over, as if I'm looking through a viewfinder and eventually the image will change. I notice one whole seam is torn enough that I can make out a few lines written in my mother's handwriting. I look up, frowning, at Sloane Emily.

"I didn't open it," she says quickly. She looks nervous but is trying for a smile. "It looked like that when it got here."

"I don't care," I say, a chill creeping into my voice. I drop the whole stack into the black leather satchel that belongs to Sloane Emily—the bag I'm carrying around like it's mine. It probably cost more than my mother's stint in rehab.

She's still looking at me expectantly, as though she's Oprah and expects me to pour my heart out to her.

"If you ever want to talk or anything . . . ," she says.

"I *don't*."

She looks down at her nails, which now look just as bad as mine. "Families suck," she says. "But at least your family's trying."

"You don't know *anything* about my family," I say icily. She stares at me for a second, then checks her phone.

"I should probably be getting back," she says just as coldly. "Early-morning run with the team."

"Good idea," I reply. The final competition is only two nights away, which means Andy is scheduling more and more extra practices.

On the walk home, my bag somehow feels heavy, as if the letters have added weight. I wrestle them out of my bag and stare at them, at the handwriting I've seen in countless birthday cards, permission slips, and notes in my lunch bag. Does she have an explanation? Is she sorry? Is she coming back? I want to know, but I'm afraid of what she'll say.

She took her time sending them. I think I'll take my time opening them. Now I just need to figure out where to stash the letters so Ivy doesn't find them, even if she goes on a little snooping adventure.

If ever I needed a distraction, it's now. I take a deep

breath and scroll through my call log. Just hearing Nando's voice will make me feel better. I dial his number and my heart skips when it rings. Once, twice—then the phone clicks abruptly over to voice mail. Huh, that's weird. I try it again, and this time it only rings once before the voice mail picks up.

Is he screening my call?

As I round the corner to BSI, I'm surprised to see his car parked in front of the main building. At first I think maybe it's wishful thinking or some kind of hallucination, but then I spot him: leaning back on the passenger-side door, his hands shoved deep in the pockets of his worn-in jeans. With boots and a flannel shirt on, staring down at the curb, he looks sort of like some kind of modern cowboy. Just the sight of him makes me warm from the inside out.

"Hey," I say, a huge smile spreading across my face. "I was just calling you."

Nando pushes off from the side of the car. His face is completely blank, almost hard, and there's no trace of any of the warmth from last night. He blinks a few times, glancing down at his brown boots, then back up at me.

"Are you okay?" I ask.

"I know that yesterday may have—I don't know—freaked you out or something. Maybe I shouldn't have unloaded all my problems on you. But I figured you knew," he says.

"What?" I ask. I'm so confused, my head feels like it's one of those shaken-up snow globes. "Knew what?"

"That I liked you." He shakes his head, and my heart melts a little. "And I thought maybe you liked me too."

"I . . . I do," I reply. My heart is a puddle of pudding, and yet it's managing to pound so loudly I think it might burst from my chest.

Nando isn't smiling. "You have a boyfriend," he says. His mouth is set in a straight line; his brown eyes are dull.

"No, I don't," I say, and for a second I have the completely ludicrous fear that somehow Dylan is spreading rumors we're still together, and that somehow Nando found out.

"That's not what Matt O'Neill said," he says flatly.

"*Who?*"

"Matt O'Neill," he says, crossing his arms. "You don't remember him? He came into the bar tonight. Going on and on about this amazing girl he's dating. Her name's Sloane, he says. Sloane Jacobs. She's gorgeous, with dark hair. She skates. Scar on her chin. Plays a hell of a game of hockey. Sound familiar?"

I feel like I'm standing in quicksand, and I'm in danger of getting sucked down into the ground. "But I don't—" I'm starting to feel too hot, and my stomach turns over too fast. *It's not possible. It's a huge city. There's no way.* "I mean, it must be someone else. . . ."

"Are you kidding me, Sloane?" he bursts out. "Do you think I'm an idiot? You *knew* I liked you. You let me act like an idiot, letting me whine, and the whole time you were with this *Matt* guy." He shakes his head. "I should never have trusted you."

I feel like I'm going to throw up right on his boots. "Nando, it's not like that. I *do* like you." He doesn't look at me, and I hear myself pleading with him. "It's complicated. . . ."

He finally looks at me. His eyes are cold and steely and angry in a way I never imagined they could be. "Unless there's another dark-haired skater with a scar on her chin and the name Sloane Jacobs, I don't want to hear it."

"Actually—"

"Jesus, Sloane, seriously, how stupid do you think I am?" He kicks at a small pile of gravel with the inside of his boot, and the little rocks go skittering across the pavement in all directions.

"Not stupid at all," I reply, but my voice is so low I don't think he hears. It doesn't matter anyway. He's already turned around, yanked open the car door, and practically thrown himself inside.

I want to run in front of the car, stop him from leaving, make him listen to the whole story. But I just stand where I am, feet glued to the ground, while he goes tearing out of the driveway in a spray of exhaust and gravel.

Either way, I lied to him. And how would he react if he knew I was running away from hockey? The hockey—the fact that I play, the fact that I love it—is what made him like me in the first place. He might be so mad that he tells someone about our switch. Better Nando think I'm a cheater than an imposter.

I know I have to text Sloane Emily to tell her what's

up. She'll need to make sure Nando didn't say anything to Matt. But when I go to start typing, my heart is pounding and my fingers are shaking so much that my attempt at a text looks more like alphabet soup than a coherent thought. I erase the message and try again.

Matt met someone I know. Someone I like. We're screwed.

CHAPTER 21

Sloane emily

Sloane Devon's text freaked me out so much I thought I was going to hurl. I called her back ASAP for more details, and even though she wouldn't tell me much about Mystery Man, she sounded shaky enough that I knew it was a big deal.

I had to stop myself from pounding on his door first thing this morning. I didn't want to arouse any kind of suspicion if he doesn't actually know anything about the switch. Instead, I'd calmly showered and made my way to breakfast like it was any other day.

I manage to choke down one bite of toast, which seems to lodge itself in my throat as soon as I spot Matt. He takes the seat across from me and begins assembling a breakfast sandwich, piling eggs, bacon, and home fries between two toaster waffles. He uses a layer of syrup as some sort of epoxy to hold the whole mess together, and then takes a bite so large it cracks into the fourth row of waffle squares. Three weeks ago, watching the boy I'm kissing sit across a table and eat something like that would have made my stomach turn. But a lot has changed since I became Sloane Devon three weeks ago.

I swallow a gulp of orange juice. It's now or never.

"So, how was your night?" I hope I sound casual and not like a duck being throttled by a manatee.

"Awesome," Matt says. "We found a great pub where we got crazy-cheap cheeseburgers, and Jake and I wrote up some plays that will totally destroy the opposing team. We're going to dominate for sure."

Either he's got an incredible poker face, or he doesn't know anything. But I have to try one more time, or I'll be sick with worry all day.

"Anything . . . exciting happen?"

"Not really," he says. He chugs the rest of his orange juice and slams the glass down on the table like he's just won a contest. "Actually, there was one thing."

My stomach drops into my butt.

"Malloy had a fake ID, which he's apparently never used, because it only took him a beer and a half to get completely wasted. He tried to do the 'Single Ladies' dance on the bar, and the bartender threw him out. It was insane."

The mention of the bartender—the one Sloane Devon knows—has my stomach turning somersaults. "Anything *else* exciting happen?" I ask, giving it one last shot.

Matt sighs. "Sloane, you can trust me, remember? Nothing happened."

Oh my God. He thinks I'm worried he hooked up with another girl. Which honestly would be better than if he learned the truth. But apparently neither happened.

And with that, all the fears and nerves fizzle out like a sparkler. I feel like someone is filling me with helium. I'm so happy I could float away.

Cameron practically skips up to our table, half a bagel in one perfectly manicured hand, her dreads held back with a vintage-looking terry-cloth headband. Matching Adidas track pants complete the look. I once again marvel at her ability to take workout clothes and turn them into a *Vogue* spread.

"What are you so pumped about?" I ask. "And if you say the three-mile run before lunch, I'm going to reach across the table and slap you."

"I saw Hannah leaving the dining room with a folder!" she squeaks. I just shrug and stare at her. She's bouncing so hard in her chair I worry she's going to fall out of it. "The lists! They're posting the final lists!"

Matt drops the last bite of his breakfast sandwich onto his plate, where it lands with a heavy, syrupy thud. "Dude, I gotta go see," he says. He licks his fingers and jumps out of his chair. "You coming?"

"Oh please, golden boy, as if you even have to look," Cameron says. "You're going to make a varsity team."

"Yeah, but I want to be captain this year," Matt says. He

picks up his plate and scoots in his chair (*such* good manners). He leans down and plants a quick-yet-perfect kiss on my lips. "See you out there?"

"Absolutely," I reply. I don't know what's waiting out there, but if it's more kisses from Matt, I'd gladly sign on to sing the lead in an end-of-summer performance of *Grease 2*. Matt trots away. Most of my fellow campers are leaving their breakfasts half eaten to file out to the lobby.

"Are you coming?" Cameron shoves the last bite of bagel into her mouth and cocks her head toward the door. I sigh and push back from the table.

"Okay, what is the big deal? What's the list?"

"The teams for the last week of camp, which are also the teams for the final game of the summer. Two varsity teams will compete, and two JV teams will compete. And each team gets a captain, someone who the coaches think is the best in their group. It's a huge honor to captain one of the teams."

All my excitement drains away. I already know which team I made. JV, of course. There's no freaking way I made varsity. But I don't care; it's a miracle I survived until now, much less learned how to play the game.

The lists are posted on the corkboard between the two elevators, and there's a crowd of campers gathered around them. They take their turns stepping up to the neon-green sheets of paper and running their fingers down the lists until they land on their names. Some yip excitedly or yell; others shake their heads and shuffle away.

Cameron skips the line entirely and shimmies her way through the crowd right up to the front, hauling me with her. The first list says "Junior Varsity" across the top in big block letters, and I run my finger down it. Cameron skips that list and goes straight to varsity. As I scan, I don't see my name. My stomach drops. Is it possible not to make *either* team? Am I that terrible? I scan the list again, but despite my wishing and hoping and squinting at the letters, my name still doesn't appear. This is very bad.

"Yes!" Cameron hops back from the list, causing a junior guy to leap out of her path. He gives her a dirty look, but Cameron doesn't notice. She's too busy fist pumping and dancing around.

"Good news?" I don't want to kill her buzz with my righteous defeat just yet.

"Hell, yes! I'm captaining the blue team, and you're on it!" She gives me a high five so hard my palm burns.

"No way," I say.

"Yes way! Look for yourself." She shoves me through the crowd toward the lists. "And meet me upstairs for a celebration when you're done!"

The second list says "Girls' Varsity Blue" in big block letters. And sure enough, there's my name. Sloane Jacobs.

"I can't believe it," I mutter.

"Believe it." Melody is standing next to me, pointing at her name at the top of another page that reads "Girls' Varsity Red." She's their captain. "You ready to go again?"

She must take my shocked silence as answer enough,

because she snorts slightly, then walks away. I'm left staring at my name on the varsity list. "No freaking *way*!" I repeat under my breath.

"Freaking way. You earned it."

I turn around and see Coach Hannah beaming at me. For a second, I think she must be talking to someone else. But no, it's me. I *earned* it. Not Sloane Devon, but *me*.

"Thanks," I manage to say.

"Don't thank me. I'm serious, you earned it." She scribbles something on the clipboard she's holding, then turns her attention back to me. "I read your file. You came here as a showboat with an anger problem, but you've turned into an excellent team player. Positive, smart, always putting your teammates and the game above your own individual glory. Your teammates this summer have a lot to thank you for. You stay cool and focus on the basics. That wins games. And gets you on the varsity roster. So good job."

Coach Hannah nods at me, then ambles over to the side of the lobby, where Anita Hall, a sophomore who spent all of camp bragging about her skills, is sobbing into her hands. Something tells me she didn't end up on the same list as me. I feel sorry for her. I know just how it feels to expect to be the best and to fall short.

What I don't understand is *this* feeling. I didn't ride Sloane Devon's reputation. I skated my way to varsity all by myself.

Even though Anita is still crying in the corner, I can't

suppress my grin. I must look like a mental patient—but a happy one.

I reach into my bag and pull out my phone to text Sloane Devon the good news. Maybe the fact that I haven't ruined her future will cheer her up. In fact, if what Coach Hannah said is right, I may have *helped* her rep.

I press the Home button and the screen glows to life, showing a list of missed calls and texts. My stomach lurches. I've missed *six* calls: three from my mother, two from my father, and one from a number I don't recognize. My first thought is that someone died. *Oh God, did James bungee jump or drown in a whitewater rafting accident? Did Dad finally kill him for joining the Georgetown Young Democrats?*

I dial into my voice mail with shaking hands. The voice in the first message is halting and quiet, but I recognize it immediately. It's Amy, my dad's press secretary.

"Sloane, I need you to call in. We've got a situation and, well, it's sensitive. And . . . um." There's a long pause where I can hear her breathe in and out slowly. *"On a personal note, well, I just wanted to say, um, I'm so sorry. I wish this hadn't happened like this. But, um, please call the office when you get this. I'm sorry. Um, sorry."*

The memory comes flooding back like a tidal wave, and I have to blink several times to make sure I'm still standing in the lobby of my dorm and not being pulled under and out to sea. I bolt for the bathroom just off the lobby—a onesie, thankfully. I twist the lock hard behind me and press my forehead onto the cold metal of the door.

I'd gone to his office to try to talk him out of sending me to figure skating camp. I had a whole plan. I'd take on some volunteer hours this summer, something public like cleaning up a park or working for Habitat that would get me photographed (*gag*). Maybe I could even teach skating lessons to some inner-city kids. He could plaster the photos all over his newsletter, maybe even trot them out at an interview. I'd been thinking so hard about the plan that I didn't even stop to —

There's a loud knock on the bathroom door, and I jump. "Occupied!" I shout. The person on the other side of the door mumbles something and shuffles away. I triple-check the door. Still locked.

Locked. Why didn't Dad just lock the damn door? Why didn't I knock? Why did I just barge in? I've thought about it a million times, and how much easier it would be if I had knocked. Then I would never have known — I would never have seen.

I picture how Amy leapt back from him and started manically smoothing out her skirt, as if she could brush away what had happened if she could just get her skirt wrinkle-free. And Dad. How his face went from a look of sheer and total panic to relief. Relief! As if he was happy I wasn't another staffer or rival politico, or worse, a reporter.

I didn't wait to hear what she'd say or what he'd say or what they'd do. I just ran.

I stare down at my phone. I still have voice mails from my mom and my dad, along with a handful of text messages.

A lump builds in my throat. Unfair. This is why I switched with Sloane Devon in the first place, to get away from Amy, from my dad, from the stupid pressures of my stupid family.

I'm not ready to go back. Not yet.

I shove my phone back into my purse and push out of the bathroom, taking the stairs two at a time toward Cameron's room. Like Coach Hannah said, I earned this.

CHAPTER 22

Sloane Devon

I can hear the music.

Okay, I can't *hear* the music, since it's not playing. But Andy's made me listen to the damn song so much that it pretty much lives in my brain at this point. He keeps telling me I have to *live* it, that artistry is what will save me since it's unlikely I'll actually be able to learn any serious jumps or tricks. And so I've been falling asleep every night listening to it. When I wake up, I wedge my earbuds back in and start it over. I listen to it for hours on end during our practices. I hum it in the shower. I think about it over dinner.

Carrying the Harry Potter song on a loop in my brain should drive me crazy, except for the fact that it crowds out thoughts of Nando and memories of his face, hurt and angry. I've tried getting in touch with him, but he screens every call. I even went to the community rink the other day to try to find him, but he wasn't there. He doesn't want to be found. He doesn't want to talk to me. And what would I say, anyway?

So I'm focusing all my energy on my routine, and now, running through our routine in front of the rest of our pairs class, I can hear the music drumming through my head.

We've managed to get two good lifts down pat. My single axel is strong, and I can execute a waltz jump easily (which is why there are six of them in the program). Andy's choreography is perfect. There's a lot of fast skating and footwork, which is no problem, since I practically grew up on ice skates. And with the way he's turned our music into my own personal ear worm, I think I'm actually getting this artistry thing he keeps yammering on about.

We go into the final lift of our piece: Andy brings me high over his head, and I float through the air, arms and legs extended, completely unafraid that Andy will drop me and I'll plummet to the ice, smashing my face to smithereens. I've got my arms out, soft like he showed me, working it all the way down to the tips of my fingers. When Andy finally places me gently back on the ice, we do our final spin, then stop hard on our toe picks, arms raised gracefully yet triumphantly over our heads. The rest of the class breaks into applause. Katinka gives a polite golf clap, and even Sergei replaces his usual grunt with a slight nod.

"Eet ees good. A leetle stiff, but very good," Katinka says. "Zat ees all for today, class. You have free time, which of course means you go to practice rooms and work harder than you work in class, no?"

She's right. As the weeks have worn on, the schedule has become more open, but the work has just gotten harder. It seems like "free time" is some kind of challenge to these people. Figure skating training is no joke, that's for sure.

Andy and I follow the rest of our class toward the door on the side of the rink, where the women's singles class is waiting to take the ice for their time with Katinka and Sergei. Ivy is first in line, looking like a stick of bubble gum in her hot-pink unitard and dainty black gloves. When I catch her eye, the look she gives me nearly lights my messy bun on fire. She looks *pissed*.

She skates past me, bumping my shoulder with her skinny, bony one. I stumble back a little, and Andy places a firm hand on the small of my back to steady me.

"Ignore it," he whispers.

"Ivy, I hope you watch Sloane. Her interpretation of music ees perfect. You learn thing or two, no? Eet take more than jumps to win." I glance over at Katinka. Is she trying to get me killed? I take a peek at Ivy, who looks like her brain is melting and will, at any minute, shoot out of her ears. I decide not to wave a red flag at the bull by sticking around any longer than I need to, and hustle off the ice.

Andy and I spend the rest of the afternoon holed up in a practice room working on our side-by-side jumps in sneakers. Constant work is the only thing that can distract me from thoughts of Nando. I'm landing the single axel perfectly, mostly because it's a cleaner version of a sloppy trick jump my team and I used to practice when we were clowning around. A double salchow, however, is a whole other story. But after hours of jumps and spins, Andy breaking it down, and me falling on my butt on the gym mats, I feel ready to try it on the ice. Tomorrow morning we have another one of our extra sessions with Katinka, and we decide we'll give it a shot. What's the worst that could happen? I break my leg, and then I can't embarrass myself in front of a crowd at the end-of-summer show.

By dinner I'm sore, exhausted, and starving. I skip a shower and head straight down to the dining hall. I'm midway through my second plate of gluten-free rice noodles and tofu meatballs in marinara when a magazine slams down on the table next to my plate. The shock of it causes me to drop my fork, and a meatless ball rolls across the parquet floor next to me.

"Jeez, Ivy. Wear a bell."

"You do not want to mess with me right now," she says, her Southern accent out in all its venomous glory.

"I beg to differ," I mutter. I stab at another tofu ball, but it skitters off my plate and rolls across the table. Ivy takes a swipe at it, sending it careening clear onto the floor.

"I *knew* there was something off about you." Ivy shoves the magazine closer to me. It's an issue of *People*. In one of the sidebars on the cover is a picture of a man with an army-close haircut and an expensive-looking suit. Underneath his picture is a screaming white headline: SENATOR'S STEAMY SECRET. I try to read the blurb below it, but Ivy snatches the magazine away.

"I figured you were just hiding from that pathetic performance at nationals. Or maybe you actually *had* lost it. But that's not it at all, is it? You never lost it, because you never had it. Because you're not *her* at all, are you?"

Ivy flips the magazine open with such force that the cover page tears a little. She whips through to a page she's marked by folding down the corner. Then she slams a pink-polished finger down onto a page so hard her finger nearly tears through. The ink below it smudges, but it doesn't matter. All I can focus on is the headline, in big black letters, all capitalized, so that it's practically screaming: JACOBS'S AFFAIR WITH STAFFER HAS WASHINGTON TONGUES WAGGING. Accompanying it is a family photo, one of those formal posed ones in front of a soft gray background. The father and mother are seated in ornate mahogany chairs, and the children stand behind them, their smiles as wooden as the furniture, their hands placed stiffly on their parents' shoulders.

I only recognize one face: Sloane Emily. The picture must be from a couple of years ago, because Sloane Emily's hair is shorter, just skimming her shoulders, and she's wearing a plaid dress with a stiff white collar that only a mother could have picked out. Her openmouthed grin shows off an imperfect smile, with her two front teeth slightly apart, the left one a bit crooked.

I look up at Ivy, then back down at the picture, then back up at Ivy again. Her eyes are narrowed, but she's smiling. I can see a spot where her lipstick is escaping her lips and creeping down the corner of her mouth. I focus on it, because it makes the overall impression of her seem a lot less terrifying.

"What are you going to do?" I say finally.

"That depends." Her voice drops to a whispered growl. "I don't know who you are, but you don't belong here. I knew it from the first moment I saw you, and now I know why. You have two options: fake a broken ankle and drop out of the show, or pack your bags and take your trailer-trash ass out of here before I take this magazine to the director."

My heart is pounding so hard I feel it in my fingertips. In that moment, I feel this weird tug inside me. My blood is boiling. I may have become an ice princess, but my hockey instincts are still there. Maybe Ivy thought that just because there are people around, I wouldn't make a scene. That I'd bow my head and slink away quietly so she can take all the glory. And I'm ready to do it. I can swallow my anger. I can put away my fight face. I can walk away. I look up at her.

She's still smiling smugly. "So what's it gonna be? Are you gonna go home like a good girl, or do I have to *make* you go home?"

And then she winks at me.

Without even thinking I reach for the plate of pasta floating in a river of bright red sauce. In one swift, rather graceful movement that I can only attribute to my weeks of training, I lift the plate over Ivy's head and turn, sending pasta and sauce cascading down her blond locks.

Her voice comes out low and growling, and if her

cheeks weren't already stained the color of marinara, I bet I'd see heat rising in them. "You trailer trash bitch," she says through clenched teeth.

I snap. I lunge first at the magazine, and when I can't get it out of her hands, I tackle her. She pitches over backward, landing flat on her butt with a thud and a loud "Oof!" I catch a glimpse of her face, which conveys total shock.

She's about to meet the *real* Sloane Jacobs.

Ivy clutches the magazine with one hand, but she frees up the other to grab my ponytail. She gives it a hard yank, which throws me off balance. I roll to one side of her, and she scrambles to her feet. Before she can run, I grab one of the straps on her stupid sandals. A sparkly flower comes off in my hand. It's enough to send her stumbling forward again. Instead of running, though, she turns and starts swatting me with the magazine. I reach for it, but she yanks it away.

A crowd is gathering, and I hear people shouting my name. But all I can think about is getting that magazine.

I lunge for her, but she slides backward on her butt until she's practically under one of the tables. I grab a chair and fling it aside, ready to go in after her, but I feel a firm grip on the waistband of my jeans. In seconds, I'm being dragged back. I make one final reach for Ivy and the magazine, but it's too late.

I feel a hand wrap around my arm and jerk me to my feet.

"What ees going on here?" It's Sergei. He reaches under

the table, grabs Ivy's arm, and in one move has her out and on her feet. She glares at me.

"Yeah, *Sloane*, what's going on here?"

I look around and see my fellow campers. Bee is staring at me with a wide-eyed, horrified look. Andy is standing slightly back from the crowd, one hand over his face while he shakes his head. The others just stare openmouthed.

I swallow hard and blink, but nothing comes. I have no explanation, not even a lie. I don't know what to say.

"Well?" Sergei asks, and when I look up at him, I see his normally stoic face has softened a little. He doesn't look angry, he just looks confused.

I still don't know what to say.

So I do the only thing I can think of: I turn on my heel, shove through the crowd, and bolt for the door.

CHAPTER 23

SLOANE EMILY

Matt and I are watching *Mystery, Alaska,* from the camp's collection of hockey movies during our post-lunch rest period. I've never heard of it, but Matt claims it's a classic. Honestly, we could be watching *Saw IV,* so long as I'm able to cuddle up next to him, his arm wrapped around me, his hand resting softly on my hip, my head nestled in that nook where his shoulder meets his chest. I can hear his heart thudding louder than I can hear the movie.

I'm surprised by how comfortable I feel with him. With Matt at my side, I don't worry about my dad, or all those missed calls, or playing against Melody, or what will happen when the summer's over.

I cuddle up even deeper into his side, breathing in the smell of his soap and deodorant, some kind of alpine-fresh smell that I can't get enough of. He pulls me in tighter, planting a kiss on top of my head.

"Sloane."

At the sound of my name, a bolt of terror runs down my spine. I immediately look up at Matt, even though I know he wasn't the one to speak.

The person who did speak is a girl—a girl who shouldn't be here, a girl who I'm supposed to be.

Please, God, let me have imagined it.

Matt turns around, a look of confusion on his face.

Oh crap.

I turn too. Sloane Devon is standing behind the couch. Her long dark hair is a rat's nest. It seems to be knotted and held together by something thick and red. The collar of my favorite lavender fitted tee is ripped and hangs off one shoulder, exposing her bra strap, which also shows streaks of red. There's a big red handprint across her midsection and what look like flecks of dirt on her face that, thanks to the fact that she smells like an Olive Garden, I suspect might be oregano.

All the blood in my body drains to my toes. Beads of sweat form behind my ears and underneath my eyes. It feels like someone's taking slap shots in my digestive tract.

"We need to talk," she says.

It appears the marinara has hit the fan.

"Now." Sloane Devon's eyes flit back and forth from me to Matt, who's staring at her and attempting to stifle laughter. I don't blame him; I'd be laughing too, if I didn't know what I know.

"I'll be right back," I manage to say, but it comes out in

a croaking voice that I don't recognize as my own. I leap off the couch, nearly tumbling over the coffee table to avoid looking at Matt's face, and jerk my head toward the back door. Sloane Devon shoves it open, apparently expecting the door to be made of lead. It clangs open and smacks into the outside wall.

"What are you doing here?" I say as soon as we're outside.

"Someone knows," she says. "*Ivy* knows."

"What?"

"Ivy knows."

"I heard you," I snap. "I mean *what* exactly does she know?"

"She knows I'm not you, so I'm guessing it won't be long before she fills in the blanks," Sloane Devon says. "Does it matter what *exactly* she knows? She's going to turn me in. It's only a matter of time before someone finds out you're posing as me."

"Oh my God." I take a long, deep breath. A thousand questions are whizzing through my brain, but I settle on one. "When?"

"I mean, she may want to wash the spaghetti out of her hair first, which could buy us an hour or so." Sloane Devon shakes her head. "Regardless, this thing is over."

"How?"

Sloane Devon looks down at her shoes: my favorite black flip-flops with the black rhinestones on the straps. I had the cushy black foam perfectly molded to my skater feet, the arches dipped in slightly from where I roll my feet when I walk. Not only are they now fitted to Sloane Devon's feet, but they're also caked with red sauce, which squishes between her toes. My mom always said they looked cheap and wanted me to throw them out. Looks like she'll finally get her way.

"Sloane, how did she find out?" I ask again. There's a weird throbbing starting in my head.

Her eyes finally meet mine. "There was an article in *People* about your dad," she says slowly. "It has a family photo."

The beads of sweat behind my ears are now turning into tiny rivers. My hair is starting to stick to it, and it's making me feel hot.

"What . . . what's the article about?" I can barely say it.

Sloane Devon looks back down at her toes, but this time she keeps talking. "There was some kind of scandal. With your dad. I didn't read it, but . . ." She trails off, and I fill in the blanks. I nod so she knows she can stop, and she looks relieved. "So what are we going to do?"

I make a decision immediately. "We're leaving. Both of us are getting out of here." But Sloane Devon's no longer looking at me. She's staring over my shoulder.

"Sloane, what the hell is going on?"

I turn around and see Matt, his tall frame filling the open doorway. I don't know how long he's been standing there, but from the mixture of anger, confusion, and hurt in his eyes, it was long enough. "You're not . . ." He shakes his head, as if it will help him shake some sense into this situation. "You're not Sloane?"

"I am—"

"But she said she was pretending to be you," he says. He points to Sloane Devon, and recognition flickers across his face. "I know you," he says to her. "I recognize you from that tournament in West Chester. You're the girl who high-sticked a ref."

"Allegedly," Sloane Devon snaps.

"It's really hard to explain," I say desperately.

"Just tell him. It'll be easier," Sloane Devon says. "Trust me."

I groan, then turn back to Matt. "Look, my name is Sloane Jacobs. And so is hers. We met the night before camp and we decided to switch places, so she went to figure skating camp, and I went to hockey camp, and we pretended to be each other for the summer."

Matt is staring at me with disbelief, obviously doing some mental acrobatics, trying to separate fact from fiction. It looks like the results are not coming out in my favor. His eyes narrow, and he crosses his arms tightly over his chest.

"So all this time, you've been lying to me?"

"Not really," I say. "I mean, about little things, like I'm from Philadelphia or know how to play hockey, but almost everything else is true."

"*Almost* everything else?" he echoes. "The little *things*?"

When I hear my words repeated back to me, I realize how ridiculous I sound. "Matt, it's not as bad as it seems. . . ."

"It's worse," he says. His eyes are narrowed and any trace of that easy grin is gone. "Sloane, you lied about *who you are*. You made me jump through all these hoops to show you that you could trust me, when it turns out all along you've been lying about *everything*."

"I'm really sorry," I say. Because what else can I tell him? But I realize all at once how insufficient it sounds, like I dinged his car or dropped his phone in the toilet or something else that doesn't involve lying to him about who I am.

"You're sorry?" he echoes incredulously. He rakes a hand through his hair. "So why did you do it? Why did you lie in the first place?"

"I had to!" I burst out, as if shouting it at him is going to make him understand.

"What did you think I was going to do, rat you out?"

"No. Maybe. I don't know."

"That's crap, Sloane. You lied to me because you couldn't trust me with the truth. You should have said something that first night we kissed."

A huge lump is building in my throat. "I know, I should have—"

"But you didn't," he says, and any hope that he'll forgive me fades away. "You just kept lying."

"Matt, I—"

He cuts me off. "I don't want to hear it. It seems like you guys are in kind of a hurry, anyway. You better get going."

Tears are welling up in my eyes now, and I don't try to stop them. "Can I please call you?"

"Sure," he says tonelessly, then steps out of the doorway so that Sloane Devon and I can pass through it. "I can't promise I'll answer, though."

♡ ♡ ♡

Since Ivy's told Sloane Devon she'd only turn her in if she stayed, I figure we're safe if she crashes in my room. Ivy will just think Sloane ditched out like she was told. After checking to be sure Melody isn't around, I sneak Sloane Devon into my room with strict instructions not to leave unless she has to pee, and even then, that should be somewhere around four a.m., when no one will be awake.

I find flights for us both for the following morning. With all the excitement and bustle surrounding tomorrow night's games, it should be easy for me to slip out undetected. I use the emergency credit card my mom got me when I started driving. She probably imagined me using it for gas if I was stranded, to book a hotel room if I got caught driving in a storm, or even to buy myself an emergency dress for a gala event. I'm pretty sure she never imagined she'd be facilitating my escape from a not-so-foreign country.

The thought of my mother sends my brain spiraling down a "what's going to happen now?" path that sort of drops off over a dark, stormy cliff. I have to stop my brain before I go tumbling over into an abyss so deep I can't even see a reasonable punishment at the bottom.

I can't worry about that right now. I can't think at all. I just need to go home—if there's even a home to go back to.

The next morning, I send Sloane back to figure skating camp with strict instructions to stop for no one. She has sixty minutes to pack her bags and meet me at the airport, an hour before our noon flights are scheduled to leave. It takes me about ten minutes to cram all of Sloane's clothes into her duffel and repack her gear bag, which for me feels about nine minutes too long. I want out of here. Now.

CHAPTER 24

SLOANE DEVON

When I get back to my dorm, I find Bee sitting on the plush carpet outside my door. "What in the name of Chef Boyardee happened to you?"

"You haven't heard?" I sigh. I managed to rinse the marinara out of my hair during a covert middle-of-the-night bathroom run with Sloane Emily, but my clothes are still splattered with red, and I suspect I missed a few spots around my neck.

"Yeah, I heard, but I want you to tell me."

I hesitate for a split second. Sloane Emily made me swear I would speak to no one—just hustle her things into her suitcases and take off.

"Come inside," I say. I push the door open and usher Bee in. She takes a seat on my bed and crosses her arms in the same way an assistant principal might when he or she calls you to the office.

I try to remember what Sloane Emily said to Matt. It came out really fast and easy, like ripping off a Band-Aid. I start by telling Bee that I'm not a figure skater. I tell her I play hockey, that I'm from Philadelphia, and that though my name is Sloane Jacobs, I'm not the figure skating Sloane Jacobs who's supposed to be spending her summer here. I tell her about Ivy and the magazine, careful not to mention the sex scandal, because that's not my information to share. Besides, I imagine pretty soon everyone in the world is going to know the details about Sloane Emily's family. Bee will hear about it eventually.

Then I tell her that I went to see Sloane Emily, and that we're on our way out of the country. When I finish my story, Bee's eyes are so wide they look like they're going to take over her face.

"I guess I can see why you did it. I mean, how often do you meet someone with the exact same name?"

"Exactly," I say. Man, I hope my dad and Coach Butler see it the same way. I'm reminded of the *Twilight Zone*–style vertigo I felt back at the hotel when Sloane and I first figured out we shared a name, a height, and the same dark hair.

"But you had to learn to freaking figure skate." She shakes her head. "You had to give up most of your summer. Why would you want to go through all that?"

"*That's* why," I say.

"I don't get it." She furrows her brow.

"I was trying to ignore some things, get away for a

while, you know? I wanted to give up my whole summer. I wanted to give up *me*. Which is also the reason I didn't tell anyone the truth. Because then I'd have to talk about the exact things I was trying to get away from in the first place." The words are out of my mouth before I realize they're true.

"Well, you can talk about them now," she says.

"I have to finish packing."

"Fine," she says. She stands up and flings my suitcase up onto the bed, flipping the lid open. "Pack and talk."

I start pulling articles of clothing off the hangers and shoving them into the suitcase. I take the tissue-paper-thin gray cami that I wore the first day I was Sloane Emily off the hanger. I remember thinking this whole thing was only going to last a day, two days tops. And now here I am, almost four weeks later, shocked and more than a little sad that it's actually all falling apart.

"My mom is in rehab," I blurt out. I keep my focus on the gray cami. It's the first time I've ever said it out loud, and I have to slam my mouth shut to keep a gasping sob from following it. I take a deep breath and glance over at Bee, who is still calmly and methodically folding a stack of jeans.

"It's been a couple years coming, and she finally got in an accident while she was, you know." I can't quite bring myself to say the ugly word out loud. "Drunk." It sounds so dirty and gritty, like I'm living in an episode of *The Wire*, which is probably what most of these preppy kids would think if they knew the truth about me. Bee still doesn't say anything, just places the stack of jeans in snug next to Sloane's hoodie, the only one she packed, with big block letters spelling out "Brown."

"Things have been so crappy. I haven't felt right, you know? And I kept exploding on the ice. *My* ice. I play hockey." I'm surprised by how strange it feels to say that out loud, in this nice room, surrounded by an explosion of Ivy's pink things.

Bee just nods and keeps packing, folding all the items I toss onto the bed. Now that I've started speaking, I find I can't stop.

"I got into a big fight at my last game. I started it. My coach talked to my dad, who, by the way, has barely spoken to me since Mom's accident, and the next thing I knew, I was getting shipped off, just like my mom. Only I was supposed to spend four weeks at hockey camp. And then I met Sloane — the other Sloane, I mean. She had this perfect life. You should have seen her hotel room. It was the size of my whole house! So when she suggested the switch, it seemed like the perfect solution. The best way not to think about the things that make me feel like I'm cracking up, was to not, you know, *be* me."

Bee takes the gray cami out of my hands, folds it, and places it on top of a stack in the suitcase. She flips the lid closed and pushes it back, making a space on the bed next to her. Then she turns her green eyes to mine. "Sloane, sit down."

I sit, but I'm still stiff as a board. My hands are clenched tight, as if I'm holding my tears in my palms and if I loose my grip, they'll come tumbling out.

"Sloane, I understand. I really do—more than you know. When my dad's alcoholism got bad, I would have done anything to just run away and hide from the problem."

She says it like it's nothing. "Alcoholism." Clinical, but the weight of the word makes me stop and look hard at her. She's said the word a lot, but it still hurts her a little, I can tell.

Bee finally breaks her gaze and looks down at her hands, which are folded in her lap. "Things were bad. He got so drunk at one of my brother's basketball games that he got in a fistfight with one of the other dads. It took three other parents plus two security guards to break it up, and the whole thing ended up on the local TV. It was so embarrassing. It wasn't long after that when he finally admitted what his problem was and got help."

"Did it work?"

"Well, it's not a cure, but he did the whole twelve-step thing, making amends and all that. And I couldn't forgive him right away. I still can't. But things get better a little bit every day."

"That's good," I say, barely able to breathe. I wonder if Mom's going to apologize, if we're actually going to talk about things no one has mentioned in my house for years—that I used to have to carry her up to bed. That she missed birthdays. That she put me in the car with her when she was drunk.

Bee smiles at me and squeezes my hand. "Do you want me to help you finish getting your stuff together?"

"No, thanks," I say. "I need some time alone, I think."

"All right." Bee reaches over and envelops me in a hug. A real hug, one that tests my ribs and squeezes the air out of my lungs. "I'm so bummed I won't get to see you skate. You were getting so good. I would have loved to see your big moment out there."

"Thanks, Bee," I say into a big tuft of her red curly hair.

"Stay in touch. You can call anytime. I'm happy just to listen, okay?"

"Thanks," I say again, only this time it comes out as a tiny whisper. The lump in my throat is rising dangerously high.

When Bee stands up, I swipe at my cheeks. As soon as the door closes behind her, I go to the last item in the closet, Sloane Emily's fleece jacket. I pull the stack of letters from my mother out of the pocket and sit back down on the bed. I find the one with the oldest postmark, the one that came first, then slide my finger under the seal.

> Dear Sloane,
> Before I say anything else, I need to tell you that I'm so sorry. . . .

And then the lump in my throat explodes. The tears pour out. They run down my cheeks, my neck, and pool in my collarbone. I gasp so hard from the sobs that I start hiccuping. The tears are so thick that I can barely keep reading.

But I do.

CHAPTER 25

SLOANE EMILY

The Montreal airport is a cavernous, glass-paneled building with soaring ceilings. I'm parked on a bench by the ticketing kiosks scanning the crowd for Sloane Devon. I look down at my watch: 11:20. She needs to get here in the next ten minutes if we're going to make check-in for our flights.

There's a bank of TV screens hanging over the automatic doors across from the benches. The chattering of travelers and the squeak of suitcases rolling across the floor means I can't hear, but the subtitles are nice and large.

The first screen is showing an infomercial for some product that consists of elastic bands and multicolored balls that's supposed to make you buff like Arnold Schwarzenegger. The next is showing a cartoon flashing so many colors I'm surprised children don't get seizures while watching it. The next three are all showing cable news, two from the U.S. and the third from some Canadian equivalent of CNN. As I watch, all three screens flip to the same image.

I blink a few times, but the image doesn't go away.

I guess I shouldn't be surprised. Washington loves a sex scandal.

My dad steps out of a building I don't recognize and approaches about a million microphones all pointed directly at him. I see him smooth his tie, a nervous habit he's had since his very first election. He never speaks without smoothing his tie.

His mouth starts to move, but I can't hear. It takes a moment before the closed-captioning catches up with him.

TODAY I HAVE DISGRACED MY OFFICE. I HAVE DISGRACED MY CONSTITUENCY. WORSE, I HAVE DISGRACED MY FAMILY, AND FOR THAT I AM TRULY SORRY. I UNDERSTAND THAT YOU ALL HAVE JOBS TO DO, AND THAT THIS IS A STORY YOU FEEL YOU NEED TO REPORT. I ONLY ASK THAT YOU RESPECT THE PRIVACY OF MY WIFE AND CHILDREN, WHO WILL BE HAVING A HARD ENOUGH TIME WORKING THROUGH THE HURT AND ANGUISH I'VE CAUSED THEM. THEY DO NOT DESERVE WHAT I'VE DONE TO THEM, AND THEY DO NOT DESERVE TO BE TORMENTED FOR MY MISTAKES. SUSAN, JAMES, AND SLOANE, I AM TRULY SORRY.

All three screens switch back to a studio shot, where three overly coiffed anchors immediately start dissecting his apology. I want to throw something heavy at all five TVs, the infomercials and cartoons included. I want to break things. I want to scream.

But most of all, I want to run away. I want to run farther and faster than I did four weeks ago when I decided to be someone else.

The automatic doors slide open, and Sloane Devon strides in pulling my rolling suitcase, my skate bag over her shoulder. She spots me, waves, and weaves through the crowd.

"We have to go back," I gasp.

She just stares at me. "Are you out of your mind?"

My whole body is shaking. "I just saw my dad on TV. If I go home, they're just going to stick their cameras and their microphones in my face. They're going to shout at me on the street and take my picture. I'll go to the grocery store and I'll see my stupid family pictures at the checkout line. I can't go back!"

"Okay, okay. Calm down," she says. She drops both bags and places her hands on my shoulders. "But where are we going to go?"

I hadn't gotten much farther than hiding out in the airport until security made me leave. "I don't know," I say. "I'm not ready to go home yet. I'm not ready to *leave*. I worked so hard. . . ."

Sloane Devon looks at me like I've sprouted a second head. "This is insane. There's no way I can go back! Ivy is waiting to out me to the whole world."

"Then don't let her!" I say.

"I attacked her with fake pasta product!" she practically shrieks. "I'll be lucky if they don't handcuff me on sight."

"Do what you want," I tell her. I pick up her gear bag and heave it over my shoulder. "You can fly back to Philly. But I worked too damn hard this summer to let it all go before it's done—before *I'm* done. I'm going back, and I'm going to play."

Sloane stares at me. Then, to my surprise, she starts laughing. "You really are a whole new Sloane Jacobs, aren't you?"

"And you're just the same old one running away," I say. It's mean, and I know it. Her eyes go wide like I've slapped her.

I charge through the automatic doors so fast they nearly don't open in time. I step right up to the curb and raise my hand for the next cab, which screeches to a halt in front of me. The driver scurries around the car and starts tossing my bags into the trunk. I slide into the backseat. I hear the trunk slam, and then he's back in the driver's seat.

"Where to?" he says.

I open my mouth to respond but don't get a chance.

"We're making two stops, actually," Sloane Devon says, as she slides into the seat next to me.

CHAPTER 26

SLOANE DEVON

$I$was worried someone was going to snag me the moment I walked through the front door at BSI; worried that maybe they'd even send Sergei to use some of his Ukrainian muscle to get rid of me.

But no one pays any attention to me at all.

Skaters rush past me, some already dressed in stretchy, shiny, sparkly skating costumes, skate bags slung over their shoulders and makeup kits clutched in their hands. Ella St. Clair is in the corner on one of the antique chairs with Caitlin Hanson towering over her, furiously french-braiding her hair. Two other skaters linger next to them waiting for their turn. There's a visible cloud of glitter hanging in the air like a haze.

Good. Maybe it will help me stay incognito.

A group of junior girls dart past me, probably on their way to catch the next shuttle to the rink. Today's performance will take place at a huge arena at the University of Montreal, with full lights, even a kiss-and-cry: a spot off the side of the rink where, after our performance is done, we'll sit and wait for our scores, and cry out of either happiness or total despair. I had to get Andy to explain to me what exactly that is, and I'm dreading it almost more than the actual performance itself.

Suddenly, a hand clamps down on my elbow. My first thought is that I'm busted.

"Are you okay?" Andy spins me around to face him, gripping both my arms like it's some kind of intervention, and I exhale. He's already in his solid black spandex jumpsuit, sleeveless to show off his arms. I never knew a guy could rock a unitard so hard.

"I don't know. You tell me." I have no idea if everyone heard why Ivy and I were engaged in fisticuffs, or if people just assume I'm some psycho who beats up the competition. *Dear God, please let it be the psycho theory.*

"Well, after your little food fight and your quick departure, Ivy stood there carrying on about how you were an imposter. It was an epic meltdown. Katinka shut her down and sent her off to get ready for the competition. I think thanks to her almighty hysterics, no one really heard the truth; or if they did, they don't believe it. Thank God she always was a drama queen."

"Thank God," I say, and I actually feel my pulse slow down by about half. I didn't realize my heart was staging a rave inside my chest. "Are you sure no one saw the magazine?"

"Girl, these kids have had nothing but rhinestones and lutzes on their minds for weeks. None of them are paying attention to CNN." Andy sizes me up. "Does this mean you're skating?"

"If you'll let me," I say, and I feel my pulse quicken again.

Andy raises his eyebrows practically through his forehead. "Why wouldn't I?"

"Because you could get in trouble for helping me," I say. "Or at the very least, I could make you look bad out there."

"*First* of all, I don't give a rat's ass if people know I helped you, because *second*, you're not going to make me look bad." Andy crosses his arms. "When people see what I've done for you, they're going to be *begging* me to coach them. How do you think I'm going to make a living someday? You, girl, are my golden ticket."

"No pressure, then, huh?" I try to laugh, but all that comes out is a squeak.

"Quit it with the 'woe is me' crap and go get dressed," he says. He spins me around and points me toward the stairs.

I look over my shoulder and stick my tongue out at him, and he swats me lightly on the butt. We head up the stairs and I turn left to go to my room. Andy grabs my arm again.

"No need to run into Ivy until you're actually on the ice. Why ruin the surprise? You can get ready in my room."

CHAPTER 27

SLOANE EMILY

I sprint into the arena, dodging spectators and nearly taking out a little blond girl with Sloane Devon's massive gear bag. I hike it up on my shoulder again and another small child has to duck out of my way.

I make it through the crowd on the mezzanine and push toward the stairs leading down to the ice. There's already a decent crowd in the stands, not to mention the crowd I just swam through in the mezzanine. Of all the things I'd pictured when I imagined playing this game, I never thought about the fact that there would actually be people watching me.

Oh crap.

I point my gaze at the concrete tunnel at the bottom of the stairs that leads to the locker room. *Don't worry about the crowd. You'll be okay. Get dressed. Skate.*

I hustle down the stairs and push through the heavy

metal door. Instantly, I'm greeted by a frazzled-looking Cameron, clad in full gear, her dreads braided in pigtails.

"Where have you been? You are so incredibly late!" She takes my gear bag off my shoulder and gestures for me to follow her through the maze of benches and lockers. "I thought you were dead in a ditch somewhere. I was afraid we'd have to bring Trina up from the B team."

"As long as your priorities are in order," I reply.

"You wanna joke, or you wanna play hockey? Because Trina would be psyched to be able to fall on her face with the varsity team." Trina's an okay player, except for her persistent problem of tripping over her own skates as soon as she shoots.

"Sorry, I just had to take care of a few things," I say.

A look of concern passes across her face. "Is everything okay? I asked Matt where you were, but he wouldn't give me a straight answer." We stop in front of my locker, and Cameron drops my bag at my feet. My stomach drops with it.

"What did he say?" I croak out. Matt could have told Cameron the truth. He could have told everyone the truth. For all I know, Coach Hannah is waiting by the ice to drag me away for questioning under a hot light somewhere.

Cameron shrugged. "He said if I was looking for Sloane, I needed to be more specific. Lovers' quarrel already?"

"Not exactly—" I start, but she cuts me off.

"Whatever, you can tell me later. It's game time."

I don't want to keep lying to Cameron. She's my only real friend here—or anywhere, for that matter. It really sucked to have Matt look at me like I'm a lying liar, but it would probably be worse to have Cameron hate me. I want to tell her, but I know her well enough by now to know that now is not the time. I can't confess to lying about who I am for four weeks and expect her to trust me on the ice.

"Remind me to tell you something after the game, okay?" I'm going to tell her the whole truth. I just hope we win, because she'll be too happy to care. And then maybe I can keep my friend.

"Will do. Now you need to get your game face on," she says. She pulls my jersey from the hanger that's sticking out of the locker and tosses it on top of my head. "And your jersey, too."

I pull the heavy blue jersey off my face, happy to have a task and a distraction from the nerves and the guilt and the anxiety dancing a conga line in my stomach. I look down at the fabric in my hands and see the stitched-on white block letters spelling out JACOBS. I have to keep myself from tearing up. I may be pretending, but I *am* Sloane Jacobs. That's *my* name.

I get dressed, then give myself one final once-over in the mirror. My phone rings. I dig it out of my bag and see a text from James on the screen.

Surprise! Came to see your big comeback. What time are you on?

I don't even have time to get nervous or freaked out or formulate a lie. That's all over now. Now it's just me. I tap a reply, then toss my phone back into my bag.

Come to McConnell Arena. 3883 University St.
I'm in blue. I'll explain after.

CHAPTER 28

Sloane Devon

I've been pretending to be someone else for four weeks. For four weeks I've put on someone else's clothes, I've trained in someone else's sport, and I've told someone else's life story. I really should be used to it, but looking in the mirror in Andy's room right now, I absolutely don't recognize myself.

And it's totally freaky.

Andy has used some kind of industrial sealant to slick my hair back in a high, tight bun. The effect has my eyebrows arched in a look of mild yet constant surprise. It's only accentuated by the heavy black cat's-eye liner he's painted on. My lips are coated with a color that should be called "Harlot" or "Streetwalker." I've got a sweep of bright blush on my cheeks extending almost to my hairline. And that's just above the neck.

My torso is covered in a ruched black spandex bodice with little rhinestones buried in the fabric. The top is sheer so as to make the dress appear strapless, but there are a few tiny rhinestones scattered across my shoulders. The skirt—if you can call it that, since it barely covers my behind—is A-line. No flounces, which I appreciate. Cover me in rhinestones, but don't give me a stinking ruffly skirt. That's where I draw the line.

"Now for the finishing touch," Andy says. He comes at me with a fuzzy black caterpillar-looking thing pinched between his fingers.

"Oh no you don't," I say, swatting his hand away.

"Shut up, close your eyes, and think of England," he says. Then he jams his finger into my eyes, first the left, then the right. I blink a few times, feeling like my eyelashes have been dipped in molasses. Fake eyelashes. I never, *ever* thought I'd see the day.

"You look good." Andy takes a few steps back to admire his work.

"I look like a drag queen," I say, trying to restore my normal blinking function.

"Grab your skates, RuPaul. It's time to go."

Andy and I take the last shuttle to the arena. As soon as we arrive, he shoves me into a broom closet underneath the stands. When he pops his head in to motion me out, I nearly pull the door shut again and tell him to go away. The only reason I follow is that I'm pretty sure he'll drag me out by my bun if I refuse. We make our way down the narrow hallway and around the corner that leads to the ice, both waddling like cowboys with saddle sores, thanks to our skates.

Roman and his partner, Elizabeth, are just finishing up their routine. They're in matching yellow spandex outfits, his a jumpsuit, hers a feathery minidress. They look like figure skating Big Bird impersonators. Thank God Andy has style. He took one of Sloane Emily's old white dresses and dip-dyed it black and glued on all those rhinestones himself. I can't believe I'm saying this about a spandex minidress covered in glitter, but I look pretty badass.

"You know I said all that crap about how I made you?" Andy whispers to me.

"Yeah?"

"Well, a sculptor is only as good as the clay, or whatever," Andy says. Then he reaches down and squeezes my hand. I feel a tiny lump rise in my throat, but a couple deep breaths push it away. I've become a lot of things these last few weeks, but a crier will *not* be one of them.

Roman lifts Elizabeth high over his head. As Elizabeth whizzes by, I'm nearly blinded by her toothy white grin, which serves as a reminder to me: *Must. Smile.* It's not something I've ever had to think about when playing sports before. "Game face" means something entirely different out here.

The music swells as Roman and Elizabeth enter their final footwork pattern, which will end in impressively fast camel spins. Then there will be thunderous applause. Then it will be our turn out there. I have to swallow hard to keep from throwing up in my mouth. I distract myself by removing the plastic guards from my skates and placing them on the ledge.

"You have some nerve."

The syrupy whisper jolts my jitters away.

"Get away from me," I say back to Ivy. She's standing next to me in something hot pink and glittery that manages to incorporate rhinestones, feathers, *and* tassels. She looks like a cabaret act on acid.

"What do you think you're even doing here?" Ivy's voice rises well above a whisper, but it's masked by the booming timpani of the music in the arena. It's loud enough that some people on the sidelines take notice, though, and Katinka comes striding over. Crap, an adult.

"What ees dee problem?" Katinka crosses her arms and glares at Ivy, ignoring me completely.

"She's a fraud," Ivy says. She points one long, pink-polished finger at me, so close that she's practically poking me in the eye. Thank God for those false eyelashes. They provide a bit of a buffer from Ivy's talons.

"What are you talking about?" Katinka still doesn't look at me. She just stares Ivy down so hard that Ivy drops her finger and sort of shrinks into herself. Katinka is a tiny lady with a huge dose of scary.

"She's not who she says she is." Ivy's voice is a little quieter now, but she's still spitting venom. Katinka turns to me for the first time.

"Are you Sloane Jacobs?" she asks.

I gulp. "Yes," I say, though my shaking voice makes the word six or seven syllables long. I look her right in the eye, and just as I'm about to crumble and run—not that I'd get very far in these skates—I see a faint sparkle there. She stares at me hard, just like she stared at Ivy, and for a split second I see a nearly imperceptible wink.

"But she's not the *right* Sloane Jacobs!" Ivy cries.

Katinka just holds up a slender hand. "I don't care about personal life. I care only for skater on ice. She ees Sloane Jacobs. She skate on ice. Ees enough for me."

"But—but—she's a liar!" Ivy sputters.

"Miss Loughner," Katinka says, and her voice turns so icy, for a moment I fantasize it will freeze Ivy altogether and she'll splinter like a Popsicle. "You are familiar with international skating rules, are you not?"

"Of course," Ivy spits.

"Then you know you can be disqualified for unsports-womanlike conduct, no?"

"Disqualified? But she—"

"Miss Loughner." Katinka raises an eyebrow.

Ivy sucks in a breath. She's shaking so hard I think she might explode. Finally, she turns to me. "Break a leg, Sloane," she growls with such venom that I actually think she's going to do it for me right now.

I smile sweetly at her. "Thank you, Ivy."

"And now, Sloane Jacobs and Andy Phillips, perform-ing a program to 'Hedwig's Theme.'"

My name echoes across the arena and bounces around in my head. It's *my* name, and I'm really going to do this.

"Go. And kick butt," Katinka clips in her multinational accent.

And with that, Andy and I take our first step out onto the ice.

CHAPTER 29

SLOANE EMILY

The red team is warming up on the ice. Melody has them organized in some kind of military-like drill situation, jumping and weaving in parallel lines around the rink. Watching them is just making me more nervous, so I have to turn away from the glass barrier.

The blue team is lined up around the outside of the rink. We start in five minutes; we'll have fifteen minutes to warm up. Then there will be intros, and then the buzzer will start the game. The thought of it sends my gaze straight down to my skates. I think I'm going to throw up.

"Jacobs, look alive! What, are you praying over there?" Coach Hannah strolls up and thumps me hard on the back, but I can barely feel it through the padding. I give her a weak smile, and she just laughs at me. If only she knew this isn't just game-day nerves. This is *first*-game-day nerves.

I try to take my mind off the game by people-watching

in the crowd, which is growing larger by the minute. There are plenty of friends and family, but it also looks like people have come in off the street to watch. It looks like close to two hundred spectators.

One woman catches my eye. She's sitting about six rows up. Her face is tired, and a few laugh lines betray her age, but her long hair is still jet-black and braided. She looks oddly familiar, but I can't place her.

Her arms are crossed tightly over her chest. She scans the ice, then leans over to whisper something to the man next to her, tall and sort of burly with a dark beard and a flannel shirt. The woman uncrosses her arms and uses her hand as a shield from the bright stadium lights. She's wearing a bright yellow shirt with black letters printed across the chest.

MAMA JACOBS.

Oh. My. God.

A big part of me wants to run and hide—maybe stuff myself back into a locker and let Trina have her time on the ice with varsity.

But I'm through running. And I'm through hiding. So I hop out of the rink and sprint up the stairs, ignoring the surprised looks and murmurs from the crowd.

"Mrs. Jacobs!" I say, shoving my way over to her. "Hi! It's really nice to meet you. I'm a friend of Sloane's. My name is *also* Sloane Jacobs, if you can believe that." Mrs. Jacobs just stares at me. The man next to her, who must be Sloane's dad, tilts his head slightly like a dog does when it hears a high-pitched noise.

"You—you know my daughter?" she asks. I notice how her accent spreads out the word "daughter" and ends it with an *ah* sound.

"I do," I tell her.

"Where is she? I don't see her on either team."

"She's actually not here," I say, and I see the blood start to drain from her face, signaling the start of full-on mom emergency mode. "She's fine! Don't worry. She's only a few blocks away at another arena."

"Oh, I didn't realize there were two different games," she says, looking at her husband.

"The email said all the games were here," Mr. Jacobs says. He has the same accent as Mrs. Jacobs, the same accent I heard a trace of in Sloane Devon's voice.

"Oh, well, you know—it's a long story," I say lightly, trying to laugh. I end up sounding like I've swallowed my mouth guard. "And I'm sure she'll want to tell you all about it. But you should go on over to the ice arena at the University of Montreal. Take a cab, it should only take you a few minutes."

They both stare at me for just a few seconds before gathering their things and hustling out of the arena. I hope they make it in time to see her.

A sharp whistle brings my attention back down to the ice. Back to my ice.

"Jacobs, get your butt down here!" Cameron looks like she's about to throttle me.

"I'm ready," I say. And I am.

CHAPTER 30

SLOANE DEVON

The lights are so bright that I can't see a soul in the crowd. All I can see is the white expanse of ice surrounding me.

Our music starts with a cymbal crash and a deafening timpani roll. Andy's left hand on my waist squeezes slightly, and then we're off. Our routine starts with some side-by-side footwork. Then we have our first jump early. It's just a waltz jump, nothing fancy. Andy calls it a rust-buster, but once when I was whining he told me to quit it and do "the baby jump." It's meant to get me warmed up for later, when we'll go for our double axel. As we whiz past the judges toward the far side of the ice, Andy catches my eye and gives me a wink. I relax a little. He's having fun with it. So can I.

I take a breath and extend my left foot backward. Then I swing it forward, executing a half turn in the air and landing on my right foot. It's just a small jump, but there's plenty of room for what Andy calls "pretty arms," and when I land without wobbling, I give plenty of pretty face, too. My heart is pounding so hard I can hear the blood pumping in my ears, but I'm not nervous. I'm full of adrenaline. I want to do it again, right now. We don't have another jump for about forty-five seconds, though.

It's time for our first lift. Even though Andy and I have carried it off flawlessly for the past week, I'm still nervous as I drop away from him. He grips my hand, pulls me forward, and before I can even think about falling on my butt, I'm soaring through the air. I hear the crowd applaud. I don't have to worry about remembering to smile, because there's a perma-grin plastered across my face. This is *so awesome.*

We do another single, this time a half loop, just like the waltz jump but landing on the opposite foot, and then go into side-by-side spins. Then we're off again, picking up speed. It's time for the double, nearly the end of our program. It's a double lutz, the easiest double there is—or so Andy claims.

All at once, my anxiety comes rushing back. I'll swing my left foot back, my weight on the back outside edge. Then I'll launch up, spin two and a half times, my arms tucked tight on my chest, and land on the back outside edge of the opposite foot. Or is it the inside edge? No, it's the outside edge. I think. No, I'm sure. Outside edge. Outside.

And then I feel it. The tingles start in my toes and work their way up my foot. When they hit my calf I feel my left leg go weak, and I have to concentrate hard not to wobble. No, not here. This doesn't belong here. Outside. Or inside?

Dammit, which is it?

I'm seconds from the jump when I hear Katinka's voice in my head. *Don't think. Just go with eet.*

I take a deep breath. And just before I kick my foot out to leave the ice, I close my eyes and think of nothing but ice: smooth, white, spotless ice. The tingles dissolve back down into my toes and disappear. Then I bend my knee, tuck my arms, and leap.

The not-thinking thing makes it so I barely notice I've landed the jump. I catch a glimpse of Andy's smile, and I hear the thunderous applause and even a few whoops from the crowd. I'm so shocked that I nearly fall down while skating backward, but the wobble is practically imperceptible and I pull myself together quickly.

Before I know it, Andy and I are engaged in side-by-side spins so fast I worry I might achieve liftoff. I hear the drums rolling and the horns rising in our music, and just as I hear the cymbal crash, Andy and I slam our toe picks down into the ice in unison, throwing our arms into the air.

The sound is deafening. There's applause and cheers, and flowers and stuffed animals start appearing down on the ice. Little girls in matching blue dresses skate around and start picking them up. Andy grabs my hand, then pulls me down in a deep bow. Then we spin around and bow to the other side. I blink into the lights, still unable to see individual faces in the crowd.

Andy throws his arms around me in a giant bear hug. "We did it!" he says. "You were on fire!"

I can't even respond. I'm still too shocked.

Andy grasps my hand and leads me off toward the kiss-and-cry. Long ago I vowed to neither kiss nor cry while sitting in the blue-carpet-covered area where we'll wait for our scores. I don't even care what the judges say. I feel like a perfect ten.

We step off the ice, grab our skate guards, and hobble over to the corner where Katinka is waiting. She gives me a thumbs-up, and I just nod at her. I'm not sure how much she knows, but I'm glad to have her in my corner regardless.

We have to wait a few minutes while the judges turn in their scores to the announcer. A photographer crouches in front of us and starts snapping photos. The flash blinds me even worse than the stadium lights. People are talking all around me, the crowd is still loud, and Andy is chattering on, reliving every moment of our unbelievable performance.

The announcer's voice booms out over the loudspeaker. Andy squeezes my hand so tight I worry my fingers are going to pop off. Another flash goes off in front of me, and I have to blink and look away to get my vision back.

Off to the left of the kiss-and-cry, I spot something bright yellow. At first I think it's a side effect of the flash, but then I see that it's a T-shirt. With black letters on the front. That spell out MAMA JACOBS.

"Mom?" I whisper, but apparently she reads lips, because she smiles and waves at me.

The announcer finishes calling out our scores, and they must have been good, because Andy throws his arms around me and screams right into my ear. I hang limp in his arms. I feel all the blood drain out of my body and pool in my toes and fingertips. I feel woozy, and I'm worried I'm going to fall off my skates.

"Honey, that was incredible." My mom takes me from Andy and wraps me up in a hug. This time I feel my arms rise and wrap around her neck. I pull her tight. She gives me a big kiss on the cheek.

"Mama," I say, already feeling the tears roll down my cheeks. "You're here."

And now, having both kissed and cried, I've officially been inducted into the world of figure skating.

CHAPTER 31

Sloane Emily

"**D**efenders, I need you to look alive out there," Cameron says. It's almost intermission, and we're down 1–0. She throws back her water bottle, swishes for a minute, then swallows. "Marino, keep your eye on Melody. Jacobs, I'm moving you to left wing. Get the puck to me or to Avery. Let's tie this thing up."

We put our gloves in the middle and shout a quick, loud *"Blue!"* Then we tumble through the door onto the ice.

I'm exhausted from the game, and also from the adrenaline coursing through my body. Just before the end of the second period, I finally manage to get the puck to Cameron in time for her to get a good shot. As we shuffle off toward the locker room for intermission, I glance up at the scoreboard.

1–1.

I'm just about to push through the heavy locker room door. A hand grabs my arm and pulls me back. I whip around and see Matt, already in his gear and his green jersey with the white C stitched on the front. The boys' varsity game is after ours, and the boys will hit the ice for their warm-up as soon as our buzzer sounds.

The sight of him makes me want to pee my pants, which would be a problem, if I hadn't already peed a little when Melody smashed me into the boards at around the twelve-minute mark. I never realized "hit her so hard she pees" was an actual thing, but I can tell you, it *is*.

"I don't know why you're hiding from the puck," he says. He normally towers over me, but he doesn't have his skates on yet, so we're nearly eye to eye.

"Excuse me?" I don't know if I'm hearing him correctly.

"You had possession twice with clear shots both times, and both times you passed it off," he says. He glares at me. Is he seriously coaching me right now?

"I'm—I'm doing my best," I say. What does he want to hear, that I'm not a real hockey player so there's no way in hell I'm going to waste a shot when someone else can do it better? He knows the truth. He ought to figure it out.

"No you're not," he says. "You need to take the damn shot next time." He jabs me in the chest with a gloved finger. "Have some confidence. Your team needs you."

"Okay," I reply. He nods; then we stand there staring at each other in silence for a few beats. I inhale and it all comes out in a rush: "Matt, I'm so, so sorry. I really am. I know I should have told you the truth, but I was too afraid to ruin everything. I was so happy. It felt so good to kiss you, and to be with you. But now I can see that I ruined it anyway. I'm so sorry."

His face is unreadable. When he doesn't say anything, I turn back toward the door.

"I don't hate you," he blurts out.

My heart stops. I face him again.

"I'm glad," I say, letting out a deep breath I didn't even know I was holding.

"I saw the thing about your dad on TV," he says. "They showed your picture. I get it."

I hate that he knows about my dad, because it just reminds me that *everyone* knows. I feel nauseated, and I have to stare down at my skates to keep myself from throwing up.

Matt sticks out his hand. "I'm Matt O'Neill," he says. "I'm from Philly."

I look up. His face is still composed, but his eyes are smiling. Just like when he kissed me that first time. I made him swear I could trust him, and he didn't let me down, not even when *I* let *him* down.

I let myself smile just a little. "I'm Sloane *Emily* Jacobs. I'm from Washington, DC."

"And you figure skate, right?" The corner of his mouth twitches slightly.

"Right," I say.

"And you also play hockey, right?"

"Well . . ."

"And you play hockey, *right*?" He grasps my shoulders and gives me a little shake.

"Right!" I say, laughing.

"Then get out there and kick some ass." He pulls me in and kisses me, softly. I try to get my arms around him, but there's too much padding between us. Damn hockey gear.

When Matt pulls away, he's full-on grinning. And my heart is winging up through my head. I feel like I could sprout wings and fly.

Matt spins me around and points me toward the door. "Go listen to your captain, then ignore whatever she says and take the shot. Got it?"

"You got it, Coach," I say, then push through the door to join my team.

It's been more than nineteen minutes of a brutal stalemate. We've chased each other up and down the ice in full sprints. The red team has taken six shots on the goal, the blue team five, and yet the score still sits at 1–1. With less than ten seconds on the clock, this is our last shot. We're not playing overtime today, so if no one scores, no one wins, which might as well mean we both lose.

Across the ice, I see Marino with the puck. She's looking for Cameron. This is our last chance. Score now, or end in a tie, but Cameron has two red players all over her. There's no way she has a clear shot, and Avery is on the bench sucking on her inhaler. Melody charges Marino, and in seconds, the puck is whizzing to me. I look for Cameron again, but she's still covered. I glance at the clock. Six seconds and counting. I look at the goal. I have a clear shot.

I'm scared, there's no doubt about it. It's worse than

the first time I attempted the triple-triple, and I could have actually landed on my head and *died* doing that. But it's not just the shot that scares me. It's the magazine. It's my dad on television telling the world that he betrayed us. It's my family, falling apart. It's all the things we'll have to say that I never said because I was terrified to confront my dad. It's all the lies I told—all the lies I lived—because the Jacobses are calm. They're polite. They're rational. They're—

Whack!

With all those thoughts rushing through my brain like a tsunami, I lift my arms and connect with the puck. I want to watch its path, but I blink, and it's already gone. All that's left is a flashing light, a deafening buzzer, the roar of the crowd, and five blue jerseys rushing at me at top speed. The next thing I know I'm flat on the ice and at the bottom of a pile of hockey players. I manage to pop my head out of the fray and catch sight of the scoreboard.

Blue: 2. Red: 1.

I look up and see a red jersey towering over me. It's Melody.

"Good game, Jacobs. If you'd asked me four weeks ago, I would not have predicted that," she says. I wonder if I should be insulted, but the truth is she's right. I notice that she's smiling through her helmet. Then she skates back to her team, where she starts handing out high fives. I feel as if Wayne Gretzky himself crowned me queen of the rink.

I look up into the stands and see James. And standing next to him is my mother, clad in a cream-colored pantsuit.

Wait, what?

I blink a few times, but she doesn't go away. She looks woefully out of place surrounded by parents dressed in jeans and T-shirts, crumpled boxes of popcorn all around her. She sees me looking and offers a little beauty-queen-style wave. She's smiling. And then she gives me a thumbs-up.

I look from the scoreboard to my mother giving me a thumbs-up, and back to the scoreboard again. *Am I dead? Have I died, and this is heaven? Did someone bean me in the head, knock me unconscious, and this is all a dream?*

"Damn, Jacobs! I knew you had it in you!" Matt towers over me in full gear. He offers me a hand and drags me up to my skates, then throws his arms around me in an enormous hug. "Now it's your turn to cheer me on. Get showered and get back in those stands."

CHAPTER 32

Sloane Devon

The medal around my neck is heavy. I reach down and grasp it, turning it over in my hands. It's shiny and silver.

We came in second.

When they called my name, I couldn't even believe it. I even looked around for the other Sloane Jacobs, wondering if maybe she showed up and competed too. When I realized that nope, we earned second place, I nearly passed out.

Roman and Elizabeth finished first. They deserved it. They managed to land side-by-side triple axels, which is pretty much unbeatable, but I couldn't care less. Four weeks ago I didn't even know what an axel *was*. And now I'm standing here on a podium next to Andy with a silver medal around my neck.

Un-freaking-believable.

I spot my parents in the crowd. They've retaken their

seats. Mom's been bouncing up and down and clapping and grinning since my name was first announced, and it doesn't look like she's stopping anytime soon. I grin and wave at her. She and my dad both wave back.

When I finally leave the ice, I head straight for my parents in the stands. My mom envelops me in yet another hug.

"How did you get here?" I ask. I know it's the first of about a million questions, but it seems like the easiest one right now.

"We could ask you the same question," Dad says.

"We met your friend at the hockey arena, and she sent us here," my mom says, and laughs. Her eyes are clear and sparkling. Sober. I have to ask.

"No, I mean how did you get *here*?" I say.

Mom looks down at her shoes, takes a deep breath, then looks back at me, right in the eye. It's startling, because I realize for the last year her expression has been so glazed she's barely been looking at me.

"I've been making really good progress. Two months in, if things are going well, we're able to check out for family events and things, so I decided to use my pass to come see you skate," she says. Then she gives a little wink. "I just didn't think it would be this kind of skating."

"So you're done?" I ask.

"Not quite," she says. "I have another month, so I have to go back after this. And there's really no 'done,' overall, but my progress is good."

I don't know what else to ask about rehab, or even if I should, so instead, I move on to the next line of questioning. "Am I in trouble?"

"No, honey," Dad says. He throws an arm around my shoulder and pulls me in to his side. "But we obviously have a *lot* to talk about."

I look up at Mom. I don't know what to say, or how much to say, to her right now.

"I'm sorry, Sloane," she says, cupping my face and looking me right in the eye. "I am so sorry for all that I've missed. I'm going to be spending a lot of time making up for the time I lost."

"But you're here now," I say.

"And I'm not going anywhere," she replies. It's all the reassurance I need.

CHAPTER 33

SLOane emiLY

*T*hey had to push five tables together to fit all of us.
None of the tables match. One is covered in finger-
painted flowers. Another has what looks like a giant fire-
work on the front. Yet another bears an illustration of the
solar system. They look sort of insane all together, but then
again, so do we.

I look around the table at the motley crew we've as-
sembled. There's James and Mom, looking grossly out of
place in her cream-colored pantsuit, and Sloane Devon
and her parents. I insisted on bringing Matt, and I couldn't
leave without saying goodbye to Cameron. Sloane Devon
brought her friends Bee and Andy. Dad is noticeably ab-
sent, and I feel a tug of sadness in my chest. I spent my
whole summer avoiding the thought of him, and now that
he's missing, it just feels wrong.

"Pass the napkins, please," Mom says. Matt pushes the

silver canister toward her, and she spreads two napkins out over her pants. "And a fork, please."

"Poutine is meant to be eaten with nature's utensils," Matt says, holding up a gravy-soaked fry between two fingers.

"Something tells me your mom eats pizza with a fork and knife," Sloane Devon whispers to me, and I giggle. She'd be right, except for the fact that I've never seen my mother eat pizza. My mother ignores Matt and accepts a roll of silverware from Andy.

We all dig into the plates spread out on the table. We managed to order an array of poutine, some with peas and onions, another with bacon. We even ordered a pizza poutine, with pepperoni, mushrooms, and mozzarella. Everyone is laughing and talking and shoving fries into their mouths—well, except for Mom, who is feasting on a caesar salad. James and Cameron seem to be deep in conversation about today's game. Across the table, Andy, Bee, and Sloane Devon are reliving Sloane and Andy's silver-medal-winning performance. And at the end, the adults are crowded together. They talk in hushed tones, possibly plotting some kind of punishment. I can't tell.

"So when can I see you again?" Matt leans in and swipes a fry from my hand and pops it into his mouth.

"Hey, that one was perfect!" I cry, because I don't want to think about his question. It was awful when I thought he hated me, but it's worse now that I know he likes me, because I may never see him again.

"Then you'll just have to figure out how to see that fry again," he says, and winks.

I pause. "I hope you're talking about us and not fries. Otherwise this conversation could get really disgusting."

He laughs. "Well, you can always email the french fry. And there's the phone. And there's definitely a train that runs between DC and Philadelphia, and I think tickets are pretty cheap for french fries with a valid student ID."

He leans in to kiss me, and even though my mind goes to my mother, who is watching me at the end of the table, I can't help myself. I kiss him back with my eyes closed and my hand on his cheek.

When we break away, I see that my mom is, in fact, watching us. When she catches my eye, she nods me over. I excuse myself from Matt, go to her, and bend over her shoulder.

"Will you go take care of the check?" she whispers, passing me her credit card down low by her hip. Classic Susan Jacobs move, and I'm thankful for it.

"Sure thing," I say, and skip toward the counter. I find our waitress and ask for our check. I'm leaning over, thinking about Matt and kissing him again. James ambles up beside me.

"I'm really proud of you, Seej," he says. He's smiling, and I can't tell if he's teasing me or being sincere.

"I knew you'd like me pulling one over on Mom and Dad," I say.

"That *is* pretty awesome," he concedes, shaking his

head, "but it's more than that. I saw you out there on that ice. You were fearless. You weren't afraid to get in there and really make plays. And when you took that last shot? It was incredible to watch. You didn't waver, you didn't second-guess yourself. You put it all out there."

"Thanks, James," I reply. "That really means a lot."

"So does this mean you're hanging up your figure skates?"

"I don't know," I say. I take a deep breath. "I definitely think I'm done competing. I never wanted this comeback anyway. I just wanted to skate and have fun."

James nods. "You know, St. Augusta's has a great girls' hockey team."

"I know. You brought half of them home at some point during your senior year, you heartbreaker." I poke him in the ribs and he jumps away.

I turn and start back to the table, and James grabs my arm. His face has gone serious.

"What?" I ask him.

"Look, Sloane. Things are going to suck for a while." He gestures to Mom. "She's going to need us. And he might too. I know you're not really one for the emotions and the family drama, but—"

I put my hand on his arm and squeeze. "James, I'm there. I can handle it. We'll handle it," I say. I pull him into a hug.

CHAPTER 34

SLOANE DEVON

"**Y**ou still have some serious explaining to do," Dad says. Everyone has gone back to their dorms and hotel rooms, and now it's just the three of us—Mom, Dad, and me—standing on the sidewalk. Our family car, a battered blue Corolla that my parents drove all the way from Philly, is parked in front of the restaurant.

"I know," I reply. I keep my gaze on the strip of rust over the rear wheel well.

"And you're going to have to explain it to Coach Butler," Dad says. His voice is in stern-dad lecture mode. "He had to call in a favor to get you into that camp. You owe him an apology. You'll be lucky if he doesn't bench you for the start of the season."

"I know," I say again. I stare at my shoes. I'm *not* looking forward to that conversation.

"Honey, do you still want to play hockey?" Mom asks quietly.

I can't look her in the eye. All I can do is stare at her Mama Jacobs shirt. "I don't know," I answer honestly. "I'm not even sure — I'm not even sure I can."

There's a moment of silence. Then she says: "Sloane, do you know that boy?"

I look up. Nando. I'd texted him to meet me here so I could say goodbye and explain one last time, but I never thought he'd show. The sight of him sends my stomach and all its contents churning, and for a moment I realize I was actually *hoping* he wouldn't come.

"Can I have a minute?" I ask my parents.

"Take your time, honey," Mom says. "We'll wait here."

I hug them both, then make my way down the sidewalk toward Nando.

"I'm glad you came," I say. "I just wanted to explain."

He spreads his hands, like *I'm listening.*

I take a deep breath and then pour the story out, the same way Sloane Emily did to Matt, the same way I did to Bee. I tell him about my mom, and the tingles, and how I thought I was done with hockey. I tell him about the fight that got me sent to Elite in the first place. I tell him about meeting Sloane Emily and how we agreed to change places. I tell him about her dad. And then I tell him why I lied.

"I knew how horrible it felt to lose something you love so much," I say, "something you're good at and can count on, something that can save your life." I think about his scholarship, and my own, the one that may or may not actually be coming. "When you said that you liked me because I reminded you of how much you loved to play, I was afraid the truth would hurt you. I couldn't do that to you. I wanted you to be happy."

He squints at me. "Even if you weren't?"

"Yes." I feel a tremendous weight lifting off my shoulders, and at the same time, tears forming in my eyes. I want to stop them. I try to brush them away, but within seconds they're streaming down my cheeks. "I'm sorry." I choke out the words. "For lying. For this. I never cry."

"It's okay, Sloane." He reaches out and pulls me in, and I sob all over his Canadiens T-shirt, the same one he was wearing the night I first saw him again. He rubs my back while I sob quietly into the blue fabric. When I'm finally all cried out, I take a step back. He drops his arms and grasps my hands.

I glance down the block at my parents, who are pretending to have a conversation to hide the fact that they're blatantly staring at us.

"They want to know if I'm going to play hockey anymore," I say. My voice is still all quavery.

"Are you?" He brushes a strand of dark hair behind my ear. The feel of his fingertips on my cheek sends chills up my spine.

"I don't know," I say.

"Well, I don't think I was wrong before, Sloane," he says. "I think you do love it. I think you're just scared."

"Do *you* love it?" I ask him.

He gives a soft laugh. "More than almost anything."

"Me too," I blurt out. And then I realize it's true: I love hockey. I always have. That's why I ran away from it. When my mom went away, and then it seemed like I was losing hockey, too, I couldn't face it. I ran. At first it was by being a rage freak on the ice, and then it was by becoming Sloane Emily.

But even after all of it, I still love hockey. And I want it back.

"I've been thinking that maybe this just isn't the right place for me. Not that the Canadian government or an expired student visa has anything to do with that," he says with a little laugh. "But I *have* been thinking about contacting some other schools, maybe meeting with some coaches. I don't know if I'm still good enough—"

"You are," I tell him. He reaches his arms around me and pulls me in again, close enough that I can feel his heartbeat in his chest.

"Well, it sounds like we'll *both* be looking at schools," he says, smiling.

"Maybe even making some visits together," I say.

"Sounds like a plan," he replies, and pulls me in for a kiss.

When Nando and I finally say goodbye, I walk back down the sidewalk to where my parents are waiting. They're staying in a hotel in town. Tomorrow we'll all drive back to Philly together.

"Is everything okay?" Mom asks.

I turn and catch a final glimpse of Nando's taillights as they disappear over the hill.

"Everything is perfect," I say. "Or close enough, anyway." Then we climb into the car, all three of us together, and drive off into the night.

EPILOGUE

SLOANE DEVON

I check my phone: 11:45. She was supposed to be here at 11:30. No text, either. I only have until 12:30. Then I have to meet my mom to head over to tour Mount Vernon. I might as well go ahead and order. Mom and I are here doing a little U.S. history–themed tourism trip around DC to celebrate the end of rehab. Dad couldn't come because he just started a new job.

There's no one else in line at the Starbucks in Dupont Circle, where Sloane Emily and I arranged to meet.

"I'll have a tall cinnamon latte," I tell the gangly barista behind the counter. Silver rings are stacked on his black-polished fingers.

"What kind of milk?" His speech is slow and bored.

"Skim," I reply. I check my phone again.

"Name?"

"Sloane," I say.

"Hey, that's *my* name!"

I whip around to see Sloane Emily standing behind me, looking almost exactly the same as when I last left her in Montreal, only she's cut about five inches off her hair and added some red and gold highlights to her new shaggy bob. I wonder what her mom thinks about that.

"Small world," I reply, and hug her. She orders a venti iced green tea, and the barista doesn't notice our matching names. Then we make our way over to a small round table in the window. Outside it's a warm summer day, though there's a touch of a chill in the breeze to let us know that fall is coming.

"Yay! I'm so glad we could get together," Sloane Emily says, clapping her hands.

"Yeah, my mom is so lost in the Cold War exhibit at the Smithsonian that she didn't mind if I disappeared for an hour or so." Mom is one of those museumgoers who isn't just content to look at the displays. She actually reads every single placard. It makes a stroll through a gallery last hours, and I definitely don't have the patience. I tried to be interested for as long as I could, but I was really glad to have this time to escape and catch up with Sloane Emily.

"How is your mom?" Sloane asks.

"Good," I reply. "She seems . . . better."

"Oh yeah?"

"Dad and I went out there to do some of these family sessions with her before she finished up. It was really weird. Lots of apologizing and crying. But I think it really helped," I say.

"That's really great, Sloane," Sloane Emily says.

The barista calls out "Sloane," then a brief pause, then "Sloane" again. I look up and see him double-checking the names on the cups. I start to go for the drinks, but Sloane Emily beats me to it, bounding out of her chair and over to the bar where our drinks are waiting.

Sloane emily

"So how're things with your family?" Sloane Devon asks. It's a question I've been getting over and over, from classmates and coaches and reporters, and every time it's sounded like nails on a chalkboard to me. But when Sloane Devon asks, I'm surprised to feel my body relax.

"Eh," I say, because I've never actually answered the question with anything other than "Fine" before. I'm not quite sure how to answer it honestly.

"That bad?"

I sigh. "No, it's not really bad. I mean, it's kind of awful sometimes. The Internet is having a field day with Dad. Conservative senator in a sex scandal? Those headlines practically write themselves. But he's being really stoic about it, and sort of just focusing on work."

"He's still, uh, working?"

"Yeah. He refuses to resign, so we'll see what happens in the next election." I frown. "Amy left to do PR for some movie studio in LA. Dad says that's over, but he's moved into this sad little condo in Georgetown. I don't think Mom's ready to—" I pause. I feel my lower lip start to tremble, my eyes welling up a little. I take a deep breath and wipe at the tear that's trying to escape my left eye. I take another deep breath and shake out my new short hair. It's a move I've perfected, and I do it any time I feel like I might fall to pieces. I square my shoulders, and I'm back. "Anyway, it's not great, but it's not the living worst or anything. We'll see. We're talking, at least."

"That's really good, Sloane," she says. She takes a long sip of her latte, and I have a moment to really look at her. She's back in her ratty old jeans, the ones with the holes formed through years of wear. She looks pretty much the same as she did when we first met, her long hair pulled back in a ponytail, only this time her T-shirt is a little more fitted, and . . . are those? They *are* cap sleeves! Maybe four weeks in my wardrobe did her good after all.

"Oh! I almost forgot the reason I wanted to get together," I say, reaching for my tote bag, the one I got from Brown when Mom and I took the admissions tour last week. "I mean, other than to catch up and all that." I pull the mound of blue fabric out of the bag and place it on the table.

SLOANE DEVON

"That's your camp jersey," I say. I push it back across the table at her. "That's not mine."

She looks at it and arches an eyebrow at me. "Are you sure?"

"Dude, you need some kind of souvenir from this whole thing," I reply. "Why not the jersey from the game that you totally rocked?"

"I didn't *totally* rock. More like Kenny G'ed it," she says. Her cheeks flush a bright pink.

"That's not what Matt said." I watch as a grin twitches in the corner of her mouth.

SLOANE EMILY

My stomach does a little backflip at the mention of Matt. "You saw him?"

"I ran into him at a preseason jamboree," she says. "A bunch of the high schools got together to play challenge games, and he was playing. Well, when he wasn't mooning over you. He pretty much thinks the sun shines out of your ass."

I feel my cheeks get hot again. Matt and I have been emailing, texting, G-chatting, and talking on the phone constantly since I returned from Canada. I haven't seen him at all, but next weekend he's taking the train down to DC. Just the thought of it has me buzzing out of my chair.

"Speaking of romance, how's Nando?" This time it's Sloane Devon's turn to squirm. She crosses and uncrosses her arms, shifting around in her chair like she's in an FBI interrogation, but I see a slight smile start to form.

"Good," she finally croaks, then clears her throat. "He's good."

SLOANE DEVON

"Good" doesn't even begin to cover Nando. It's like he won the life lottery these last couple weeks. Back when he was first looking at colleges, Boston University had been recruiting him hard, so when he called their coach to let him know he was looking to play again, the guy practically chartered a plane to come pick him up in Montreal. Nando flew down for a tryout, and it went really well.

But not as well as his UPenn tryout.

It turns out the UPenn team suffered a few injuries in the off-season, thanks to an ill-advised drunken rafting trip. After viewing Nando's tryout DVD from his first round of college searches, the coach promptly called him down for a meeting and an in-person tryout. And so, in three weeks, Nando will be moving down to Philly to take a couple second-session summer classes so he'll be eligible for spring hockey.

When I tell all this to Sloane Emily, she squeals so loud that a Yorkie passing by on the sidewalk barks at her.

"Dude, chill," I say, but I can barely contain the cheesy, toothy grin on my face.

"Sloane and Nando, sittin' in a tree," she sings. I toss a

hunk of banana walnut bread right at her face. She bats it away, breathing deeply to recover from her giggle fit.

SLOANE EMILY

"I still can't believe it worked," I say. I think back to my first scrimmage, when I was wearing so many pads at least no one could see me shaking like a leaf. Sure, I'd played plenty of street hockey in our driveway with James, but I never *ever* thought I'd be out on the ice for real. "Can you believe we actually did all that?"

"Not even a little bit," Sloane Devon replies. "It was worth it, though, right?"

The question hangs there in the air for a moment. Sloane Devon's gaze goes over my shoulder, out the window and into oblivion while she ponders her own question. I stare down into my iced tea, trying to find a pattern in the ice cubes floating on the top.

"Yeah, it was," I say, and as soon as it comes out, I know it's the truth. Sure, it took a couple weeks for my bruises to fade, and my knees still haven't quite forgiven me for four weeks of crash-course hockey.

But well, then there's Matt.

Across the table, I see Sloane Devon smiling, and I wonder if she's thinking about Nando. Her cheeks flush, and she shoves a giant chunk of banana walnut bread into her mouth. Yeah, definitely thinking about Nando.

"Would you do it again?" I ask.

"I don't know if we could get away with it again," she says.

"Sloane!" The barista barks out the name, holding up an iced coffee. He looks back at the side of the cup, where a name has been scrawled in black Sharpie. "Sloane J?"

I look down at my iced green tea, then over at Sloane Devon's nearly full latte.

"Did you?" I ask her.

"No, did you?" She arches an eyebrow at me.

The barista takes one last look at the cup and barks again: "Sloane J!"

ACKNOWLEDGMENTS

I'm pretty sure I'm one of the luckiest authors in the world; I am surrounded by a team of sassy, stylish, talented professionals. First and foremost, I have to thank Lexa Hillyer and Lauren Oliver. I can't imagine anyone else filling your (totally fabulous) shoes. Big thanks also goes to Beth Scorzato, who is an incredible editor and author wrangler. She kept me on track and sane during the craziest of deadlines. Everyone at Paper Lantern Lit, you guys rock! Thanks to Stephen Barbara, whom I will never stop referring to as "a baller agent." Thanks to Wendy Loggia, my editor at Delacorte Press, who is wonderful and encouraging and makes my words better. There are so many people at Delacorte who make books happen, and I'm lucky to have every one of them on my side.

Thanks to all the incredible Tweeters, bloggers, and Facebookers who have been so supportive of me, especially Tara Gonzalez (hobbitsies.net) and Sarah Blackstock (storyboundgirl.com), who have cheered me on since the beginning. Thanks to my Atlanta-area book crew, especially Vania Stoyanova, the Not So YA Book Club, and The Little Shop of Stories. Thanks to Corrie Wachob, Rachel Simon, and Mitali Dave for being readers, cheerleaders, and buddies.

Big thanks for this book goes out to my derby teams, especially the Boston Massacre and the Wicked Pissahs. Without all your training and general badassery, I certainly wouldn't have been able to write the action scenes in this book, and without hits from some of you, I wouldn't have that great passage on gross injuries. Maude Forbid, Anna Wrecksya, Shark Week, Lil Paine, Ginger Kid, and Dusty, you guys are my besties and my heroes, on skates and off. Pissah Fo' Life! BOSTON! BOSTON! PINCH PINCH PINCH!

And of course, I couldn't do any of this without the support of my family. Dad, thanks for buying me that long line of Mac laptops that helped keep the words flowing. Someday I'm going to write enough books to return the favor! Mom, thank you so much for reading drafts and spotting errors and in general helping me make a good impression on the world.

And finally to Adam, who works harder than any person should so that I can stay home, watch YouTube videos of puppies, and sometimes write books. I love you lots and lots.

ABOUT THE AUTHOR

Lauren Morrill grew up in Maryville, Tennessee, where she was a short-term Girl Scout, a (not so) proud member of the marching band, and a trouble-making editor for the school newspaper. She graduated from Indiana University with a major in history and a minor in rock and roll and lives in Macon, Georgia, with her husband and their dog, Lucy. When she's not writing, she spends a lot of hours on the track getting knocked around playing roller derby.

DON'T MISS
Lauren Morrill's
first novel!

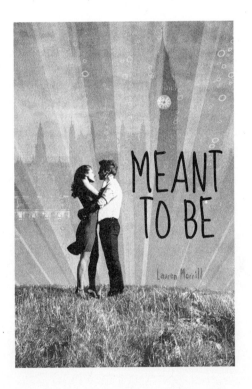

(It's funny AND romantic.)

1

Down and Dirty at Thirty Thousand Feet

Have a gr8 trip—and feel FREE to
do anything I wouldn't do :) —P

There are certain things in life that just suck. Pouring a big bowl
of Lucky Charms before realizing the milk is expired, the word
"moist," falling face-first into the salad bar in front of the entire
lacrosse team . . .

"Bird strike!"

Being on a plane with Jason Lippincott is another one of them.

Two rows ahead of me, Jason is holding his hands up in mock
prayer as our plane bounces like it's on a bungee cord. Not that I
would have any idea what bungee jumping feels like, since I would
rather compete in a spelling bee in my underpants than leap off a
crane with only a rope tied around me. At least I'd come away from
the spelling bee with a medal.

As the plane drops several hundred (thousand?) feet, I white-
knuckle the armrest. Jason's prayers may be a joke, but mine
are very, very real. *God, please deposit me safely on the ground in*

London . . . and in the process, maybe you could find a way to get Jason to shut it?

I hate to fly. Seriously. HATE. IT. It seems wrong to be hurtling through the clouds at warp speed in a metal tube. It makes about as much sense as being flung over the ocean on a slingshot.

I tuck my pocket Shakespeare into the seat back and carefully realign the magazines that have bounced out of formation on my tray table.

"We're going down!" That's Jason again, *of course*.

The plane bounces even worse than before. My knees crash into the tray table, sending my half-eaten package of peanuts and my entire stack of magazines raining into the aisle. I instinctively grab for the armrest once more, and the businessman next to me lets out a loud yelp.

Oops. Not the armrest. His thigh. (I thought it felt a little flabby.)

I mutter an apology and adjust my kung fu grip to the *real* arm-rest this time.

Breathe. Breathe. I close my eyes and try to picture Mark. Weirdly, the first image that comes into my head is his yearbook picture. He has the perfectly proportioned features of a model. A bright white smile with perfect teeth all lined up in a perfect row, except for that one tooth, three from the center, that is a teeny bit crooked, which I love, because it sort of shows off how straight the other ones are. And his thick, wavy brown hair is always in the right place, mussed just enough but not too much, without the aid of any greasy or crunchy hair product. Perfect. Just like him. I finally start to feel calm, like I'm coasting across the ocean on the back of a little songbird instead of strapped into a lumpy polyester seat.

Then Jason lets out a loud "Woooo!", shattering my Mark-inspired Zen.

I sit up straight in my seat. Jason's got his arms raised like he's on a roller coaster. A pretty flight attendant glides up the aisle toward him. Good. If God can't get Jason to shut it, maybe she can.

I crane my neck for a better view of the scolding I know is coming his way. Instead, I see the flight attendant pass him a folded-up napkin, which he immediately opens to reveal a stack of chocolate chip cookies. From the way he's handling them, all delicately, I can tell they're still warm.

The flight attendant flashes Jason a smile. He says something to her and she laughs. He acts like a jerk and *still* scores first-class snacks!

"Oh my God. He is too much. Isn't he hilarious?" It's Sarah Finder, Newton North's resident TMZ. She's elbowing her seatmate, Evie Ellston, in the ribs, nodding in Jason's direction.

"Seriously. Adorable. And the Scarlet thing is over, right?"

"*Way* over. They broke up weeks ago." Of course Sarah knows. Sarah *always* knows. So far, during the three hours and twenty-seven minutes we have been on this flight, Sarah and Evie have left no student undiscussed (except for me, possibly because the last time there was any gossip about me, it was in eighth grade, when Bryan Holloman taped a felt rose to my locker on Valentine's Day. The only reason anyone cared was that, it came out the next day, the rose was actually meant for Stephenie Kelley). From my vantage point in the seat directly behind her, I've already heard about Amber Riley's supposed nose job, Rob Diamos's recent suspension for smoking cigarettes in the janitor's closet, and the shame Laura Roberts was undergoing, having received her mother's '00 Honda instead of the brand-new Range Rover she'd been telling everyone she'd get.

"Think he's all wounded and needy? On the prowl for someone new?" Evie has one of those oversized mouths attached to an oversized face that makes all her vowels sound a mile long.

"Doubtful," Sarah answers. Then, lowering her voice: "He said he's trying to join the mile-high club."

"Seriously? Isn't that, like, when people . . . you know . . . on a *plane*?" From the way Evie's voice jumps to Mariah Carey octaves, it's hard to tell if she's horrified or interested in signing herself up as a willing partner.

"Shhh! And yes. Totally. You know how he is. Up for *anything*," Sarah says.

Gross. I say a silent prayer that God can add Sarah to the list of People to Render Temporarily Mute while he's working on keeping our plane in the sky. I mean, I am totally not one of those prudes who believe having sex as a teenager is some kind of mortal sin or social death. I don't have a problem with sex. I just don't happen to be having it. And if I *were* having sex, I certainly wouldn't be getting it on in an airplane *bathroom*. Who wants to get down and dirty in a place so . . . cramped and dirty?

I close my eyes and try to get Mark back, but Sarah's voice keeps slicing into my visions like one of those infomercial knives. *Cuts cans, shoes, and daydreams.*

Without imaginary Mark to keep me company, there's only one way to simultaneously block out Newton North's biggest mouth and chase away visions of airmageddon. I pull my iPod out of my purple leather satchel, which is tucked safely under the seat in front of me. I unwind my headphones and click on some mellow tunes (Hayward Williams being my choice music of the moment. It's like someone put gravel and butter into a blender and out came his voice). But as I reach back to put in my earbuds, I encounter something wet and sticky nested in my curls. I pull the end of my ponytail around to my face to find a wad of what looks, smells, and feels like grape Bubble Yum.

A fit of giggles erupts behind me, and I turn to see a little boy, maybe seven, wearing a Buzz Lightyear tee. He's grinning maniacally, his mother snoozing peacefully beside him.

"Did you?" I whisper, furiously shaking my hair at him.

"Oops!" he exclaims before dissolving into another fit of hysterical laughter, his fat cheeks burning red under his mop of blond curls.

Add children to the list of things I hate. Flying and children.

After several minutes of careful picking, followed by some full-on tugging (all while I thank my parents for making me an only child), it becomes clear: I am going to have to leave my seat and go to the bathroom, in total defiance of the pilot-ordered Fasten Seat Belt sign.

I don't use airplane bathrooms. As a rule. And I *really* don't like breaking rules. (It's kind of one of my rules.) I mean, if I'm going to plummet to my death, it's *not* going to be with my pants around my ankles. Then again, a big wad of grape gum in my ponytail definitely constitutes an emergency, no matter how little I care about my overchlorinated, wild chestnut waves. I carefully unfasten my seat belt, keeping my eye on the flight attendants' galley, and make a beeline for the lavatory.

As I pick at the purple gooey mess my head has become, I can hear faint giggling coming through the wall. What is it with everyone on this flight acting like it's a day at Six Flags? I'd rather be on the *Titanic* at this point. At least there I'd be traveling in comfort, with crystal glasses and warm towels.

I finally yank the last gob of gum out of my hair and step out of the lavatory, wrestling with the little sliding door, which has grabbed hold of the sleeve of my hoodie. I fumble around, bashing my elbow on the doorframe, before finally freeing myself and whipping around to leave. Right then the plane bounces hard, and I am shot out of the bathroom like a cannon ball. A pair of arms saves me from bashing my head into the narrow doorway. I look up to see Jason Lippincott steadying me on my feet.

"Book Licker!" he says, invoking my least favorite junior-high nickname. He grins, several freckles on his forehead scrunching together. "Enjoying your flight?"

I pull away from him. "It's Julia," I reply as calmly as possible, adjusting the hem of my pants, which have hooked themselves over the sole of my sneaker.

"Of course," he says, gesturing down the aisle. "After you."

"Um, thanks," I say. Maybe he can tell how badly I want to get back to my seat belt.

As I make my way down the aisle, I begin to notice my classmates' eyes on me. The looks quickly turn to snickers and then full-on laughter. Ryan Lynch, Newton North's lacrosse captain, is grinning stupidly at me. Sarah is whispering furiously to Evie, her eyes trained in my direction. I have absolutely no idea what is going on, and I immediately wonder if there is more bubble gum in my hair or it somehow landed on my face. I reach to pat my hair down when a wild gesture catches the corner of my eye. I turn to see Jason making a thrusting motion in my direction, winking at Ryan, who reaches out to give Jason a high five.

Oh my God. No way. They think it was *us,* in the bathroom, with the mile-high club and all that. They think it because he's *making* them think it! How could they think I would do *anything* with Jason Lippincott, much less anything in an airplane bathroom! My eyes dart back to Sarah, who is still in full-on gossip mode, her gaze locked on me. If Sarah knows, everyone knows, which means it's only a matter of time before the news gets back to Mark. And by then, who knows how crazy the rumor will get? Newton North is like one giant game of telephone sometimes.

One thing is certain: good, sweet, kind, thoughtful Mark is going to want nothing to do with me if he thinks I've been even semi-naked with Jason on a transatlantic flight.

Though Jason has stopped thrusting, he's still laughing and air-fiving his seatmates. Air-fiving. Yeah. First he calls me Book Licker; then he pretends I got down and dirty at thirty thousand feet!

All I can do is turn and hiss, "Stop it!" before dropping into my seat. I cram my headphones into my ears, crank the volume on my iPod, and try to drown out my humiliation with some tunes. At this point, I'm almost *hoping* for a crash.